"Excuse me," she said, stepping up to her, "but aren't you Mrs. Feinberg?"

◆

Elaine Feinberg turned slowly and gazed at Kristin with what Kristin thought were vacant eyes, the eyes of someone suffering amnesia.

"Yes," she said in a voice nearly void of expression, mechanical, uninterested.

Kristin widened her smile.

"I'm Kristin Morris. My husband and I bought your house. I know we only met for a few seconds, but—"

"What do you want?" she demanded firmly, her eyes changing quickly to those of one terrified.

"Nothing, I just . . . wanted to say how sorry I was for what happened to your husband and . . ."

"You're sorry? You don't know how sorry you will be. Unless, of course, you become one of them," she said.

"One of them? Who's them?"

"You'll find out," she replied.

NEIGHBORHOOD WATCH

Books by Andrew Neiderman

Published by POCKET BOOKS

ANDREW NEIDERMAN

NEIGHBORHOOD WATCH

POCKET STAR BOOKS

New York London Toronto Sydney Singapore

An *Original* Publication of POCKET BOOKS

A Pocket Star Book published by
POCKET BOOKS, a division of Simon & Schuster Inc.
1230 Avenue of the Americas, New York, NY 10020

Copyright © 2000 by Andrew Neiderman

ISBN: 0-671-02709-3

First Pocket Books printing January 2000

10 9 8 7 6 5 4 3 2 1

POCKET STAR BOOKS and colophon are registered
trademarks of Simon & Schuster Inc.

Front cover design and illustration by James Wang

Printed in the U.S.A.

For Brian Ingber
A friend sorely missed

NEIGHBORHOOD
WATCH

PROLOGUE

ELAINE FEINBERG FELT HER BABY stirring inside her. She interpreted the movement to be restlessness even though she was only in the beginning of her seventh month. Her child wasn't impatient in the womb, she thought; rather, he or she sensed Elaine's disquiet. In fact, it seemed more like the wind that whistled and twisted around the house had sliced through her too, making the fetus shudder. She envisioned the infant tightening its fetal position, grimacing; and then she thought she heard its tiny, but shrill cry vibrate through her bones and into her skull.

She put the palm of her hand on her enlarged stomach and pressed it as firmly as she could without causing herself any pain. She hoped to comfort her baby.

"There, there," she whispered. "It's all right. It will be all right."

Elaine put all her effort into making the words ring with sincerity and with confidence, even though she had no faith in their validity.

It wouldn't be all right.

It couldn't be all right.

Poor Sol was in his office, racking his brain, tapping out numbers on his calculator, trying to find a miraculous solution to their deep financial woe. Their little world had closed in around them like some giant hand clenching, squeezing, firming its hold, the fingers shutting down all linkage with the outside, blocking out not only the flow of money, but the flow of sympathy. More and more they found themselves alone, an island in the development, the stream of displeasure and intolerance rushing around them, creating torrents, waves so high they risked their lives merely stepping out the door.

She hardly spoke to anyone in Emerald Lakes anymore. Her hello's would echo off the faces of her neighbors, all of them one bland expression, not a smile, not a warm glint in the eyes, nothing but winter in their eyes.

I'm tired, she thought, tired of the battles.

And she knew Sol was tired, too.

She closed her eyes and tried to recall when things were different. It wasn't that long ago when there was such optimism about everything, and her pregnancy was the giant exclamation point emphasizing their rainbow future.

A stirring in the air around her snapped her eyes open. It was as if someone had slid open the patio door. Of course, that could never happen, not in Emerald Lakes. Why Emerald Lakes, Sol told her when they first moved here, was as safe as . . . as being back in the womb. Here you could be all snug and warm, never a worry.

She sighed deeply. The womb. Her baby had quieted down. The power of her hand, she thought and smiled to herself. She closed her eyes again. Surely they would get through their crisis. Surely, it would all end happily and Sol would stop aging right before her eyes.

He was working too hard, she thought, deciding to sit up. She should get him to relax. Maybe if they just sat and talked with some music playing, put on some Yanni, they would have a relaxing, stressless night for a change. Neither she nor he would toss and turn trying to slip out of the grip of worry. Maybe if they just—

It was so loud an explosion, she expected the roof to come crashing down. Later, she would say the walls vibrated. Certainly the bed did and that vibration traveled through her body, surely terrifying the baby, too. Her heart stopped and then began to pound.

"SOL!" she cried. She dropped her feet into her slippers and stood up, shaking so hard, she had to brace herself on the bed a moment. "SOL!"

She started out of the bedroom. It looked like smoke in the air around the office doorway and there was the scent of something burning.

"SOL! WHAT WAS THAT? SOL?"

She paused a moment, listened, and then walked slowly toward the office doorway, her hand pressed over her heart. She turned into the office and saw him slumped over his desk. The blood streamed freely from his temple, down his cheek, over the side of his chin to soak the papers.

Did she scream? She really couldn't remember. She did remember seeing the gun in his hand, but she also remembered thinking, we have no guns or didn't have until now. Most important, and she emphasized this when the detective arrived, most important, she would swear on a stack of Bibles that the patio door in the office was unlocked and open at least a quarter of an inch. But when the detective went to look, he said the door was closed, locked, and from the inside.

She had to have been mistaken.

But she wasn't. She insisted.

"My husband never owned a gun. I never saw that gun in the house. I don't care that his finger is on the trigger. My husband wouldn't do such a thing to us.

"Not to us. Not to me and our baby, our unborn baby."

The detective was patronizing, but he didn't believe anything she said. To him it was black and white.

Easy.

One moment Sol was alive and the next he was dead because he wanted it that way.

Who would believe otherwise? Certainly not her neighbors.

She heard the whispering.

"A terrible blight on Emerald Lakes. A suicide!"

"There's just so much we can do with people like this. Just so much the Neighborhood Watch can do to protect them and us."

"Especially if they don't cooperate."

Philip Slater leaned back in his burgundy leather, rich mahogany desk chair. He had soft gray hair and mesmerizing black onyx eyes set in a face dark enough to be Arabic. He spread his arms over the chair's armrests and curled his long fingers around the claw ends.

It was quiet, cemetery quiet, silent enough to hear the heartbeat in the miniature grandfather clock resting on the white marble mantle.

"He tell anyone he wasn't going to be here?" Philip asked.

"Not me," Nikki Stanley replied quickly. The five-foot-five petite woman narrowed her beady brown eyes to add a schoolmarm's expression of reprimand.

"Sid?"

"Not a word," Sid Levine replied.

Slater gazed at the clock furiously. Suddenly they heard the doorbell. Philip turned in his chair and leaned forward, folding his hands on his desk, and fixing his eyes on the doorway to this office. They could hear Marilyn Slater greeting Vincent McShane and then McShane's hurried steps down the marble tile corridor.

"Sorry," he said and quickly moved to his seat in front of Slater's desk. "We had a little family crisis. Mindy," he added ashamedly, "was caught smoking with some of her girlfriends in the locker room today. Just found out she was suspended for two days. Eileen is devastated."

"Peer pressure is far stronger than the influence we have on our children. That's for sure," Nikki said.

Vincent nodded and released his breath as if he had been holding it in to keep from being discovered. The passage of air over his thick lips made him sound like a horse, an embarrassing sound. He straightened up in his chair and sucked in his beer belly. Philip Slater never missed an opportunity to criticize him for it and when Philip criticized anyone in Emerald Lakes, it was open season on him. McShane had tried to lose weight. He knew that five feet eight, one hundred and ninety pounds was a bell ringer, but those damn Rob Roys at his business lunches, and the food he consumed at those lunches—all held at the best gourmet restaurants in Manhattan—made it very difficult to diet.

"Did I miss anything?" he asked sheepishly.

"We didn't start. We needed a quorum," Philip said,

"and you knew Larry Sommers was out of town this week."

"Sorry. Eileen was crying and . . ."

"What are you going to do about Mindy?" Sid Levine asked with the curious tone of someone who expected to be in similar circumstances shortly.

"We grounded her for two months . . . no movies, no dates. Directly home after school."

Nikki nodded.

"That's all they understand . . . losing privileges."

"All right, we'd better start the meeting," Philip Slater said. He and Marilyn had lost their only child, Bradley, to a blood disease when Bradley was six. Philip wasn't interested in the problems related to bringing up teenagers.

"Sid?" Philip Slater said.

Sid Levine leaned over in his chair to look down at his notepad. He adjusted his thick lens glasses, and cleared his throat. With his free hand, he brushed back the sides of his pearl black hair. Other men in their early forties, especially those who were in the same stressful line of work, showed more signs of age. Sid had no receding hairline, no deep wrinkles or dark circles around his dark gray eyes, and managed to keep his five-foot-ten-inch frame rather trim, which was something Vincent McShane coveted.

"Well, as I predicted last month," Sid began, his voice a bit nasal, "the landscaper has asked for an eight percent raise. I had only one brief conversation with Pirnos, but I think he'll settle for five percent. Our water bill for the commons is expected to rise along with the raise in rates. Someone backed over a floodlight off the north gate entrance. I had it replaced at a cost of fifty-four dollars and thirty-seven cents."

"Didn't that happen once before?" Nikki asked quickly. As soon as she asked the question, she looked at Philip Slater to see if he would appreciate her recollection.

"Yes, two years ago," Sid said flipping pages back, "in March."

"Just about the same time," Nikki added and nodded.

"Sid?" Philip Slater said, raising his eyebrows.

"None of the homeowners saw anything," Sid replied defensively. "Or at least, no one's made a complaint to me."

"Don't we have the same man in the security booth there and doesn't he park his car just to the right of that broken floodlight?" Nikki asked sharply.

"Well, I don't know if it's the same man, but whoever mans the gate does park his car near it, yes," Sid replied.

Nikki looked as satisfied as a trial lawyer who had driven home a major point.

"I'll speak to Siegler," Philip Slater said. "If one of his men is responsible, they'll pay for the light. Go on, Sid."

"We have a working balance of twelve thousand two hundred dollars and fifty-four cents. Our bonds are presently earning eight and a quarter and I'm just about to move the money we received in fines from Barry and Susan Lester into our working capital account," he concluded.

"Okay," Philip Slater said. "A motion to approve the treasurer's report?"

"So moved," Vincent snapped.

"Any objections?" No one even breathed loud. "Good. Let's move on. Neighborhood Watch. Nikki?"

Nikki Stanley tucked a loose section of her skirt

under her legs and opened a pad that looked like the ticket pads meter maids used.

"Saragossa Drive, number 2341, the Kimbles. They've had their garage door open during the daylight hours for upwards of four hours at a time," she said in a venomous voice.

"Yeah, I've seen it that way almost every time I've driven by," Vincent McShane said.

"Then why haven't you ever called me on it?" Nikki demanded instantly. She spun around on him. He looked quickly at Philip Slater, who stared without expression.

"I . . . just assumed you would see it and put it down," he sputtered.

There was a deep moment of silence.

"As trustees of the homeowners board, we're all officers of the Neighborhood Watch," Philip Slater said slowly, patiently. "Even though Nikki is the chairman, it's not fair to load her down with the full burden."

"No. Of course not," Vincent agreed. "I'm sorry, Nikki. I should have told you sooner," he said. She smirked to suggest that his apology, no matter how sincere it sounded, did nothing to compensate for his failure. He pulled his lips in and sat back quickly.

"Go on, Nikki. Please," Philip Slater said.

"I have cited them and advised them of article eight, section one. They apologized and promised to be more diligent."

"Fine," Philip Slater said. "Go on."

"Maracabo Circle, 5467, the Mateos. Twice this month they put out garbage bags that were so full, they couldn't close their bin. On March twenty-first," she said, referring to her notes, "one of those bags came unraveled and some debris was seen around the bin. It took two phone calls to get them to clean it up."

"Gentlemen? And Mrs. Stanley?" Philip Slater asked.

"Ten dollars, first offense," Sid replied. "I think that's fair."

"It's not a first offense," Nikki snapped.

"But it is the first time they've been so cited," Sid insisted.

"Sid's right, Nikki. Send them a ten-dollar fine. Continue."

"Courtney Street, 5768, the Dimases."

"What could they have done?" Vincent asked.

"They," Nikki said curtly, "didn't do anything. They complained about the Del Marcos' children tying a garbage can on a rope and dropping it from their house roof to use as a makeshift basketball hoop. The bottom of the can had been beaten out."

"Rather ingenious," Sid Levine said.

"Yes," Philip Slater said. "But quite unsightly, I imagine."

"As well as noisy," Nikki added.

"What happened?"

"They claim they phoned Mrs. Del Marco twice about it, but she did nothing. She said the boys have a right to play around their own home."

"And?" Philip Slater asked.

"I paid her a visit and read her article thirteen, subsection two, concerning decorations on the outside walls. She was quite cantankerous and refused to consider the hanging garbage can a decoration. I then referred her to article twelve, section one concerning noise. She pointed out the boys don't play after eight P.M."

"Mrs. Del Marco has a point there," Vincent said.

"What's the situation as of today?" Philip Slater asked.

"Charles Dimas seeks relief and has asked us to render a finding," Nikki said.

Philip Slater leaned forward slowly into the light revealing his finely chiseled strong features.

"The question before the committee is does a hanging garbage can used as a makeshift basketball hoop constitute an outside decoration? If so, it will fall under the regulations as set forth in article thirteen. What's your pleasure?"

"It's certainly not intended to be a decorative piece," Vincent said. "The kids are just amusing themselves. It could be worse; they could be throwing things into my garbage can," he quipped, but no one laughed.

"I would agree, but it is unsightly," Sid commented. "Anything that adds or detracts from the overall appearance of one of our homes must fall under article thirteen, whether the homeowner considers it formally as a decoration or not. It's the effect it has."

"Very good point, Sid," Philip said.

"I move the Del Marcos be cited," Nikki said quickly. She glared at Vincent.

"Second," Sid added.

"Vincent?"

"If it's the majority feeling . . ."

"Don't you have a mind of your own?" Phil Slater snapped.

"Sure. I just thought . . . right. I agree."

"Nikki, send the Del Marcos our finding and give them the usual twenty-four hours," Slater said.

She nodded with satisfaction.

"We have a request," she continued. "From Paul and Kay Meltzer. Seems that a nearby satellite television company has come up with a new product—a dish that is well camouflaged by serving as a table umbrella as well. They would like us to reconsider article nine, section three, concerning antennas and other metal objects outside the home."

"I read about that," Vincent said. "It doesn't look bad."

"Have you seen one firsthand?" Philip Slater demanded quickly. He turned his gaze on him with a fury that made the investment banker shrink in his seat.

"No, but—"

"Then let's form a committee of two to gather information about it before we make any decision we might later regret," Philip Slater said. "Sid, would you accompany Nikki at your first opportunity?"

"Of course," Sid Levine said.

"Fine. Nikki?"

"That's all I have," she said closing her notepad. "Except to report that the Feinberg home is up for sale. It was advertised yesterday."

"Horrible," Vincent muttered. Philip spun around to face him.

"It's horrible, but we're lucky to be rid of such a negative resident." Philip smiled, his lips stretching so quickly they looked as if they cut new space in his cheeks. "Emerald Lakes has a way of weeding out the rotten apples or," he said, relaxing, "encouraging them to weed themselves out." There was a heavy silence. "Anyone have anything else?" No one spoke. "Well then, I invite a motion to adjourn," he said.

"So moved," Vincent said quickly. He was always the most eager to end the meetings, a fact not lost on Nikki who shook her head with her usual expression of disapproval.

In the living room, Marilyn Slater rose from her

seat and went out to the corridor just as the directors began to emerge from Philip Slater's office.

"Can I make coffee?" she offered. She was an attractive brunette with hazel green eyes and a svelte figure. Always nicely dressed, not a strand of her styled hair out of place, she personified elegance to the rest of the women at Emerald Lakes. Her makeup and jewelry, while striking, was a bit understated, subtle.

Everyone looked at Philip whose face registered disapproval.

"Not for me," Nikki said.

"I've got to get home," Vincent said mournfully.

"Me too," Sid replied.

"Next time, maybe. Good night," Marilyn said. She watched them leave and then turned to Philip. "Productive meeting?"

Philip nodded.

"Yeah, but it's a battle," he said. "Why is it we have to convince people, punish people, so they will do what's only good for themselves?"

"I don't know, Philip," Marilyn said. "But if there's anyone who can get them to do the right things, it's you."

He gazed at her askance for a moment, not quite sure she had meant it as a compliment. Then he shook off the doubts and went to have some coffee.

1

◆

"OH, THIS IS WONDERFUL!" Kristin Morris exclaimed the moment she, Teddy, and their five-year-old daughter, Jennifer, stepped through the front door onto the travertine marble entryway. From there, there were three steps down to the enormous sunken living room. The room was practically as big as their entire apartment in Commack. There was a white marble fireplace against the far wall, not to mention all of the upscale furniture and expensive wall hangings. Teddy tugged on his daughter's hand, and he and she stepped back as if they had inadvertently entered the wrong house.

"This is . . . er . . . this has got to be beyond our budget," he said. Michele Lancaster, their forty-two-year-old real estate agent, smiled, revealing thousands of dollars of orthodontic work. Being fifteen or so pounds overweight, she attempted to hide her midriff bulge by wearing a very loose fitting one-piece with a billowing skirt. She wore a soft white leather jacket and dangling pearl shell earrings. Not a strand of her dark brown hair was out of place. Teddy thought it resembled a helmet.

"It isn't," she said. She leaned toward him to deliver

a secret. "In fact, I'm sure we can get it for a price that will keep the mortgage payments in your budget."

"How can that be?" Teddy asked, looking around again as if his first glimpse had fooled him.

Michele didn't respond. She simply held her smile. Looking over the elaborate artificial flower display in the flower box in front of him, Teddy could see a woman, presumably the present owner's wife, sitting at a breakfast table with her back to them. She was gazing out of the French doors, her attention so concentrated on something amid the gardens and fountains that she didn't hear them enter or even hear their conversation now.

Teddy shifted his blue flecked green eyes toward Kristin. His twenty-nine-year-old wife widened her brown eyes and shrugged. She brushed her light brown hair over her right shoulder in a swift, graceful motion. Although it was a rather warm late-April day, she wore a white cable knit sweater over her dark brown slacks because she felt she looked like she was in her eighth month, instead of her fourth. It did no good for Teddy to swear that no one could tell she was pregnant simply by looking at her.

"I wouldn't have any problem finding a place for my piano in here," Kristin commented.

"No kidding," Teddy said. "You could fit an orchestra in here."

"What's an orchestra, Daddy?" Jennifer asked.

"A whole group of people playing different musical instruments," he explained patiently. He smiled at Michele. "She's up to two hundred and fifty questions an hour."

"Adorable," Michele said smiling and nodding at Jennifer. "And a wonderful place to bring up children," she added widening her eyes.

Kristin looked at Teddy with an I-told-you-so expression. He closed his eyes with a silly grin.

"Right this way," Michele said, and led them down the steps and into the living room. Still reluctant, Teddy closed the dark oak door behind them and shook his head. They had driven nearly three hours from Long Island to this housing development in the Mid-Hudson Valley, and they had to drive the three hours back. There really wasn't all that much time to waste.

"That is a working wood-burning fireplace with a gas starter," Michele explained as she took them over the thick beige Berber carpet. The carpet was so plush, the real estate woman's two-inch heels sank with every step, making her appear to wobble. Teddy thought the ceilings were rather high for a home in the Northeast, where people were more concerned about the cost of heating, but he had to admit he loved the sense of space and openness in this house.

"It's beautiful," Kristin said. "Isn't it, Jennifer?"

"Uh-huh," the five-year-old said and gaped with interest at everything around her.

"Looks like it's never been used," Teddy added. Michele winked and tilted her head toward Elaine Feinberg. She had still not turned their way.

"Elaine, dear," Michele finally said. "The Morrises are here to see the house."

Teddy and Kristin watched curiously as the thirty-year-old brunette turned slowly toward them. Jennifer instinctively drew closer to her father. From this angle they could see that Elaine Feinberg was easily in her last trimester of pregnancy and she was the sort who carried well. There was no puffiness in her face. She wasn't an unattractive woman, but she looked like someone who had been up for days: her eyelids drooped, her lower lip hung listlessly, and the very flesh in her cheeks seemed to sag. She didn't smile. She simply nodded and reached for the cigarette burning in the ashtray. Teddy noted how her hand trembled. Was this a case of someone being terminally ill? Was that the reason for the possible low buying price?

"Would it be all right for me to take them through?" Michele asked softly.

"You know it is," Elaine Feinberg said curtly and shifted her gaze away quickly. Why wasn't she interested in being introduced to them? he wondered. Even more so, why didn't Michele think of doing that?

Kristin, never the shy one, moved forward anyway.

"How many months are you?" she asked.

"I'm ending my seventh," Elaine Feinberg said.

"I'm in my fourth," Kristin replied smiling. She anticipated more conversation, but Elaine Feinberg simply turned to direct her gaze out the French doors again.

Teddy knew his wife, knew it was on the tip of her tongue to ask Elaine Feinberg why she was smoking while she was pregnant. Kristin's second pregnancy had ended in a miscarriage. She had been in a depression for a long period following the miscarriage, which was another reason for the move and their new start.

This time Kristin was having a good pregnancy; it made her even more radiant, and the potential of a new home only sharpened and intensified the brightness in her eyes and the flush in her cheeks.

But her directness had gotten her into trouble before and he anticipated her cross-examination of Mrs. Feinberg. He cleared his throat.

"We really should be moving along," he said quickly.

"Right this way," Michele indicated and took them into the kitchen. Elaine Feinberg continued to sit and stare, smoking very sluggishly, her cheeks collapsing as she drew in the smoke. It was as if she were condemned to move in slow motion, all her movements heavy and full of effort. Jennifer looked back at her with curiosity, the questions titillating her, but Teddy pulled her along before she could start.

"Oh, Teddy, look at this kitchen," Kristin said spinning around like a child in a candy store. She didn't know which appliance to check out first—the Sub-Zero refrigerator and freezer, the digital microwave oven, the double ovens, the built-in Mixmaster, the computerized dishwasher. "Do all these houses come with garbage compactors?" she asked.

"Yes," Michele said. "And the Genaire ranges. Mr. Slater, the developer, insisted that there be no corners cut in his homes. You pay for quality and you get it. Besides, every electrical appliance in this house comes with a built-in ten-year service contract, renewable after ten years. There are no homeowner headaches at Emerald Lakes," she said.

"How old is this house?" Teddy asked. The fireplace and the kitchen appliances looked barely used.

"Less than a year," Michele said, obviously proud to be the real estate agent with this listing.

"Less than a year? But . . ." He turned and gazed at Elaine Feinberg again. Why would she and her husband want to sell so soon? Especially since they were expecting a child in a few months? It must be economic disaster, he thought. Her husband lost his job and they can't make the payments. But to take such a loss . . .

"Let's look at the bedrooms," Kristin cried. "Okay, Jennifer?" Jennifer nodded and Kristin took her hand. Then they started down the corridor. Teddy hesitated a moment, shrugged and followed. Throughout the inspection, he was always a room behind Kristin, Jennifer, and Michele because when he got to the master bedroom and stood looking out the patio doors at the tiled portico and tiled cement swimming pool and whirlpool, he simply stared in disbelief.

This wasn't the first house they had considered. He knew something about the present real estate market. This house had to be . . . what, over four hundred thousand, maybe five. He had been talking two, two-fifty. To buy it at a price that would keep his mortgage payments in the ballpark he had suggested meant they'd get a steal. Unless, of course, this house wasn't worth as much as he thought.

But why wouldn't it be? Look where it was located: an upscale residential gated community of thirty-five homes built around a mile-wide and two-mile-long lake surrounded by a wonderful forest of pine, birch, maple, and hickory. The water, reflecting the greenery, took on a rich shade of lime. When the lake was calm and there was barely a breeze, and when it was the height of spring as it was now, it looked like a sea of emeralds sparkling in the sunlight. All the homes were built on acre-size lots. They were only sixty-odd miles from Manhattan. And the house was easily thirty-five hundred square feet, maybe even four thousand!

"Teddy," Kristin called from down the corridor. He poked his head out and saw her. "Look at your office."

"My office?"

He hurried down to where she and Jennifer stood

and gazed in at a room with built-in oak bookcases, a large oak desk and a leather swivel chair, a matching settee, dark oak tables and a worktable with a fax machine and copier. The office had a bay window that opened on a view of the lake. It was breathtaking.

"Teddy?" Kristin said, her eyes brightening with the inner exhilaration he had come to recognize, an expression of excitement that usually titillated him. Kristin was a very sexy woman with her dark eyes and nearly caramel tinted skin. Being four months pregnant hadn't slowed her down either. She tilted her head slightly and pursed her lips. The quickening of his heartbeat threw him into an embarrassing fluster. He was sure Michele Lancaster could see the flush in his cheeks and could sense the erotic electricity passing between Kristin and himself.

"The monthly payments," he said holding his hand out, palm down and waving it slightly, "they would be in our ballpark?"

"If the board of directors approves you, you'll qualify for a low-cost mortgage loan from the Hudson Valley Bank. Mr. Slater is the president of the board of directors of that bank and Mr. Stanley, who lives two doors down, is the bank president.

"I should explain," she continued, "that part of the reason this house falls into your budget range lies with the fact that the land is lease land."

"Lease land?"

"No resident owns the property on which his house is built, individually owns it, that is. All of the property is owned by the Emerald Lakes homeowners association to which each resident pays a lease rent, built into your homeowner's fee. It's rather nominal rent."

"What an odd setup," Teddy said.

"It's the way Mr. Slater designed the complex. This way everyone really is an owner and everyone has more reason to feel responsible for each other's property."

"It's like a luxury commune."

"Precisely. But it enables you to have a diminished up-front cost. Simply put, Teddy, this house wouldn't cost you a dollar more a month than the figure you gave me on the telephone."

He nodded and looked at Kristin. She was trying desperately to control her exuberance.

"We didn't figure in the extra furniture we would have to buy because we didn't consider buying a house this big," he said. Despite what Michele was telling them, he felt obligated to remind Kristin of every negative.

"Oh, the price we're talking about includes the furniture you see," Michele said.

"What?"

"And the wall hangings, I should add."

Kristin finally looked astounded and skeptical herself.

"These people aren't leaving," Teddy muttered, gazing about at their good fortune, "they're fleeing. Why?" Teddy asked. "What's going on? Has there been a discovery of nuclear waste beneath these homes or something?"

"Hardly," Michele said laughing. "There isn't a more ideal location for a residential community. All sorts of environmental studies were done here before Mr. Slater broke ground. You'll get a copy of everything." Her face turned somber. "Mr. Feinberg committed suicide just a little over a week ago."

"Oh my God," Kristin said.

"What's suicide, Mommy?" Jennifer asked.

"I'll tell you later, sweetheart. Just let Mommy and Daddy talk, okay?"

Reluctantly, Jennifer retreated, but her steely blue eyes revealed her displeasure at being relegated to the back burner.

"How did it happen?" Teddy asked.

"He shot himself."

"Here?" Kristin followed, grimacing.

"Yes. I would have told you. We're required to disclose such things."

"How dreadful," Kristin whispered, so Jennifer wouldn't hear. She gazed toward the kitchen. "Especially with her being pregnant."

"Do they know why? Were there health problems?"

"A combination of things, I gather—money problems, marital problems. Naturally, it's all hush-hush now. Anyway, that's why she's what we call 'a motivated seller.'"

"I feel as if we're taking advantage," Kristin said.

"Don't be silly," Michele said quickly. "If you don't buy this place, someone else surely will. Why shouldn't it be you? And Mrs. Feinberg wants to get out desperately."

"Where did he do it?" Kristin asked.

"The office. You'd never know anything like that happened in there. I mean . . . we took on the responsibility of being sure it was spotless. I assure you, if you weren't told, you'd never know," she added.

"Teddy?" Kristin asked again.

He thought a moment.

"It's not like I'm buying a car someone got killed in or I'm sleeping in a bed someone died in," he rationalized.

"Precisely," Michele said.

"This is such a beautiful house," Kristin said gazing around. "It's such a shame."

"If you walk away from it, someone else will walk into it tomorrow," Michele threatened. Teddy nodded. Despite the tragic circumstances, he felt like he and Kristin had just won the lottery.

"What was this stipulation you mentioned before? Something about being approved by the board of directors?" he asked.

"Yes, but you shouldn't have any problems: an optometrist—"

"Ophthalmologist," Teddy corrected. "I deal with diseases of the eye; I don't prescribe glasses."

"Teddy is very sensitive about that. Most people don't know the difference," Kristin explained.

"Which is considerable. I have a medical degree," he added, trying not to sound superior.

But he couldn't help feeling that being an eye specialist made him a little superior. The ancients believed that the eyes were the gateways to the soul. Ever since he was a child, he had been infatuated with that part of human anatomy. To him the eyes were the most miraculous part of life. It was this holy and devoted respect of the human eye that gave him the energy and excitement in his work and made him stand out as an ophthalmologist. Teachers and other doctors saw it immediately. It had taken a mere twenty-five minutes for the doctors at the medical group in Middletown, a small city just a few miles north, to see the potential in him and offer him a position.

The Mid-Hudson Valley had always been an area both he and Kristin admired, not only because of its proximity to New York City but because of its environmental beauty. They wouldn't be far from her parents, who lived in Yonkers, nor his, who lived in Queens.

"Well, you're even more qualified than I thought," Michele said laughing. "Which is more reason why I wouldn't anticipate any problems. The directors favor professionals. Mr. Slater knows so many people. I'm sure he's familiar with the doctors and medical group you're joining."

"I've never heard of being approved by a board of directors before I could buy a house," Teddy mused. "I know it's done with co-ops, but a single family residence . . ."

"It relates to the special lease land arrangement, and the directors of Emerald Lakes pride themselves on how well managed this development is. Surely, if you have been looking at real estate recently, you can see the difference. It's not just in the state-of-the-art security; it's the maintenance, the upkeep of the common grounds and the homes themselves."

"I've never seen such picture-perfect streets and lawns," Kristin remarked. "And it's so quiet."

"My wife's a composer," Teddy explained.

"Oh, Teddy, don't exaggerate. I dabble on the piano, but I haven't placed any of my pieces yet."

"Anyway, she works at home and appreciates a peaceful neighborhood," Teddy continued.

"Of course," Michele said. "Everyone here does. Oh, some people object to the strict enforcement of the codes at first, but they soon see the value and many of them eventually become champions of the very regulations they first thought too stringent."

"Really?" Teddy nodded at Kristin. "What are some of these regulations?" he asked.

"Nothing more than you will find in other developments; the difference being Emerald Lakes enforces them. You know, rules about where and how to put out your garbage so it doesn't become unsightly, rules against such things as repainting your house bright pink . . ." She laughed. "In short, anything that would hurt the property values of your neighbors and yourself. Most of it is just common courtesy."

"That sounds reasonable," Teddy said.

"Shall we go back to my office then and get out the papers? You won't have any real obligation, just a refundable deposit, which would be returned if you should change your minds within the next week or in the unlikely event you don't get approval from the board."

"What do you think, Teddy?" Kristin shifted her weight from foot to foot like a little girl who had to go tinkle. He smiled and turned to Jennifer.

"What do *you* think, Pumpkin? Would you like to live here in this big house?"

Jennifer narrowed her eyes and pursed her lips as she thought. She gazed up at Michele and then looked at her parents and shook her head.

"What?" Kristin said. "Why not?"

"I wanna go home," she moaned.

"Oh, honey, this could be a wonderful new home for you, with lots more room to play and . . ." She turned to Michele. "There are other children here, aren't there?"

"Of course, and some right around her age, too."

"See? You'll make new friends."

"I wanna go home," she repeated and lunged forward to embrace Teddy's knee. He looked at Michele and smiled.

"She's not usually this shy . . . the prospect of moving . . . it's traumatic even for a child this age."

"Of course."

"Well, I can't imagine us finding anything better than this for the money we've been discussing," he said nodding.

"No," Michele replied. "You won't." She led them out. When they reached the breakfast table, they discovered Mrs. Feinberg was gone. Teddy hesitated.

"Shouldn't we talk to her and let her know of our intention to buy her home?" he asked.

"Mrs. Feinberg hasn't been feeling well these days, with the way her life has been jolted, her being pregnant and all. I'm sure you can appreciate the emotional strain," she said to Kristin, who nodded. "Anyway," Michele added, "Mrs. Feinberg has every expectation that you will buy the house." She followed with a thin laugh. "Can you blame her?"

"I can't help having mixed feelings," Kristin said gazing around again. "It's too good to be true and yet . . . that poor, poor woman."

"Occasionally, Kristin, home buyers do come upon a bargain. You're just lucky you arrived first," Michele said.

"I suppose," Kristin said.

Teddy took her hand while Jennifer clung to his other. Then they followed Michele out.

At the real estate office, they signed all the necessary documents and Teddy wrote out the deposit check. Michele took down all the information she felt was pertinent for the directors of Emerald Lakes.

"The committee will review all this before the interview," Michele said.

"Interview?" Kristin asked. She looked at Teddy who shrugged.

"Oh. Didn't I mention that? The board's new residents committee interviews prospective buyers. They used to rely on a private detective, but found this more palatable. Can I schedule you for this coming Tuesday about ten o'clock? I'd like to move everything along as quickly as possible," she added.

Teddy looked at Kristin.

"I guess that's fine," he said. "Where?"

"Right here in our conference room," she said. "I'll go ahead and set it up."

Kristin and Teddy had plenty of time for the trip back to Long Island and they were able to stop at a nice restaurant for a relaxing dinner. Neither of them could stop talking about their house and the development. Only Jennifer held on to her reluctance. It made Teddy think.

"We really didn't look around enough," he remarked. "We didn't even see the entire complex, the whole lake . . . the dock. I took longer to buy a dehumidifier last year. But we would have been crazy to pass it up."

"I know. Life's funny. Someone's misfortune becomes someone else's good luck."

"What's mis . . . mis?"

"Bad luck, honey," Kristin explained.

"The old yin-yang," Teddy said. He reached across the table to take Kristin's hand. "But if you feel that bad about it . . ."

"I can't help this ambivalence about the house, Teddy. But I'm sure I'll get over it," she said quickly.

"Why do you have to get over it, Mommy?" Jennifer asked.

They laughed.

"Don't forget," Teddy warned. "We still have to pass inspection."

*   *   *

When they returned on the following Tuesday, they couldn't help being nervous.

"It's like we're auditioning," Kristin commented. She had deliberately chosen one of her more conservative dresses. Teddy wore a tie and jacket, and they had bought Jennifer a new outfit. "Don't we look like Mr. and Mrs. Middle-Class America?" she quipped.

"That's who we are, honey," Teddy said smiling. "And I'm not ashamed of it."

Michele greeted them at the office and led them into the conference room where Philip Slater, Nikki Stanley, and Sid Levine waited.

"Morning," Philip Slater said, standing and extending his hand. "I'm Philip Slater and this is Nikki Stanley and Sid Levine, two members of our homeowners board of trustees."

Teddy shook his hand.

"Teddy Morris. My wife, Kristin, and daughter, Jennifer."

Kristin shook Philip Slater's hand. He looked younger than she had envisioned, although he was a man with a strong, hard look that reminded her of chiseled granite. He gazed at her with piercing dark eyes that under different circumstances might very well be attractive. Now they seemed more like lenses specifically for microscopic scrutinizing.

"Please, have a seat Doctor Morris. We appreciate your making the special trip."

"Not at all. We're excited about the house and the development."

"I'm glad. Your prospective new home is one of my favorites. I designed it myself."

"Did you? Good job."

"Thank you. Let me explain our setup here first. We feel it's our unique community government that has made Emerald Lakes the real jewel of upstate New York, maybe of the entire East Coast. We're zealots of a new sort, paying homage to the simplest and yet the most important aspects of development life, everything geared primarily to one thing—maintaining and improving the value of our homes.

"At the risk of sounding preachy," Philip continued, "a home is more than a mere structure consisting of wood, metal, and mortar. It's an environment. How that environment is shaped will determine how the residents are shaped. One acts upon the other." He smiled. "A simple fact of life, yet one so often ignored by other homeowners associations."

Teddy nodded, but Kristin just stared at Slater. He directed himself to her.

"I understand you compose music."

"Oh, I just tinker."

"Did you know that one of our residents, Claude Simmons, is a theatrical agent? He might know where and to whom you should submit your creations."

"Oh, I'm not good enough to—"

"That would be great," Teddy said. "Kristin is far too modest. I'll do the promoting."

"That's a nice quality to see in a woman these days," Philip Slater said. Kristin tipped her head and smiled with a question on her lips. "Modesty," he explained. "Anyway, we just have a few questions for you. Nikki?"

Nikki Stanley gazed at her notepad and then looked up with beady eyes.

"What do you expect from a development like this?" she asked.

"Expect?" Teddy looked at Kristin. "Oh, I suppose good relationships with our neighbors, for one thing.

Sort of a camaraderie," he added. Philip Slater nodded. "And all the other things like security. We've never lived in a gated community before. It does give you a more secure feeling."

"I'm impressed with how well the streets and grounds are kept. It's picture perfect," Kristin said.

"Yes, it is," Philip said proudly.

"You don't mind following rules that keep it that way?" Nikki demanded.

"Of course not. Why should we?" Teddy responded. "I agree with what Mr. Slater said."

"Call me Philip, please. Enough people call me Mr. Slater at work."

"Philip. Real estate values are directly related to what the grounds and surroundings are like."

"Tell us what your experiences with your present home have been like, your neighbors, your community. What annoyed you? What do you want to see continued?" Nikki asked.

Kristin smiled. It was like some sort of an oral exam, an audition.

They talked for nearly an hour. Some of the questions seemed silly, but she didn't, as she was tempted to do at times, belittle them or reply sarcastically. Finally, Philip nodded and rose.

"I think we've heard enough. Just give us a minute, please," he said.

Teddy and Kristin left the room with Jennifer, who had behaved better than they had hoped, partly because she was fascinated with the event herself. Not more than five minutes later, Philip Slater emerged to shake Teddy's hand.

"Welcome to Emerald Lakes," he said. "My committee is in full agreement. You will be a real asset."

Exactly twenty-five days later, after what was a remarkably fast and problem-free escrow period, Teddy and Kristin Morris and their five-year-old daughter moved their clothes and other essential possessions into their new home. The only pieces of furniture they moved was Kristin's piano and Jennifer's bedroom furniture.

When they arrived, they were given a report as to what had been done: the carpets had been steam cleaned, moldings repainted, windows washed, furniture polished, appliances tuned and cleaned, and the bulbs in lamps and outside fixtures replaced with new ones whether they needed them or not. Kristin even discovered relined drawers and cabinets.

"I think they even removed their fingerprints," she quipped.

After they had settled in, Kristin decided they should do their supermarket shopping and see a little of the surrounding area. One of the things they had noted when they had first pulled up to the main entrance of the development was that the security guard at the gate had to open the gate to let them out.

"I don't understand this," Kristin said. "Why worry about people leaving? They had to have checked them on the way in, right?"

"I suppose."

The security guard came out of the booth with his clipboard.

"Hello, Mr. Morris. Going to be gone long?"

"Long as it takes to shop for food," Teddy said smiling.

"Why do you stop cars going out?" Kristin asked.

"Prevent anyone from stealing your car, for one thing. Over at Whispering Pines some teenager breached the security gate and swiped a car just last week. People leave their keys in their vehicles in developments like this."

"But you knew it was us."

"So I will open the gate," he said and stood back. "Have a good day," he added.

Teddy drove out, a shit-eating grin on his face.

"I still don't like it," Kristin said. "It makes it feel a little like a prison."

"Are we in jail, Daddy?" Jennifer asked quickly.

"No, honey," Teddy said. "Mommy's just kidding." He turned to Kristin. "You heard him. In this day and age you can't complain about having too much security," he remarked.

"I suppose, but sometimes it makes you more nervous. I mean, it gets you worrying too much."

"Sometimes worrying is good," Teddy said. "It's like good preventive medicine."

Kristin shrugged. She sat back and concentrated on the scenery.

The roads leading to and from Emerald Lakes were all quite rural in character. There were no streetlights until they reached the business district of nearby Sandburg, a hamlet with a population of just over ten thousand. On the way they passed moderately priced homes, some old farmhouses, and much undeveloped land and uncleared forest. They pointed out the school to Jennifer, a sweet looking, old fashioned red-brick structure with immaculate grounds and a full playground in the rear.

"You're going to love going to school here, honey," Kristin said, and for the first time, Jennifer did seem pleased.

Sandburg's business area wasn't much different in character from its immediate surroundings. There were only two streetlights on the main thoroughfare and there were no parking meters or parking restrictions, other than not parking in front of driveways or hydrants. They found a space in the supermarket parking lot quickly. Inside, they divided the list and parted when Kristin sent Teddy and Jennifer to fetch some bread crumbs while she went after the dairy goods. Just as she made the turn to the refrigerated section, she paused.

At first she thought the woman in the supermarket looked like someone she knew from Commack, but when Kristin saw her face fully, her heart began to pound.

"Excuse me," she said, stepping up to her, "but aren't you Mrs. Feinberg?" Her skepticism stemmed from the fact that this woman was not pregnant.

Elaine Feinberg turned slowly and gazed at Kristin with what Kristin thought were vacant eyes, the eyes of someone suffering amnesia.

"Yes," she said in a voice nearly void of expression, mechanical, uninterested.

Kristin widened her smile.

"I'm Kristin Morris. My husband and I bought your house. I know we met only for a few seconds, but—"

"What do you want?" she demanded firmly, her eyes changing quickly to those of one terrified.

"Nothing, I just . . . wanted to say how sorry I was for what happened to your husband and . . ."

"You're sorry? You don't know how sorry you will be. Unless of course, you become one of them,"she said.

"One of them? Who's them?"

"You'll find out," she replied.

Kristin watched her pluck a package of frozen mixed vegetables out of the freezer and drop it in her cart.

"You've given birth," Kristin said. "What did you have?"

"I had a miscarriage," Elaine Feinberg said. She turned and smiled coldly. "The baby was born dead," she added and pushed past her.

Kristin couldn't move. She was standing in the same spot when Teddy and Jennifer found her. As she told him whom she had met and what was said, the cold air from the refrigerator case chilled her. Jennifer gazed up with a look of dismay.

"How can a baby be born dead, Daddy?" she asked.

"You remember, honey. It happens sometimes. It happened to Mommy," he said quickly, avoiding Kristin's eyes. They always tried to avoid discussing her miscarriage, which Jennifer was too young at the time to realize.

"Will Mommy's new baby be born dead again?" Jennifer asked. Kristin flashed a look of panic at him.

"No, honey. The baby is fine. We had it checked just recently. Don't worry."

"Didn't that lady have her baby checked?"

"Jennifer . . ."

"Let's finish up our shopping and get going," he said, and Kristin nodded.

"She was so cold, speaking to me like someone in a trance, Teddy, warning me I'd become one of them. One of what?"

"Don't think about it. The miscarriage must have been caused by the emotional aftermath of what happened to her husband," he said.

"That poor woman." Kristin shuddered and embraced herself. "Now I'm very glad they cleaned and polished our home so thoroughly," she said. "It would give me the creeps to be reminded that my new house was once occupied by a suicide victim and by a woman who suffered a miscarriage," she added pointedly.

"Was there a dead baby in our new house, Mommy?" Jennifer asked.

"What? Oh no, honey. Damn," she muttered. "That woman surprised and shocked me. I didn't think. I shouldn't have said anything in front of Jennifer. Now she'll have nightmares."

"Come on, honey," Teddy said, taking Jennifer's hand. "Help me get the cereals."

Kristin thought for a moment and then hurried after them.

She wanted to tell Teddy more; she wanted to tell him how the woman, Mrs. Feinberg, had accusation in her eyes when she spoke. But she knew what Teddy would say—she was exaggerating, imagining, reading more into someone's gaze than was actually there.

Perhaps Teddy was right, she thought. After all, of course it was ridiculous. How could she and Teddy be in any way to blame for her husband's death and her subsequent miscarriage? All they had done was come along and offer to buy her home.

2

◇

MARILYN SLATER SAT IN THE light cherry wood rocker and gazed out the living-room window. From this corner of the room, she could look down Slater Court to the corner of Courtney Street and see the house in which the Feinbergs had lived. She saw the new family move in, their comings and goings, passing like transition scenes in some soap opera. In a real sense, the activities of the residents of Emerald Lakes had become her entertainment and her windows had become her television screens. She couldn't even say how many hours she spent gazing out of them. Sometimes she felt as if she were in a big bubble smack down in the middle of the development. She ventured out so rarely these days, she might as well be confined to a germ-free environment.

In her right hand she held her glass of water spiked with Absolut vodka. Philip rarely drank so he had no idea how much alcohol they had and how much she drank. Marilyn disguised her breath with mints and gum and made sure to wash her glasses thoroughly. It didn't surprise her that Philip knew so little about what she did now. He seldom asked her about her day, just assuming she filled it with care of the house, shopping for their needs, reading, watching television, visiting with the few friends she had outside of the development.

The truth was she had lost contact with nearly all but one, Ann Cassil, and only because Ann was as lonely as she was most of the time. Ann called herself a sports widow. Her husband was either golfing, skiing, or watching football games with his friends.

"I don't know what drew us to each other," she revealed to Marilyn during one recent phone conversation. "We don't even like to eat the same things. How," she wondered rhetorically, "does something like this happen?"

Indeed, Marilyn thought as she rocked, how does it happen? She tried to recall her own romance, tried to understand what it was about herself as a young woman in her twenties that made her vulnerable and easy prey for Philip, for that was the way she thought of herself now, easy prey.

He was—and still is—a man of great strength, she thought. Perhaps her coming from a family in which the man of the household was weak caused her to be attracted to Philip's strength. She saw how her mother had suffered because of her father's frailties. Her father was easily intimidated by other men, was anything but aggressive in the workplace and often was passed over for promotions by younger, more vigorous men. He was the sort who would just shrug and accept it if he were overcharged or given a defective product. Her mother had to fight all the battles and it aged her and wore her down until she withered away prematurely in her early sixties and succumbed to heart disease. Ironically, Dad was still alive and in a home, the cost for which Philip paid.

Philip was generous when it came to worldly things

and he loved to be in charge, the one responsible, the one who looked after everyone. He never stopped her from buying anything. Actually, he was always after her to buy herself more, insisting that she keep up with the styles and look wealthier than anyone else in the development. After all, she was Mrs. Philip Slater, wasn't she? That required looking and acting a certain, expected way.

That went for the house as well as for her. Philip encouraged her to shop for art, to update the furnishings, to change the drapes and shades, to redo rooms. He insisted she make the house her career, and she had.

She had gone to college and had graduated with a major in English, but she had no intention of being a teacher or a writer. Philip, who was two years older, had started to date her when she was a sophomore. She had many opportunities to go out with other men, but Philip was overwhelming in those days, not that he wasn't as overwhelming now. It was just . . . different.

It was almost as if he had become another person, or the person she fell in love with had either slipped away or been drawn down into him and buried somewhere under this darker, colder, sterner man. But maybe he wasn't all that different. Maybe she deliberately had overlooked and ignored this part of him. Maybe she had dreamed she would change him instead of him changing her. She had been too immature to realize or care back then and now it was too late.

It was too late because she had more of her father than her mother in her. Direct confrontation was difficult if not impossible for her. Just the thought of getting into arguments with Philip made her tremble and gave her an upset stomach. Of course, all this was worse since Bradley's death. Whatever fragility she possessed before, intensified. She would cry at the slightest provocation.

The fact was, she was comfortable with Philip's domination and control. There wasn't a problem, no matter how small, that he wouldn't assume and solve. Could he be protecting her? Was it because he saw what she had become and he wanted to spare her any more pain? She liked to think so, although the affection between them had run down until there was barely a perfunctory kiss on the cheek, a stroke of her hair, a quick embrace at the door. The flow of her love life, whatever there had been of one, was down to a drip . . . drip . . . drip.

Philip Slater, however, was not the sort of man who admitted to mistakes, whether they occurred in business or with people, especially with people. He prided himself on his perception when it came to people. He loved to play the development game, as he called it. When he was in an amusing mood in the evening, he would sit by this window, too, and look out at the streets of Emerald Lakes. Then he would begin. He would go through each and every man and woman residing here, detailing their personality, what they would do and not do. Sometimes to amuse himself, or maybe because he thought it might amuse her, he would imagine different wives with different husbands, predicting what the relationship would be, who would dominate, how they would speak to each other, even how they would make love.

"Now you take Nikki Stanley," he would say. "She would most assuredly always assume the top position if she were married to Vincent McShane. Don't you think?"

She would say nothing, but that didn't matter to Philip. He heard what he expected, what he wanted to hear, and just continued as if she had spoken.

At times she wondered if she were really here. Maybe she was a ghost. Maybe she had died with Bradley. Philip often looked at her as if he were looking through her, thinking about something else, and if she did tell him something new, he would either have already learned about it or act as if he hadn't heard her speak. Unless it was something about his precious Emerald Lakes, of course. That would perk him up and get her his strict attention.

Emerald Lakes had become his life. It was his church, his school, his world. He lost his only child so he made everyone here his children, even if he or she were older than he was. Philip had to have someone to look after and she wasn't enough for him. She was too easy.

Maybe I am dead, she thought. Maybe this is hell. She gulped her drink and wiped her mouth with the back of her hand roughly. Philip would have a hemorrhage if he saw her do anything that wasn't dainty or ladylike. But seriously, she wondered—how do you really know if you're alive? How do you really know where you are?

She thought for a moment as she gazed at the Feinberg house. Marilyn had watched that new family and she had seen their excitement. Her attention was focused on the little girl. Bradley was about that age when he died. Or was he younger? What was happening to her mind? How could she forget even the slightest detail about her own child, much less his age? She had trouble remembering his face now. What mother had trouble remembering her child's face?

She rose slowly and put the glass down on the coaster on the marble table. Then she went to the basement door, opened it and flicked on the light before descending the wooden steps.

The basement was finished in a light pine. They had a pool table and a beautiful white marble bar, but it was never used. Philip and she didn't entertain, and especially never invited any of the residents of Emerald Lakes to a social occasion. It was as if Philip saw them and his life here as all business and he didn't want to mix business with pleasure.

At the back of the basement was a storage room with everything in it organized neatly on shelves and in boxes. It, too, had a tightly woven grayish white Berber rug. She flicked on the storage-room light and squatted beside a carton at the rear of the room, just under the bottom shelf and began to dig through the carton until she found an album buried under a pile of Philip's old work shirts. Sitting back on her haunches, she opened the album and began to look at the photographs that had captured the stages of development of their little boy.

He had such a troubled face, she thought, even at the age of two or three. She turned the pages lethargically, the tears starting again. Her little boy, her baby . . . it was Philip's fault that she had trouble remembering. He never liked to talk about Bradley. It was better to pretend he had never existed, none of it had ever happened.

But there were the pictures of her and her child on the lawn or in the back by the swings Philip had long since removed. There were pictures from birthday parties and the pictures from their vacations. Bradley looked so fragile in all these pictures, small for his age and underdeveloped because of the illness. Philip used to hate her to tell people what their child's actual age was. He was ashamed of the child's illness. It was a detraction from his strong, successful image. How could he be the father of such a sickly little boy?

She slammed the photograph album closed and buried it again in the carton. Got to keep it hidden like this, she thought, or Philip will get angry. He'll say I'm doting on the tragedy and therefore making it last longer.

But when does a tragedy like this end? she wondered. She got to her feet and walked up the stairway, flicking off the lights behind her and moving slowly, like one in a daze, toward the bedroom. She sat on Philip's side of the bed, just staring down at the floor. After a moment she reached over and opened the nightstand drawer. When she felt the metal, she wrapped her hand around it and brought it out slowly. Then she gazed down at the pistol in her lap.

A bullet would come from the barrel of this gun to tear into my flesh and drive my soul out of my body and into whatever oblivion awaits us all, she thought. This was the ticket, the vehicle of passage, this was the key that unlocked the door of darkness.

There were bullets in it. She knew that. She lifted the gun and placed the barrel against her left temple. Marilyn had done this before and she had counted as high as seven, the point being that when she reached ten, she would pull the trigger. One, she began. This time she reached eight before her hand began to shake and the tremors traveled through her body into her feet. Weakened by them, she barely had enough strength to put the pistol back and close the drawer.

Then she stood up, took a deep breath and returned to the chair by the window. She sipped her drink and stared out again, waiting, watching, wondering: Am I alive? Where am I? Is this hell?

An hour later after she had washed her glass thoroughly and started to prepare their dinner, she had forgotten she had made a visit to the basement. Philip was right. It was better to block it out.

Philip Slater cradled the receiver of his office telephone and sat back to read the cost analysis for the new house he wanted to construct on lot thirty-eight in Emerald Lakes. Erik Richard, his architect, had come up with a design that was more original than anything yet constructed in the development. It departed considerably from the traditional ranch, employing characteristics of Greek revival: a gabled, low-pitched roof, a full-width porch supported by prominent rounded Doric columns; but the most dramatic departure from the other homes was the fact that this would be a two-story home. To build it, he would have to get his homeowners committee to approve a variance on the height restriction. Because of its location on the lake, however, it wouldn't block anyone's view, and he had been toying with the idea of selling his own house and moving into this. He deserved it, deserved to stand out and above the others. Besides, his present home was cluttered with too many painful memories. Marilyn needed another start, a fresh view. It would do both of them a world of good.

Of course, he would have no trouble getting the committee to agree. It was just that later on someone else might ask for a similar variance and he would have to find a reason to deny it. He would be accused of being treated specially, but what of it, he should be treated specially. This development and just about everything in it was his baby. Whatever pleasure and security these residents enjoyed, they enjoyed because of him.

The buzzer sounded and he tapped his intercom button. Philip didn't have a plush office in his construction company. It was spartan, a workplace and not a showplace. He had a handsome enough dark oak desk and an orthopedically designed desk chair. There were bookcases, primarily for the building codes, books on house design and books on construction practices and materials.

Directly behind him and above the desk was a portrait of his father, John Thomas Slater, from whom Philip had inherited his sharply chiseled features and his black onyx eyes. It was his mother from whom he had inherited his competitive drive, his ambition and determination, but all the pictures he had of her were small. She always let his father believe he was the head of the household, the power and authority, even though it was she who came up with the strategies that made them wealthy. It was actually his mother who had given Philip the idea to develop a picturesque, secure community around Emerald Lake. Too bad she never lived to see the dream become a reality.

To the right of the desk was a drafting table upon which was a scaled model of Emerald Lakes. Sometimes Philip would stand over it and gaze down on the miniature homes, feeling like a god, gigantic. He was filled with a sense of power and control. Anytime he wanted, he could add a street here, change a street there, extend a fence, build a wall, turn lights on and off, plant grass on the common grounds or change the landscaping. Across his office on the far wall was a large aerial photograph of

Emerald Lakes—the development, the lake, and the surrounding roads—which reinforced this deific feeling.

Aside from that photo, some architectural plans on the cork board, and a few plaques he had been given by community organizations for his contributions and achievements, the walls were bare. Across from his desk were two nail-head brown leather chairs and a brown leather settee. There were no ashtrays. Philip forbid smoking in his presence.

He leaned forward to speak into the intercom.

"Yes, Lorraine?"

"Mrs. Del Marco is here to see you. She says it's urgent."

"Send her right in," he said and put his documents down only a moment before Angela Del Marco thrust open his office door and marched in, her sharp, high heels clicking over the hardwood floor. The tall, dark-haired woman fixed her furious eyes on him. Her lips were pressed so firmly together, the corners of her mouth whitened. She was a bit taller than Marilyn, but stouter and far less graceful. Right now she looked like she might lunge over the desk at him and tackle him like a football defensive end.

"What can I do for you, Angela?" he asked, twisting his lips into a tight smile.

"You can do something about this," she said and thrust the citation at him. It floated quickly down on his desk. Although he knew what it was, he picked it up and read it.

"Actually," he said, sitting back, "you're the only one who can do anything about it now. Make out a check and get it over with." He put the citation down as close to the edge of the desk as he could.

"This is ridiculous. Who does Nikki Stanley think she is sending me a . . . a fine?"

"It's legal and correct, Angela, and it isn't Nikki Stanley; it's the Neighborhood Watch committee after a unanimous decision, I might add."

"But—"

"As I understand it, and correct me if I'm wrong, Nikki did attempt to settle this with you beforehand."

"And I told her my children have a right to play at their own home."

"Of course they do, Angela, but that's not the issue, is it? Just imagine for a moment, if everyone in the development dangled old cans and baskets from their house roofs. You've ridden along some of these country roads where the zoning laws are so loose people can do almost anything they want. You've seen the houses with broken-down automobiles on their front lawns, houses with cheap signs advertising some home business, houses with mangy lawns, rusted swings, and you know what it's like for people who have nice homes nearby. Their real estate values go in the sewer and their equity and life savings along with it."

"But all we're doing—"

"Is hanging a basket off a roof, I know. But a flood starts with a little leak, doesn't it, and then the leak grows bigger and bigger until what do you have?" he asked in a reasonable tone of voice.

"Now," he continued, pulling out his lower right desk drawer and reaching in to bring out a Xeroxed pamphlet. "If you go back into your Emerald Lakes suggested yard items, you will note that we included a basketball pole and net. It's on page four and there are even stores suggested."

"Steve was the one who suggested the homemade hoop to the boys. He said when he was growing up, that's what he and his friends had, and we thought it was good that the boys learned to make do with things and not have us buy them expensive toys and equipment all the time. Steve says—"

"That was fine for Steve when he was growing up in an urban neighborhood, but Steve's a man of some stature in the community now and you live in the most desirable development in the area, if not in the whole state. It's different," Philip said firmly. "Frankly, I was disappointed to hear Nikki tell me about your attitude. We're only trying to ensure that your home, as well as our homes, maintains its value. The people in Emerald Lakes, including your family, have a great deal of their financial well-being invested in their houses."

Angela relaxed her shoulders and picked up the citation.

"The fine's not going to break us, but I resent it," she insisted.

"Fines are the only way to urge people to do what's best for themselves as well as for the rest of us. Unfortunately," he added.

"I still resent it," she said. "Nikki Stanley enjoys doing this."

"Enjoys it?" Philip shook his head. "Angela, don't you think Nikki resented your attitude? She's not being paid to serve on the Neighborhood Watch committee. She and the others volunteer their time, time they could devote to their own families and their own self-interests."

"I thought you said it was in all our self-interests to live up to the Covenants, Conditions, and Restrictions," Angela snapped. Philip felt himself redden.

"It is, but it still takes some sacrifice to devote the time and the energy for the good of us all," he said. "Besides," he concluded, sitting back again, "if you have any disagreements with the committee's finding, you can attend the next meeting of the trustees and appeal the decision."

"It's the same group of people!" she exclaimed, holding out her hands. Philip was silent. "And besides, Philip, you know as well as everyone else in the development that what you decide is what the committee decides."

Philip's eyes widened with indignation.

"That's not true. Everyone on my committee has a mind of his or her own and—"

"Everyone on YOUR committee." Angela stuffed the citation into her purse. "I'll send in the money. I wouldn't want to cause any more major trouble and upset *your* committee. Thanks for your help," she said and spun around. He watched her leave, closing the door hard behind her.

He wasn't as angry with her as he was with himself. Philip had misjudged the Del Marcos and this was his second mistake. He never counted the Ricks as a mistake because they had built and bought before the formation of the homeowners association and the Neighborhood Watch. Once he realized what they were going to be like, he simply bought them out. He had to give them a handsome profit, but in the long run, the investment was worth it. But the Feinbergs and now the Del Marcos, they were different. They were permitted to become members of Emerald Lakes homeowners association.

Actually, he shouldn't be so hard on himself, he thought. The Feinbergs and the Del Marcos were residents before he and the committee had established the new preview procedures. They learned too late about Sol Feinberg and now he was learning too late about Steve Del Marco. He thought the man was more dominant in his household and Angela was a team player. Why did Steve permit his wife to come here to argue with him? The fact that Steve didn't call to complain or come with his wife proved that his heart wasn't in rebellion and defiance.

Steve Del Marco was one of the more successful insurance agents in the area. Philip had directed a great deal of business his way. He didn't expect anything for it. It was important to him that his residents be financially successful. But as an insurance man, Steve should realize how important maintaining the value of property was.

Of course, Philip couldn't move in with these people to see what their home lives were really like, but he could see now that he couldn't make any logical conclusions. People didn't act logically or reasonably, even if the outcome would benefit them. That's why they needed the best CC and R's and why they needed all the preview procedures. It was important to know as much about the prospective residents as possible, and in this, the day and age of computer tracking, he would send out his detective to penetrate the walls of privacy as much as possible.

Actually, Philip admitted to himself, he was furious. Who did she think she was barging in on him like that and then slamming the door on the way out? And all that sarcasm . . . why did he have to endure it? Spoiled, selfish, immature behavior, that's what it was. And damn if he would tolerate it.

He reached for the Emerald Lakes directory, which was always just to his right on his desk, and looked up Steve Del Marco's work number. He poked out the combination quickly and leaned back in his chair.

"Steve Del Marco, please," he said when the receptionist answered. "Tell him Philip Slater." He drummed the arm of his chair with his fingers, his gaze focusing on the tiny spot in the aerial photograph that he knew to be the Del Marcos' residence. "Steve. Sorry to bother you at work, but I was just interrupted myself, and by your wife."

"Oh," Steve Del Marco said, his voice quickly losing whatever light tone it had. "I'm sorry. She threatened to do that this morning, but I thought I had talked her out of it. I'm sorry, Philip."

"There's a time and a place for these things," Philip said sternly, not satisfied with the repentance. "I'm the president of our homeowners association, but that's not my full-time job. I have a company to run."

"I know. I'm sorry. I'll speak to her."

"I wish you would and I wish you would talk to her about her attitude. We're all in this together, Steve."

"Understood."

"What's good for one is good for everyone at Emerald Lakes, and what's good for everyone is good for one. It's always been that way and it always will be. No one's out to discriminate against an individual resident."

"I know. I'm sorry, Philip."

"We're always trying to help each other," Philip continued. He knew that sometimes he sounded like an evangelist, preaching to his residents, but from time to time, they needed a little preaching.

"You're right. She was overreacting. She's been a little on edge lately. Her younger brother's getting a divorce. He's got three children, all under ten, and—"

"I'm sorry to hear that, but my committee is not anyone's whipping boy."

"Of course not."

"Cooperation, that's the key word at Emerald

Lakes. I wish you would have a little discussion with Angela about it," he insisted.

"I will."

Philip felt his anger recede, and as always when he had a compliant resident who offered no resistance, no arguments after a dressing down, he began to feel a bit generous, as generous as a father who had driven his lesson home and now wanted his child to love him again.

"I'm sending someone over to see you later today," he said. "Bob Morrison. He's managing a small printing company in Wurtsboro and I think he's paying too much for employee health insurance. I told him you were the man to see."

"Thank you, Philip. I appreciate the referral. I'll be happy to help him. I'm really sorry about Angela. It won't happen again."

"Good. I like Angela, and Marilyn always says nice things about her, too. It bothers me whenever we have any dissension at Emerald Lakes, especially since the ugly business with Sol Feinberg," Philip said. Steve was silent. "Well, I don't want to take up any more of your time or any more of my own with this."

"I understand," Steve said. "Thanks again."

Philip cradled the phone and clasped his hands as he put his elbows on the desk. He lowered his chin to his knuckles and stared at the aerial photograph. Viewing it from the air, the way the property was delineated, it took on the shape of a head, a shape similar to his own, he thought. Was that just accidental or was it some divine sign?

He shifted his eyes slowly to the space on the wall where his little boy's picture had once hung. He stared at it, blinking rapidly. Marilyn didn't want to try to have another child. She harbored a fear that he or she would be taken, too. Or was that his fear?

If there was only a way to build a wall so high nothing evil could enter Emerald Lakes, no disease as well as no criminal element.

Damn that Angela Del Marco. Why couldn't she see what he wanted for all of them: a wall, protection, a sense of security which meant that they could harvest happiness in their homes? Philip wasn't confident about her husband bringing the message home and getting her with the program. He would need help. But that was all right. Help was at hand.

He lifted the receiver and tapped out a number.

"Hello, Philip," Nikki said. He smiled, knowing she had one of those identification devices so she could see who was calling before she picked up the receiver. She didn't let the phone ring twice when she realized it was him.

"Nikki, Angela Del Marco just left my office, upset with the citation."

"That doesn't surprise me," Nikki said.

"Well, it does me," he said sharply. "It always surprises and disappoints me when one of our own residents is uncooperative."

"I understand, Philip. It upsets me, too," she admitted once she saw his gist.

"I want the Del Marcos to know how lucky they are to have a Neighborhood Watch committee looking after their interests as well as everyone else's."

"Of course, Philip."

"And the best way to drive that home is to scrutinize them even more closely for a while so they understand completely where they are."

"All right. I'll speak with the others and have everyone give them a second and third look from time to time. I know their backyard fence is overdue for a whitewash."

"See that they know that and give them a deadline. We can be lenient only with those who appreciate leniency and respect our codes and property values."

"I will, Philip."

"Thank you, Nikki. Thank you for your time and effort. I do appreciate it, even though some might not."

He could almost hear her beaming with pride.

"Thank you," she said.

"I'll speak to you later about this matter and a few others."

"Fine," she said and hung up.

Philip cradled the receiver. He felt no guilt, no remorse. He had to do what he had to do for the good of the development. It came with the responsibility, the burden of leadership. They should be grateful they had a man like him. Most of them were. He took a deep breath, a breath of pride, and, after a moment more of thought, returned to his cost analysis for the building on lot thirty-eight.

3

"WHAT'S THIS?" Teddy said as they pulled up to their driveway.

Nikki Stanley and a vibrant redhead who wore her hair in a neat pageboy sat on Teddy and Kristin's front steps chatting nonchalantly. The redhead had skin as clear and white as fresh milk, spotted on the tops of her cheeks with tiny orange freckles. Her lips had that same bright orange tint that made wearing lipstick unnecessary. When they both stood up, Nikki Stanley appeared almost childlike in height and size beside her companion. Teddy pressed the remote to open the garage door but stopped on the driveway.

The two women started toward them. Nikki wore a far more serious expression, her eyes small and intent. The redhead was long legged with slim shoulders and a full bosom that announced itself proudly against her white cotton three-quarter-length-sleeve sweater. Nikki wore an ankle-length peasant skirt, dark blue blouse, and blue cardigan sweater.

"Hello," Nikki Stanley said as Teddy, Kristin, and Jennifer emerged from their brown Skylark. The two-year-old moderately priced vehicle and Kristin's Ford Escort seemed out of place in the large two-car garage attached to this expensive home. Teddy's earlier quick perusal of the vehicles in front or in the garages of the other homes revealed Mercedes, Cadillacs, and a Lexus. He had also spotted a Jag.

"Hi," Kristin said. Jennifer, as always, drew as close as possible to her parents when confronting strangers. She fixed her eyes on the two women and held Kristin's hand.

"This is Jeannette Levine," Nikki Stanley said. "She lives right across the street."

"Everyone simply calls me Jean. We're here to welcome you to Emerald Lakes." She had a warm smile and soft blue eyes. Nikki flashed a perfunctory smile.

"Pleased to meet you," Kristin said shaking her hand. Teddy extended his.

"I'm Teddy Morris. This is my wife, Kristin, and our daughter, Jennifer," Teddy said.

Kristin pulled Jennifer in front of her and rested her hands on Jennifer's shoulders.

"Hi, Jennifer," Jeannette said. "How old are you?"

"Five," Jennifer replied.

"Five? That's wonderful. Terri Sue is six. She finally has a friend close to her age. Her nine-year-old brother, George, is getting a bit too rough for her," Jean said, smiling at Kristin and Teddy.

"You hear that, honey? You'll have a new friend," Kristin said. Jennifer drew back, still eyeing Nikki Stanley suspiciously.

Teddy opened the car trunk. "First thing you do when you move into a new home is go to the supermarket," he said. Nikki's eyes went to their car.

"Let us help you with your groceries," she offered.

"Oh, that's very kind of you," Kristin said. "But—"

"It's all right. We don't mind," Nikki said anticipating Kristin's response.

"Thanks," Kristin said shrugging. The women gathered around the car trunk and Teddy began taking out the bags.

"Me too, Daddy," Jennifer said, holding out her arms. He chose the smallest and lightest bag and placed it in her hands. She clung to it proudly and started toward the open garage.

"You shouldn't be lifting one that heavy," Nikki said, practically seizing the bag Kristin had started to accept.

"Oh, nothing's that heavy," Kristin said, surprised her neighbor had spotted her pregnancy so quickly. The women took two bags a piece and followed Teddy through the side door from the garage into the kitchen. They placed the bags on the counter.

"I'll get the rest," Teddy said. "Thanks."

"I'll help you, Daddy," Jennifer cried and raced out behind him.

"It's so convenient to shop here," Kristin began. "Just a few minutes away, no problems parking, no lines at the checkout counter . . ."

"Yes," Jean said, "and Farmer's, a small market in Sandburg, will even deliver if you can't get to the store yourself."

"Oh?"

"But they charge considerably more for everything," Nikki added, her lips twisting with obvious disapproval. Without instruction, she began unloading the bags of groceries. She went directly to the cabinet in the right corner and began putting away the staples. Kristin stepped back and smiled quizzically. How did she know I wanted them there? she wondered. When Nikki turned to get some more, she saw the look on Kristin's face.

"Oh, I'm sorry," she said. "I just assumed you wanted them in here."

"Well, I suppose that's fine," Kristin said.

"It's where Elaine kept her staple items," Jean explained.

"Oh?"

"It's where they belong anyway," Nikki said. "You should keep your cold cereals in here. This cabinet is perfect for the jar goods," she continued as if she were selling the house. "You can display a lot and they're easy to reach."

"That's where we keep ours," Jean added.

"You mean you have the same kitchen cabinets, the same design?" Kristin asked.

"Practically. My home is the one across the street and to the right," Jean said. "Nikki lives two houses up."

"They're both beautiful houses," Kristin said.

"Thank you," Nikki said. "Actually, all the homes in Emerald Lakes are exceptional," she added as if it were a crime to lord your house over another in the development.

"Here's all of it," Teddy announced, struggling to get the last three bags on the counter. Jean rushed forward to grab the middle one. "Thanks. I feel like a contortionist," he said, moving his hip against the counter. He placed the bags carefully and looked at Kristin, discerning a strange expression on her face. "Everything all right?" he asked instinctively.

"Fine," she said. "Nikki and Jean were just showing me exactly where to put everything."

"Oh?"

"An organized kitchen makes it all so much easier," Nikki said. "These houses were all designed to be as efficient as possible when it comes to domestic chores. If you employ a cleaning girl, even on a part-time basis, you'll want to hire one from the Marsh

Agency. They're all pretty well schooled in how our homes are organized—where the vacuums and cleaning materials are kept, where to put the bath towels for the guest rooms, how to organize your dishes, pans, and pottery . . ."

"You mean everyone does it all the same way?" Teddy asked, smiling.

"Essentially. As I said, it's the way the homes were designed," Nikki replied.

"Some diversity on the outside, but conformity on the inside," Jean Levine recited as if it were the motto of Emerald Lakes.

"Um, interesting," Teddy said, folding his arms and leaning against the counter. "So, how long have you guys been here?"

"Nikki was here at the very beginning. What's that, about five years, Nikki?"

"Five years and seven months this May 5th."

"Sid and I moved in four years ago. Nikki's on the board of directors," Jean added.

"They know that already, Jean," Nikki snapped. Teddy considered the diminutive woman. He hadn't really looked at her closely at the interview, directing himself more to Philip Slater. She had a firmness which made her size deceptive, and her eyes had that no-nonsense look.

"Oh," he repeated, the name sinking in. "You're Bill Stanley's wife? The banker?"

"Around here, Bill's known as Nikki's husband," Jean quipped. Nikki shot her a look of displeasure, but Jean only laughed. "My husband's a broker with Gantz and Gantz on Wall Street," Jean said.

"How long is his commute?" Kristin asked.

"About an hour and ten, which isn't bad when you consider what he comes home to," she added. Teddy raised his eyebrows and smiled. "Oh, I didn't mean . . ." She looked again at Nikki who smirked with clear disapproval. "I meant our home, this beautiful development, the lake . . ."

"Of course," Teddy said. "But I'm sure he looks forward to all of it," he added with an impish grin. Jean's cream complexion tinted crimson.

"Teddy, you're embarrassing her," Kristin chastised. "You know she didn't mean that."

"Jean often has trouble saying what she means," Nikki commented, her eyes fixed on the tall redhead, who giggled nervously again.

"Do you have any children, Nikki?" Kristin asked.

"Bill and I have an eight-year-old son, Graham, and a ten-year-old daughter, Heather," she said quickly.

"I love those names. That's what we've got to start doing," Kristin said turning to Teddy, "going through that book of names again."

"Do you know what you're having?" Nikki asked.

"No. We didn't opt for that. Surprise is still important," Teddy said. "Of course, Jennifer would like a little brother, right, Peanut?"

She nodded.

"And what name would you like him to have if your mother does have a boy?" Jean asked her.

Jennifer shrugged and then said, "Kermit."

"Kermit?"

Jennifer looked up at Kristin to see if she had said something wrong.

"Like the frog," Kristin added for her.

"Oh. Ooooo, of course. Kermit." Jean stopped smiling. "You wouldn't . . ." She shook her head.

"No," Kristin said laughing. "We're going to do the research and come up with something we both like."

"We'd be glad to help," Jean said. "Everyone loves poking his or her nose into everyone else's business here."

"Jean makes it sound as if we're all a bunch of gossips. We're just eager to help each other. The residents of Emerald Lakes are like an extended family."

"Yes, we're a kibbutz," Jean joked. Teddy laughed. He liked her and enjoyed the way she obviously annoyed her more sober friend from time to time.

"We had better put the perishables away," Nikki reminded them, and plucked the quart of low-fat milk from the bag.

"Right," Kristin said digging in.

"Oh, you bought Grain Flakes," Jean said holding up the box. "Isn't that funny? We're all buying that these days."

"It's got the best fiber content and nutrition," Nikki said with a tone of approval.

"Yes. Eileen found it first, didn't she?" Jean asked.

"No, I did," Nikki claimed.

"Are you sure? I recall her list had it underlined."

"Because I told her about it," Nikki insisted. Jean nodded but she still looked skeptical. "You can ask her yourself," Nikki snapped.

Jean smiled at the surprised Morrises, who stood back watching and listening to them argue about who should get credit for discovering a good cold cereal.

"We often share our grocery list, pointing out bargains and better products," she explained.

"That's very nice," Teddy said quickly.

"How do you do that?" Kristin asked. Teddy raised his eyes. He could hear the underlying tone of ridicule in her voice. These Stepford Wives were about to confront Mrs. Ralph Waldo Emerson. It was on her lips: "Conformity is the hobgoblin of little minds."

"We call each other, tell each other, often go shopping together when we can," Jean said.

"And the Neighborhood Watch committee puts out a monthly newsletter filled with valuable information like that," Nikki added.

"I see," Kristin said shifting her gaze to Teddy. He pretended to be interested in a cabinet door.

"This brand of cranberry juice has too much corn syrup in it," Nikki announced.

"It's my favorite," Kristin said smiling. "Actually, I have a weakness for corn syrup."

"You've got to watch your diet now that you're pregnant," Jean warned.

"You see, Teddy Morris, I do show," Kristin joked.

"Oh, you don't show at all," Jean remarked. "One would never know."

"You did."

"Well, I read your application," Jean revealed. Teddy looked up.

"Oh?"

"But we didn't put down my pregnancy on our application," Kristin remarked. "Why would we?"

"That's right," Teddy said turning to Nikki. They gazed at each other.

"I don't recall saying anything about it at the interview either," Kristin added.

"Well, we must have heard from . . . from the real estate agent. It's standard procedure," Nikki explained. "All of the residents of Emerald Lakes are required to learn as much as they can about a new resident."

"Required?" Kristin said.

"Not exactly required, encouraged," Nikki corrected.

"Well, that puts us at a disadvantage then," Teddy said.

"Pardon?" Nikki's eyes blinked rapidly. She's not the kind who likes being confused or likes lacking understanding, Teddy thought. Very competitive.

"We don't know very much about you," he said.

"You will," she predicted "Jean?"

"Oh dear, I left it outside on the front stoop!" Jean Levine cried and hurried through the house and out the front door.

"Jean can be so scatterbrained sometimes," Nikki said.

"What's scatterbrained, Mommy?" Jennifer asked.

"Not now, honey."

"She has little notes pasted all over her house to remind her to do the most basic things," Nikki continued. "I swear, if Nature didn't insist, she would forget to go to the bathroom."

Teddy laughed.

"How can she forget to go to the bathroom?" Jennifer said.

"What did she leave out there?" Kristin asked, giving her daughter a reprimanding look simultaneously.

Instead of replying, Nikki turned to watch Jean rush back inside. She held a leather bound, thick file.

"We're always updating," she said handing it to Kristin, "but this is the most recent."

Teddy moved alongside Kristin to look at the document. The cover simply read "Emerald Lakes Directory." Kristin opened the book and they gazed at the table of contents. Every current resident was listed. Teddy looked up after Kristin turned to the first page, The Andersens.

"This is a book containing personal information about each and every resident?" he asked.

"Yes. As personal as we're allowed to be, that is," Nikki said. "I'm the editor," she added proudly. "Jean does some of the writing. So, the purpose of part of this visit is to make an appointment with you to get pertinent information. We'd like to add you to the book as quickly as possible. Needless to say, everyone's waiting to get to know you."

"It seems a rather impersonal way to do it," Kristin said. "Couldn't we just have a cocktail party or something?"

"Those things never work well," Nikki said firmly. Teddy noticed that she closed her eyes and held them closed a second whenever someone said or did something that annoyed or challenged her. "People misunderstand, spread misinformation, develop nasty rumors. We have been able to avoid all that with the book," Nikki said. "How about this coming weekend, say Sunday at two?" she asked. Kristin didn't reply. "Are you free?"

"Can we let you know?" Teddy asked quickly.

"Of course. Our telephone numbers are in the book, as well as the time of day we're usually at home," Nikki said.

"Eileen McShane is on our welcoming committee and would have been here with us, but she's a dental hygienist and had to work today. But she wanted me to tell you welcome," Jean reported. "She works for Doctor Baxter, who happens to be an excellent dentist."

"We can help you with all those things," Nikki said. "Doctors, dentists, lawyers . . ."

"We know a great obstetrician," Jean said. "And it couldn't be better for you. He lives in Emerald Lakes, Doctor Hoffman."

"Thank you," Kristin said, her voice drier. "We're so overwhelmed with everything at the moment."

"Of course you are," Nikki said jumping on the admission. "That's why we're here. We've all been through it and know what it's like to scurry about looking for all these necessary services."

"Oh, look at the time," Jean said eyeing the round wall clock above the sink. "I'd better get home. My two will be arriving home from school any minute. Welcome to Emerald Lakes."

"Thank you."

"Yes, welcome," Nikki said. "I'd better be going, too."

"Thanks again for your help," Teddy called as they started toward the front door.

"You're welcome. And please, don't forget to phone as soon as you can about Sunday."

"We won't." He stood beside Kristin, watching them leave. Jennifer came up beside them. When the door closed, Kristin turned slowly and looked at him and then at the book.

"The Emerald Lakes directory?"

Without warning, they both broke into laughter.

"What's so funny, Mommy?" Jennifer asked.

"Nothing, honey," she said, but she started to laugh again, holding her stomach as she did so.

"Stop, Mommy, or you'll shake the baby out," Jennifer cried.

"You mean, Kermit?"

Teddy couldn't contain himself. The two of them flopped on the couch. Then Teddy held out his arms and Jennifer ran to him, the three hugging, all of them overwhelmed with the excitement of a new home.

After dinner and after they had put Jennifer to bed, Kristin began her attempt to personalize their home. Since so much of what they had inherited with this house was so valuable, it was difficult, if not impossible to discard many things; but as expensive as some of the artwork was, it just wasn't her or Teddy's taste. She sauntered through the house and considered what could be moved, what could be replaced. The problem was that this house, as apparently most of the homes in Emerald Lakes, had been arranged by a professional designer. It was perfect, every room completed. Everything fit where it was because of color or size.

"It's great, but it's almost like being forced to wear someone else's shoes," Kristin complained. "You're the same size, but not the same style."

"Um. Maybe we could get a trade-in value on some of this stuff. It's worth a try," Teddy said.

"I know. It's just that once I start with something in a room, I'll have to replace or rearrange everything else in that room. I guess this is the downside of finding a homeowner's dream bargain," she realized. "The first time you look at something, you're overwhelmed with the value, but then, when you have to live with it day after day . . . I mean, I know you have to make some compromises when you buy instead of build to your own specifications, but I can't help feeling I'm sleeping in the Feinberg's bed. Do you know what I mean?" she asked, grimacing. She hated inserting a negative note so soon, but she couldn't help it.

Teddy nodded.

"After a while it will be our bed, our furniture. You'll see," he promised. "Possession is nine-tenths of identity," he quipped. Kristin laughed.

"I'm glad Jennifer has her own things at least. That makes her feel at home faster. For me," she said folding her arms under her breasts and gazing around, "it will take a while."

"Come on," he said. "You're just tired after a long day. Let's go lie down in our—and I stress *our*—king-size bed and I'll rub your tummy."

"Which leads to other things," Kristin said.

"Every new house . . ."

"Has to be broken in. I know."

"Besides, this is safe sex. You can't get pregnant because you already are."

Kristin laughed.

"I remember when I was about twelve I had this idea that if a pregnant woman made love, she could have twins as a result."

"Only one three or four months younger?"

"Who thought out the specifics? It seemed logical at the time," she said. "I asked my grandmother who told me she had heard a story back in Hungary about a woman who had gotten pregnant when she was already six months pregnant and gave birth to another baby six months after the first. It was one of those folktales."

Teddy nodded.

"It sounds like something that belongs in the Emerald Lakes directory."

Kristin laughed.

"You're joking but you might be right," she added.

They started for the bedroom, putting out lights behind them as they went, when they were interrupted by the sound of the doorbell.

"Oh no, not another welcoming committee," Kristin moaned. She waited in the living room as Teddy went to the front door.

"Good evening, Mr. Morris," she heard a deep-voiced man say. She moved toward the door because whoever it was kept himself outside.

"Any problems?" Teddy asked. He looked out at the uniformed security guard. The name tag just over his right breast pocket read "Spier." He looked more like a barroom bouncer with his thick shoulders and wrestler's neck. He had large facial features, thick lips, and dull gray eyes.

"No problems, sir. I just came on duty and noted in the day book that you and your wife just moved in today. My name's Harold Spier. I take care of the main gate tonight, along with my assistant Carl Stark. I wanted to introduce myself because at eleven-thirty I make door rounds and I didn't want to frighten you."

"Door rounds?"

"Who is it, Teddy?" Kristin asked, even though she had heard most of it. She came up behind him. Spier took off his hat, revealing a closely cropped military-style haircut and nodded.

"Evening, ma'am. I'm Harold Spier. As I was telling your husband, either me or someone else makes door rounds every night about eleven-thirty."

"What are door rounds?"

"Just to be sure you've locked your doors for the evening. I'll check every door in your house," he replied without smiling. He looked like a man without a sense of humor, especially when it came to his work.

"Really?"

"Yes, ma'am."

"That's something I thought police do in towns, check stores," Kristin said.

"We're not police, ma'am. We're the development's security personnel. This is just our regular protocol."

"What if we don't come home until after eleven-thirty?" she asked. She wasn't sure she liked someone rattling her doorknobs.

"We'd know that, ma'am, because you would have come in the gate. In that case we give you ten minutes or so and then we check your house especially."

"Have there been many burglaries around here?" Teddy asked quickly.

Spier straightened up with pride. "Not a single one in Emerald Lakes, sir, because our security system is well respected by the criminal element. If you need us for anything, just dial two-one-one. Everyone's phone is programmed so you can call the booth in an emergency.

"Anyway, welcome to Emerald Lakes. I'm glad I met both of you. It makes it a lot easier for me when I recognize faces."

"Yeah, I don't want to get shot if I take a walk around here at night," Kristin quipped with a tone of annoyance that surprised Teddy.

"We'll get to know your peculiar habits after a while, ma'am. Have no fear about that," Spier said, his face tightening. He continued to keep his gaze fixed on Kristin. "I understand you're in your fourth month, ma'am."

"What is it, a national news flash?" she asked with a wry smile.

"No, ma'am, but it helps for us to know these sort of things just in case some sort of related emergency should arise. It's for your own well-being, and I assure you, no one outside of the development knows anyone's personal business because of us. Just one more question and I'll leave you two be," he added, reaching into his back pocket for a notepad. He flicked it open. "Do you have any weapons in the house?"

"Weapons?" Teddy repeated.

"Particularly guns, sir, pistols, rifles. We like to keep that sort of thing on file for obvious reasons."

"No, we don't," Teddy said.

"Do we have to go through this again with the day-time security, too?" Kristin demanded.

"Oh, no," Spier said. "We share everything. In a few days, it will be as if you've lived here for years." He put his hat on. "Well, thank you again," he said, nodded with the firmness of a salute, and turned to go. Teddy closed the door.

"Why were you so sarcastic, honey?" Teddy asked.

"Was I?"

"Were you? 'I don't want to get shot taking a walk at night'? You should have heard yourself."

"I don't know. All this Big Brother stuff. And since you mentioned it, what about that crack about my peculiar habits? What's so peculiar about taking a walk at night?"

"I don't think he meant peculiar in the pejorative sense."

"Pejorative? Well, well, counselor," Kristin kidded.

"Besides, we're paying for all this attention with our homeowner's dues," Teddy said. "I listened when Michele explained all that."

"I know."

"It's all for our benefit, isn't it?" he asked gently. "And with one five-year-old and another child on the way . . ."

"Right, right. I guess I'm just tired and irritable."

"Oh, yes, I was going to rub your pregnant tummy."

He took her hand and continued their retreat toward the master bedroom. The patio door drapes were still open. Just past the pool and the hedges at the rear of their backyard, the surface of Emerald Lake glistened in the moonlight like a brand-new silver coin.

"Isn't that beautiful?" Teddy said, walking up to the patio doors. Kristin came up beside him and he kissed her on the neck. "What a romantic setting. And it's ours."

He turned her to him and they kissed. Then, without speaking, they began to undress. As they lay beside each other and petted and kissed, the moonlight began its nocturnal journey from one side of the lake to the other, eventually reaching their patio with its illumination. The lunar light was so bright, it was as if they had left a light on in the room. Now it was their naked bodies that glistened as they made love softly, tenderly but with a sensuality that brought them both to a satisfying conclusion.

Afterward, they lay beside each other until their heartbeats slowed and their breathing became regular. The moonlight passed over the house. The lake looked inky, but they could see the stars that had been washed out by the moon's brightness before.

"I think we're going to be very happy here, Kristin. Don't you?"

"I hope so," she said. She stared out at the shadows in their backyard. Suddenly, she thought one took shape and became the silhouette of a man. She sat up in bed and studied the scene.

"Something wrong?"

For a moment she didn't reply. He sat up, too.

"What is it, Kristin?"

"I thought someone was standing out there watching us, but I guess it was just the movement of shadows."

"Where?"

"It's nothing," she said and lay down again. He stared a moment and then shrugged and reclined again, too. Then he smiled at her and ran the palm of his hand gingerly over her slightly raised stomach.

"I guess now we're going to have twins, honey."

"All right, Teddy Morris. I won't ever confess my childhood fantasies to you again if you tease me."

He laughed but her eyes returned to the patio windows.

"Maybe we shouldn't leave our drapes open so wide."

"Why not? You can't be afraid of Peeping Toms here. Our security forces would mow them down with machine guns," he said.

"Unless our security forces were the Peeping Toms," she replied.

He laughed.

"Considering what goes on here, we might be the best show in town."

"Right," she said and gazed at the window.

"Relax. We're in paradise," he said and snuggled closer. He was the first to fall asleep, his breathing becoming deep and heavy, but she kept her eyes open, her attention fixed on the backyard. Was it only her imagination or had someone been spying on them? It wasn't the sort of thing she wanted to bring up on their first night in a new house, she thought, especially a house in which the former owner had taken his own life. She shook off the memory of Elaine Feinberg's accusatory eyes as quickly as it had returned. I've got to stop this, she thought, realizing she was spooking herself.

After a while, she rose, went to the bathroom, brushed her teeth, checked on Jennifer, and returned. Before she got into bed, she peered out and studied the darkness again to be sure there was no one there. Then she closed the drapes so the morning light wouldn't wake them too early. When she crawled into bed beside Teddy, she was comforted by the warmth of his body and felt herself finally relax.

But at exactly eleven thirty-eight, she heard the doors being checked. Spier hadn't been exaggerating. He even came around and tried the patio doors. Now that could be embarrassing if they ever began making love at eleven-thirty or so and left those drapes open again, she thought. Amazingly, Teddy didn't waken. She listened until she was sure the security guard had moved off.

Why should all this wonderful security bother her? she wondered. True, there was some tradeoff of privacy, but on the other hand, one bad incident could make it all well worth it, she thought. She should be grateful. Few people had the luxury of knowing their children, their homes, their cars, their very lives were this vigorously protected day and night.

Kristin closed her eyes and almost immediately conjured Harold Spier with his firm, military posture, his cold politeness, and his stone gray eyes. There was such a look of purpose, such a rigid diligence and stiff intensity. It was as if the man had been designed for a single purpose and put all his energy into one thing like some sort of a human watchdog.

But that's what security men were supposed to be, weren't they: watchdogs dedicated to protecting their

masters. Teddy would just say it was better that a
man like Spier was working for them. Right?

She hoped so.

The Neighborhood Watch, the Emerald Lakes directory, the best cold cereal, door checks . . . I'm in
my new home, she thought. Better get used to it.

She fell asleep, dreaming of the new baby.

4

ADJUSTING TO HER NEW LIFE in Emerald Lakes proved easier than Kristin had anticipated, especially because of the way their immediate neighbors accepted them and offered to help them. Kristin appreciated it, even though she thought they took themselves too seriously at times. However, she was well aware that in this day and age, for whatever reasons sociologists determined, people were more aloof and private. Friends and relatives who lived in other developments and similar communities, in other states as well as New York, often remarked how they had lived in the same house for years and not so much as exchanged pleasantries with some of their neighbors. If they did greet them and get to know them on a "good morning" basis, they hardly, if ever, saw or spoke to them much more than that.

Emerald Lakes was definitely different. Jean Levine brought her little girl to meet Jennifer the day after they had moved in, and when the two hit it off, Jean invited Jennifer to have dinner with Terri Sue that night. The following day Jean and Nikki offered to accompany Kristin to the elementary school to register Jennifer, but she explained it was something she and Teddy wanted to do together. Now, Kristin no sooner emerged from her house to carry a small bag of garbage from the compactor to her bin, which was exactly two feet from the left corner of the driveway at every house, when Jean Levine came tearing across the street as if she had been at her doorway waiting to pounce the moment Kristin showed herself.

The bright redhead wore a white silk blouse with gold shoulder pads and gold silk pants. A pair of gold-leaf earrings swung beneath her lobes and a diamond-studded heart on a gold chain lay firmly in the valley of her breasts. All of the women Kristin had already met here always looked so well dressed and put together, no matter what time of the day she saw them. Kristin felt sloppy and a bit embarrassed to have herself caught in her old rolled-up jeans and Teddy's college sweatshirt. She had simply tied her hair up, rather than brush it out, and she wore no makeup, not even a trace of lipstick.

"Hi," Jean cried smiling.

"Hi."

"Well," Jean began, "tell me what it's been like."

Kristin paused and smiled. The radiant sunlight of a nearly cloudless blue morning turned the windows of the houses into sparkling mirrors. Even the immaculate street gleamed.

"Been like? What do you mean?"

"The first few nights in your new home," Jean wailed, not disguising her disappointment in having to explain.

"Oh. I'm sorry. I wasn't thinking."

"Well?" Jean asked impatiently.

Kristin gazed at her new friend, who looked as anxious as a reporter getting an exclusive from some celebrity. She looked at the sprawling red maple trees, the trim hedges, the beds of flowers and nodded.

"It's quite meditative."

"That's right," Jean said, smiling widely again. Kristin got the impression she had just passed some entry exam. "And how about Jennifer? She's such a sweet, polite little girl. Is she still a little afraid?"

"Afraid? Is that what she told you?"

Jean nodded. "Something about hearing a dead baby cry. She has quite an imagination," Jean added, nodding with wide eyes.

"Oh? Oh," Kristin said, realizing that "Jennifer was there when I met Mrs. Feinberg in the supermarket and found out about what had happened to her." Jean Levine's smile wilted.

"What about Mrs. Feinberg?"

"Didn't you know? She had a miscarriage. This is such a small town," Kristin continued when it was obvious Jean did not know. "I just assumed you would have heard."

"We don't know about people outside of Emerald Lakes."

"Pardon?" The way Jean said *people outside of Emerald Lakes* made it sound as if they were in another country.

"There's so much to keep up with here, I just don't involve myself in the gossip concerning outsiders, especially an ex–Emerald Lakes homeowner," she remarked disdainfully.

"Oh? You weren't friendly with her?"

"In the beginning, but her husband and she became quite undesirable after a while. It's rare, but sometimes, the committee makes a mistake."

"Makes a mistake? I don't understand," Kristin said, a puzzled smile on her face.

"Approving a new homeowner, silly. Anyway, I just hate to hear about bad things happening to children." She paused and drew closer to whisper. "We don't gossip and talk about each other's misfortunes in Emerald Lakes, but you probably know about Philip and Marilyn Slater's tragedy."

"No," Kristin said shaking her head. "I have yet to meet Mrs. Slater."

"Oh. Well, Nikki would scold me for telling you, but you should know . . . they lost their little boy a few years ago. He was only six."

"How horrible. How?"

"Leukemia, I think. Nikki knows exactly."

Kristin thought a moment and then went to put her bag in the can.

"Oh, no, don't do that," Jean said sharply, so sharply for a moment Kristin thought she was putting her garbage into someone else's can. She pulled her arm up.

"What?"

"See the *C* painted on the other can. That's the can that takes the compactor bags," Jean explained.

"Oh. Oh, yes." She dropped the bag into the correct can.

"You didn't read your 'Welcome to Emerald Lakes' letter, did you?" Jean said accusingly while waving her right forefinger. "Naughty, naughty. The board of directors spent a great deal of time designing that orientation package for new residents. We're all very proud of it."

"No one coming around to give me a test soon, are they?" Kristin asked without disguising her note of annoyance. Jean looked devastated. "I'm sorry. I'm just kidding. No, I didn't get to it yet, but I will this morning." Jean's smile returned.

"Your other can is for things that can be recycled," Jean instructed.

"Oh. Of course."

"We're very environmentally conscious here. Our water is constantly monitored, our septic systems checked, and only the most environment-friendly lawn fertilizers and chemicals are permitted. Watch your catalytic converter," Jean warned with a smile and that right forefinger again.

"Pardon?"

"You know . . . that thing on your car that keeps it from polluting the air. The Del Marcos"—she gazed down the street toward a brown and white ranch-style house—"not only had a faulty converter, but apparently their car had a nasty oil leak. It wasn't only their own driveway that got spotted, but our street too. Daytime security discovered it during a routine check of our little neighborhood."

"I see. They have a pretty house," Kristin said gazing at the house Jean had focused on so intently. "I noticed it the first time we drove in to look at ours," Kristin remarked, "and wished that was the one for sale." She didn't mean to reveal that she preferred the more styled design.

"Thou shalt not covet thy neighbor's house, grounds, or cars," Jean preached. Although she was smiling, she looked serious.

"Is that in the orientation packet, too?" Kristin asked. Jean started to look insulted but suddenly, with the abruptness of a schizophrenic, changed her expression to a light, even childish smile. She stepped closer to whisper like a coconspirator.

"You're funny," she said, "but don't do it in front of the others, especially not Nikki. They take their work very seriously."

"If you can't make fun of yourself, you're in trouble," Kristin said. Jean laughed.

"Want a cup of coffee?"

"No thanks. I don't mean to be unfriendly; it's just that I like to work in the morning."

"Work?" Jean pronounced, and grimaced as if it were one of the most distasteful words in the dictionary.

"I try to compose music . . . write songs on the piano."

"Oh, right. Will you let me hear one?"

"Maybe later."

"Call me. Anytime you're ready. Really. I just have such admiration for anyone with an ounce of creativity. I'm one of those people born without any talent, except the talent to manage our home, love my husband, and raise our children, the new Trinity."

Kristin laughed.

"Nowadays, that's a lot more talent and a great deal more important than you might think," she said.

Jean shrugged.

"Don't forget to call me to hear one of your songs," she sang and began to retreat. Kristin stared after her for a moment and then reentered her house. She didn't know whether to laugh or cry. Jean Levine was friendly, but she was no great intellect. And there was a strange note of fear behind some of the things she said. Kristin was sure Jean meant it when she chastised her for not reading the orientation letter.

Where was that stupid thing?

She went to the office and found it with the pile of new house papers: the mortgage and escrow documents, titles, environmental studies, etc. It was a two-page document with a cover page that read "Welcome to Emerald Lakes, for New Residents." Kristin flipped it open. A disclaimer emphasized that "this letter is not a substitute for, nor do any of its recommendations and rules nullify or supersede, the homeowners Covenants, Conditions, and Restrictions. Rather, the purpose is to give the new residents a quick lesson in the basic things they will have to know." There it was . . . a list of simple do's and don't's concerning garbage, cable hookups, entrance and exit through the main gates, some of the things the security guard explained to them the other night, and a list of emergency telephone numbers.

Oh well, Kristin thought. It was nice to find a place so well organized, a place where newcomers didn't have to flounder and fumble their way through initial things. She brought the letter out to the kitchen and pinned it up by the telephone. She accepted this little code of behavior even though she wasn't one who felt comfortable with any sort of regimentation.

For as long as she could remember, she was something of a rebel, sometimes defying rules and orders simply because they were imposed on her. Her father always justified her rebelliousness by saying it was a by-product of her creativity. But her mom never really bought the excuses. Kristin took advantage; she was the first to admit that now. She was a daddy's girl and relied on him to bail her out time after time, and time after time he did, whether it was her insubordinate acts in high school or her membership in college protest organizations.

But she was on her own now. If she put that compactor garbage bag in the wrong can, she thought, Daddy couldn't save her from the wrath of the Emerald Lakes homeowners association. She laughed aloud. Then she went to her piano and began to tinker with the new melody that had been replaying it-

self in her mind ever since the first day they had set
foot on the grounds of Emerald Lakes. It was somewhat heavier music than she was accustomed to creating, but it was interesting and the notes she was
composing were taking her to places she had never
been. She lost herself so completely in the work that
she didn't realize the passage of time until the phone
rang and Teddy started to describe the nice little
restaurant Doctor Porter had taken him to in
Middletown. She was shocked to discover it was after
two.

"You had your lunch already?"

"Hey, honey. Don't tell me you forgot to eat again.
You've got more than one mouth to feed these days,
remember," he chastised gently.

"Right. I'll have something now."

"I guess I don't have to ask if you're making yourself at home. How's it going?"

"Good. I'm . . ."—her eyes fell on the orientation
letter—"learning how to live and play in Emerald Lakes."

Teddy laughed.

"I'll see you later. Oh," he said before cradling the
receiver. "I nearly forgot. I got a phone call this morning from Phil Slater, our president."

"Our president?"

"Of the homeowners association and the chief
stockholder in the bank from which we got that great
mortgage," he added for emphasis. "Remember?"

"How could I forget? Jean Levine just told me
about the Slater's little boy."

"What about him?"

"They lost him. He was only six. She thinks it was
leukemia. She wasn't sure about the details. They
have some unwritten rule here about gossiping and
telling about each other's misfortunes."

"Really. Wow. Sad. Anyway, he asked if he and his wife could drop by this evening to welcome us personally. They bought us a housewarming gift. I thought it would be all right about eight."

"Our first guests. Oooo, I'm all flustered. I'd better check to see if there are any rules about how to entertain your first guest."

"Huh?"

"In the orientation letter you buried with everything else, Teddy. If Nikki Stanley found out how cavalier you were with this document, you'd be on her shit list."

"Right. Don't blow up the neighborhood before I get home," he said. "Bye."

She laughed to herself after she hung up and then remembered she was hungry. She smeared gobs of peanut butter on toasted English muffins and chased them down with two full glasses of milk. It was funny how she could get so involved in her music that she would ignore her hunger, but once she remembered and began to eat, she was like a ravenous animal.

Noticing the time, she realized Jennifer, along with the other children in Emerald Lakes, would be brought by the school bus to the front gate any minute. This would be her second trip home on the bus. Kristin had gone to the gate to wait for her the day before and discovered she was the only mother to do so. The other children gazed at her as if meeting her daughter at the gate was the weirdest thing to do. Today, she decided to take her time and let Jennifer walk more than half the way to the house before greeting her.

Even though she hadn't been here long, one of the things she had realized about Emerald Lakes was how quiet it was around the homes during long portions of the afternoon, and especially the early evening. She understood that many of the other husbands and wives who lived here both worked, but she had yet to find anyone taking spontaneous walks or simply sitting outside. She discovered through a conversation with Jean and Nikki that all lawn and garden work around the homes was done on specific days and at specific times. It was so prescribed in the regulations. When she commented about the regimentation, Nikki brought up the economic reasons.

"We negotiate bids and proposals with private contractors through the homeowners association for all our residents. That way, we ensure that we will all get the best possible service for the lowest possible price. Then we tell them when to do the work so no one is disturbed by it.

"Believe me," she emphasized, "other homeowner associations are starting to imitate us. I get calls constantly requesting information about how we do this and how we do that. We set the standards for development life in upstate New York, and it didn't surprise us to learn that other homeowners in other states have already heard about us through relatives who visit."

"That's right," Jean chorused. "My cousin Nancy lives in a development in Hidden Hills, California, and they have requested a copy of our CC and R's."

"But we don't give that to just anyone who asks for it," Nikki pointed out sharply. "That's something the committee discusses and approves first."

Recalling the conversation, Kristin smiled to herself as she walked toward the front entrance. She liked Jean, but Nikki was like someone who had suffered a great deal in her early life and had forgotten what it was to laugh, to joke, even to smile.

The security guard opened the gate and the children of Emerald Lakes bounced down the school bus steps and hurriedly entered the development. The older ones who had been laughing and shouting instantly quieted down, some glancing back at the security guard who looked more like a customs agent checking to be sure none of them were smuggling in contraband. Jennifer appeared and walked quickly to keep up with Terri Sue Levine and her brother George. Kristin stopped and waited.

Something about the way the children walked to their various homes seemed odd. This was an elementary school bus so the children varied in ages from five to eleven. They were all dressed nicely, looking like children from affluent homes, and on the surface didn't appear any different from the hundreds of children Kristin had seen walking home from schools everywhere else. What was it? she wondered and tilted her head as she thought.

It occurred to her when the first two children split away to go to their house. It was the way the young people walked through the development: so orderly, keeping to the right, staying out of the road. Absent was the elation most children exhibited when they were free from the constraints of school and their school buses. There were no bursts of laughter; there was no horsing around, no screams and shouts, no running and jumping. It was as if an invisible chaperon trotted alongside them, waiting for one of them to violate the rules for pedestrians in Emerald Lakes.

Kristin waved.

"Jennifer!"

Her daughter did not wave back. Terri Sue and George glanced at her and she looked back at them.

She did not burst forth to leave the pack. She kept her pace: controlled, orderly, patient.

"Hi, honey," Kristin said when the group of children reached her. It was then, after glancing at Terri Sue and George once more, that Jennifer shot forward to embrace Kristin. "Hi, Terri, George," Kristin said.

"Hello, Mrs. Morris," George said.

"Hi," Terri offered shyly, but they didn't pause to walk along with her.

Kristin took Jennifer's hand and started back to the house.

"How was school today, honey?"

"Good."

"Do you like the bus ride?"

"Uh-huh."

"Everyone seems so well behaved today. Did the bus driver bawl them out or something?" Kristin asked.

"No. His name is Mr. Tooey. He told me where to sit and he said I can't put my hand out the window," Jennifer explained.

"That's for safety reasons."

"I know." Jennifer paused and looked up at Kristin. "You don't have to wait for me, Mommy. You can wait inside like everyone else's mommy. I know how to go home already."

"Do you? That's nice, sweetheart, but I like to meet you. I miss you. Do you mind?"

Jennifer, to Kristin's surprise, nodded.

"You do mind?"

"You're supposed to wait inside like the other mommies," she insisted.

"Who said such a thing?"

"Everyone. They laughed at me."

"That's silly, honey. Why do I have to wait for you?"

Jennifer shrugged.

"Next time they laugh at you, you tell them your mommy is a different kind of mommy," Kristin said, her ire rising. "You tell them your mommy has a mind of her own. Can you remember that, honey?"

Jennifer shook her head.

"I'll remind you," Kristin said.

In front of their house, the Levine kids paused to watch Kristin and Jennifer walk by. Then they hurried inside as if they couldn't wait to tell. Surprised at how furious such a simple thing made her feel, Kristin deliberately swung Jennifer's hand back and forth and took her time returning to the house.

At eight o'clock sharp the doorbell sounded. Kristin looked up from the apple pie she had baked. Despite what Teddy had told her, she had decided to be prepared. What sort of a host has nothing to offer, especially to her first important visitors?

"Oh, I'm sorry," she heard Teddy say at the door. "Please, come in."

Kristin hurried around to greet the Slaters and was surprised to see only Philip enter. Despite the hour he was still dressed in a silver and black suit and tie, but he looked as fresh as he would if he had just put on those clothes. He carried a gift-wrapped package under his right arm.

"Evening, Kristin. Sorry. Marilyn couldn't come. She gets this terrible migraine occasionally, and unfortunately tonight is one of those occasions."

"Oh, I'm sorry."

"But don't let me put a dark cloud over your arrival," Philip said quickly. He smiled. "I hope you've had an easy time of it."

"And how," Teddy said enthusiastically. He gazed at Kristin, urging her to chorus.

"Yes. The neighbors have been so helpful and all of the things the association does to help new residents are wonderful," she added. "Please. Come in," Kristin said. "Teddy told me you specifically requested there be no coffee and cake. I hope you don't mind coffee and pie."

Philip Slater's smile widened.

"I must confess the aroma of freshly baked apple pie hit me as soon as I turned up your walkway. My mother was a great homemaker. I miss it," he concluded and stepped down, Teddy right behind him, beaming.

"Mommy!" they heard and all turned to see Jennifer come in with a drawing she had just completed. Everyone in her class had been asked to draw the thing that they loved the most in their rooms at home. She drew her giant stuffed Mickey Mouse sitting in her little wicker rocker.

"Jennifer, you remember Mr. Slater, don't you? Come say hello, honey."

Jennifer stopped in the living room and looked up at Philip Slater. Her deliberate hesitation brought a smile of puzzlement to Kristin.

"Jennifer?"

"I don't wanna," she cried as she turned and ran back to her room.

"Jennifer!"

"I don't believe that," Teddy said. "She's bashful, but not that bashful. I'll go get her."

"Please," Philip said seizing his arm. "Let her be. She'll get used to seeing me around and be more comfortable with me as time goes by. Anyway, let me give you this."

He handed the gift to Kristin and smiled conspira-
torially at Teddy.

"This is very nice of you. Should I open it now?"

"Please do," Philip said. Kristin went to the coffee
table and put the package down. She tore off the gift
wrapping neatly and revealed a new doorbell chime,
one that played a few bars of music instead of sounding an anonymous *ding dong*.

"Oh, how sweet," Kristin said.

"We can hook it right up," Philip said winking at
Teddy. "It's designed to simply plug into wires for the
one that's already here."

"We don't have to do it right now," Kristin said.

"No problem," Teddy said. "While you're getting
the coffee and pie, we'll see to it."

"Okay," she said. Teddy still had that silly grin on
his lips. She started for the kitchen and the two men
went to work. Less than ten minutes later, just as
Kristin had the coffee ready to pour, Teddy announced the chime was ready for its first test run.

He called Jennifer, who was tempted out of her
room to participate in the festivities.

"You can push the doorbell, Jen. Okay?" She nodded, gazing tentatively toward Philip Slater. "Go
ahead, honey."

She ran to the front excitedly and opened the door.
"Push it, babe," Teddy ordered and she did.

Kristin's eyes widened with delighted surprise as
soon as she heard the first two notes. It was one of
her tunes, Teddy's favorite, from a song she had enti-
tled "Every Beat of My Heart." She squealed with de-
light and Jennifer came running back.

"How did you do that?"

Teddy and Philip Slater laughed.

"Philip was the one who came up with the idea. He

told me he wanted to do something special, something personal."

"It's so nice of you."

"It was no big deal. I have a friend who manufactures these things. I'm glad you're happy."

"Did you hear that melody, honey? It's one of Mommy's songs," Kristin told Jennifer.

"Can I push the button again, Mommy? Can I?"

"Oh no," Teddy said. "I'll be hearing the tune in my dreams."

"Not such a bad thing to hear in your dreams, is it?" Philip said.

Kristin blushed.

"Thank you, really. It's a very special gift. And please, tell your wife thank you, too."

"I will." He smiled at Jennifer. The excitement left her face.

"I wanna go color," she said quickly and ran back to her room.

"I don't know what's got into her tonight," Kristin said.

"I'm sure it's just the strangeness of being in a new world," Philip said and narrowed his eyes as he looked after Jennifer. There was a heavy silence. Kristin looked at Teddy who gestured with his eyes toward the dining room.

"Well, why don't we have that coffee and let me try my pie on our captured guinea pig," she said.

"Good idea," Teddy said.

Philip smiled.

"From the aroma, I know it's going to be delicious."

Kristin served the pie and coffee, and they talked. Phil Slater described his background and how he had come to build the development. He asked polite questions, but made no attempt to get too personal. If he did ask something that could be construed as such, he quickly apologized.

"That's all right, Philip," Kristin said. "We should be preparing ourselves for the interview on Sunday."

"Interview?"

"For the Emerald Lakes directory."

"Oh." Philip smiled. "One of my committee's pet projects. Actually, it's turned out very well and proven to be very useful. I hope you'll get involved with some of our other activities. We're always looking for fresh blood and new ideas."

"Oh, if I know Kristin, she'll come up with new ideas," Teddy warned.

"Well, a little controversy is a good thing as long as it stimulates healthy discussion and results in improvement. But, I must say, I have a talent for reading people accurately. Like you, Teddy, I am intrigued with eyes," he explained. "I gaze into the eyes of someone and I sense their true personalities. Looking into Kristin's, I see only compassion and kindness," he said fixing his gaze on her.

To Kristin it was like he had put his hand under her blouse and cupped her breast. She felt a sudden tingle, an instant of electricity flow through her veins and arteries and clamp itself around her heart to make it skip a beat. It was as if the tips of his fingers freely explored the very essence of her inner being. She felt her face fill with warmth, a warmth that traveled down her neck and over her bosom. The nearly five-month-old fetus within her womb stirred as if it, too, had been nudged in its most secret places.

"I'm sure you'll be one of our best residents, Kristin." Philip Slater said. "Well, I'd better get home and see how Marilyn's doing. Thank you for a most delicious and unexpected treat. These days, I'm very rarely surprised by anyone," he added and stood up.

Teddy and Kristin rose.

"Once again, welcome," he said offering Kristin his hand.

"Thank you," she said. Teddy accompanied Philip Slater to the door where he bid him good night. After Philip Slater left, Teddy hurried down the steps and back to the dining room. Kristin was clearing the table, looking like she was in deep thought.

"Well?" Teddy said.

"Very sneaky, Theodore Morris. But it was a very thoughtful gift. It was nice of him."

"Great guy."

She turned slowly. "Sad about their only child."

"I know."

"He never mentioned anything about it, but I kept feeling as if I should say something."

"I suppose it's not easy for him to talk about it," Teddy said and turned to see Jennifer inching her way up the corridor toward them.

"Hey, Peanut. What's the matter? Why were you so frightened of the nice man?"

Kristin turned to look at her.

"Jen?"

"I don't like him," she moaned.

"Oh, Jen, why?" Kristin said moving toward her. Teddy stepped up behind.

"He's just a nice neighbor, honey," he said. She shook her head and continued to cringe.

"He's got eyes that move," she complained.

"Move? Everyone's eyes move, honey," Teddy explained. "We've got little muscles behind them and—"

"His move out of his head," she explained.

"Out of his head? Jennifer, what are you saying?" Kristin asked. Jennifer shook her head.

"They moved toward me."

"Oh, Jen." Kristin embraced her and looked at Teddy. "She's been having nightmares. Jean Levine told me she told her about a dead baby crying."

"Oh," Teddy said.

"Everything's all right, honey. You just had a bad dream," Kristin said.

"But I was awake, Mommy."

"You can dream while you're awake," Teddy told her. "It's called daydreaming, honey."

"So you see," Kristin said, smiling, "you shouldn't be afraid of Mr. Slater. Come on. Show me your drawing now," she coaxed. Jennifer glanced at Teddy timidly and then hurried back to her room to get her drawing.

"What an idea . . . eyes moved out of his head. Little kids have such wild imaginations," Teddy remarked.

"Oh, I don't know," Kristin said. "The first time you saw me, you said your eyes popped out of your head."

He laughed.

"They did. Luckily I'm an ophthalmologist, so I knew how to fix it."

They both turned excitedly, prepared to lavish compliments when Jennifer hurried back with her drawing.

Later in bed, Kristin lay awake with her eyes open for the longest time. Teddy looked like he fell asleep as soon as his head hit the pillow, but in the darkness, she imagined two eyes peering down at her and thought about Jennifer's bizarre claim. It made her shudder and she slid her body closer to Teddy.

"You all right?" he asked.

"Yes." Her voice was small, like a child's. He kissed

her forehead. "Not getting romantic, are you?" he asked.

"No. I just want to feel you beside me," she said. He embraced her and she fell asleep in the crook of his arm, opening her eyes for an instant when she heard the distinct sound of their doors being checked by the ever present, efficient security service that kept the residents of Emerald Lakes feeling secure and safe.

For some inexplicable reason, tonight Kristin didn't feel that way. She fell asleep wondering why.

5

◈

"HELLO," Teddy called from the foyer. "Anyone home?"

"Daddy!"

Jennifer came running down the hallway and across the living room. Kristin, who had been on the back patio, slid the door open and entered.

"Where were you?" she asked before he came down the marble steps. "I called the office nearly an hour ago and they said you had just left."

"Stopped to pick something up," he said cryptically. He scooped Jennifer into his arms and kissed her.

"I got a gold star today, Daddy."

"Really? For what?"

"Desk neatness."

"Well, what do you know? Must take after your mother. My desk was always a mess and still is." He paused and looked at Kristin. "Everything all right?" From the look on her face, he already knew the answer. "What's wrong?"

"I've been outside reading the directory. Our copy was delivered by one of the security guards."

"Directory?"

"Our interview, remember? Look at this. I never

told them this, did you?" She thrust the booklet toward him.

He took it with his free hand and gazed at the paragraph. Then he looked up sharply and lowered Jennifer to the floor.

"I never told them that either."

"How would they know I had a miscarriage last year, Teddy?" He shrugged.

"Maybe you let it slip somehow. I remember Jean was rattling on about her children and Nikki asked a lot of questions about our earlier days together, but . . ."

"Even if I had referred to it, which I didn't, why put something like that in here?"

"I don't know," he said shaking his head. "Maybe they're frustrated journalists." He shrugged. "Well, it's over and done. No sense—"

"I want it out. I want you to call Mr. Slater and tell him how upset I am."

"If it's already been printed and delivered, Kristin, what good will a retraction do?"

"Maybe everyone doesn't consider this a best-seller and everyone hasn't dipped right into it, Teddy. I'm just not happy about it being there. How do you think it makes me feel to open this thing and read it in black and white, and know that these strangers know some intimate details about our lives? I knew this whole thing was a stupid idea. I just knew it."

"All right. Don't get yourself worked up."

"What?"

"I'll call. I will," he added when she gazed at him furiously. "I promise," he said. "Anything else in here I should see?"

"It's all stupid. Calling me an amateur composer with dreams of being another Andrew Lloyd Webber.

I never even mentioned his name. I write ballads, not musicals."

"They fancy themselves writers and took some creative license, I suppose."

"They don't have to be creative with my background and my life. It's . . . it's like standing naked in the street. If I want people to know my fantasies, I'll tell them myself." She widened her eyes with emphasis. Her face had turned crimson with indignation.

"All right. It's not like anyone but the people who live here will see it," Teddy said as calmly as he could. But the more relaxed and coolly he behaved, the more infuriated Kristin became.

"How do we know that? The way Nikki Stanley talks, everyone in America is dying to read and hear about the people of Emerald Lakes."

"Well, this is a model community. Hank Porter was telling me that even when the real estate market took a dip two years ago, the property values continued to escalate in Emerald Lakes."

"So why doesn't he live here then?"

"He already had built a house in another development and they're happy there, but he says if there ever comes a time . . ."

"Does his development have a directory?"

"I don't know. All I know is he talks very highly about ours, as does just about everyone I've met who learned we're living here. They're impressed," he said. "Look, everyone has some rough times making a move. Up until now, you have to admit, it's been great. This is really the first glitch. Let's not blow it out of proportion, honey. I'll take care of it and we'll correct it."

She relaxed and gazed at Jennifer who stared with a mixture of fear and curiosity. She didn't see Kristin angry very often, and she had no idea why her mother was so angry now. It was the child's expression that made Kristin feel a little foolish haranguing Teddy this long.

"Where did you say you were?"

"Oh. I forgot." He retreated to the front door and returned carrying a large box with holes in it.

A scratching noise started and the distinct sound of whimpering. Kristin's eyes widened.

"What's that, Daddy?" Jennifer asked, drawing closer.

"Open it up," Teddy said, lowering the box to the floor by her feet.

Jennifer squatted and carefully pulled on the flaps. Then she gasped. She was gazing down at a two-month-old brown toy poodle with a white spot on its forehead.

"A puppy! Daddy bought us a puppy!"

"Teddy, he's adorable," Kristin said. "Is it a he?"

"Yes."

"What's his name?" Jennifer asked.

"You have to give him a name, honey."

The puppy sniffed at her cheeks and she giggled.

"Careful, honey. He's just a baby."

Jennifer put the puppy down and it sniffed at her shoes and whimpered.

"All he does is sniff and sniff," she said.

"So, call him Mr. Sniffles."

"Yes. Mr. Sniffles."

"We need to make him a comfortable little bed. I'll cut up this carton and we'll find some old blanket for the time being," Kristin suggested.

"Can he sleep in my room, Mommy? Can he?"

"We'll see, Jennifer. Take him outside for now. He might want to piddle."

"What's piddle?"

"Make pee pee," Kristin explained.

Jennifer opened and closed her mouth, nodded, and gently lifted Mr. Sniffles into her arms.

"What got into you, Mr. Morris?" Kristin asked.

"Thought we needed something around here to make life more exciting. Until the new baby comes, that is." He held up the directory. "I'll take care of this right away."

He went to his office and called Phil Slater. The thin, soft voice of Marilyn Slater surprised him. She sounded as weak and feeble as a woman in her nineties.

"I'm sorry, Philip isn't at home," she said. "Please give me your name and number, and I'll have him call as soon as he arrives."

He told her and when she didn't say anything, he added, "We're the newcomers." He thought if he lightened the tone, she might be more receptive.

"Yes, I know," she said. When she didn't add another word, he thanked her and hung up. Kristin was in the kitchen, preparing dinner. "He wasn't home yet," he said as soon as she looked at him. "I spoke to his wife."

"So?"

"Nothing except she sounded like she was in a tunnel . . . you know, distant, small," he said. Kristin thought a moment.

"I haven't seen her, have you?"

"No. Maybe their tragedy messed her up."

"It's understandable," Kristin said.

Less than an hour later, Phil Slater called and Teddy explained why he and Kristin were upset.

"I'm sorry that happened. I'll speak to Nikki and have the changes made and the pages replaced. My committee gets a little too enthusiastic sometimes. But it's a good fault," he added, "especially when you see how uninvolved and indifferent other people are in other communities."

"The thing about it is," Teddy pursued, "neither Kristin nor I recall ever mentioning the miscarriage. How would they know that?"

Phil Slater was silent a moment.

"You must have referred to it somehow," he finally replied.

"Not that either of us can recall."

"Um. Well, I'll phone Nikki right now and get this taken care of. Please give Kristin my apologies."

"Thank you."

He related the conversation to Kristin.

"Even if we did refer to it cryptically and they made the conclusion, I thought they don't spread that sort of gossip in Emerald Lakes. That's what Jean told me. That's why she was reluctant to talk about what had happened to his child." Teddy didn't reply. She thought a moment and then went to the telephone.

"What are you doing?"

"I don't like wondering," she said. She opened the directory, found the number she wanted and punched it out by vehemently stabbing the pad with her forefinger. After two rings, Nikki Stanley answered.

"It's Kristin Morris," Kristin said.

"Oh, I knew it was you."

"Why? Were you expecting my call?"

"No. We have caller I.D. Anyway, I know why you're calling and I've already started to take care of it. Sorry."

"That's nice, but what I would like to know is how did you two find out about my miscarriage? I didn't say anything about it and neither did Teddy."

"You must have," Nikki replied firmly. "How else would we know?"

"That's what I'd like to know. You didn't find out from my doctor, did you?"

"Of course not. Why would we ask him about such a thing and why would he tell us? I regret it was included. Jean gets a little over the top with her writing and I didn't proofread it as closely as I should have. I apologize, but you don't need to get paranoid about it."

"Paranoid? Neither of us mentioned a fact and that fact occurs in the directory. All I want to know is how? That doesn't make me paranoid. That makes me curious and quite upset."

"I'll call Jean and see if she remembers anything that gave her the information. It might have been something she read between the lines and concluded."

"Between the lines of what? I don't recall us giving our medical history to the real estate agent or the bank. Where could she possibly have read such a thing, between the lines or otherwise?"

"I don't propose to remain on the phone conjecturing about the source of a verifiable fact. It was unfortunate that it was included. I'm sorry," Nikki said, obviously peeved that she had to repeat the apology. "Let this be the biggest problem you have," she added caustically.

"Yes, let it," Kristin said. "Thank you." She hung up sharply. Teddy widened his eyes.

"What did she say?"

"She said she was sorry. She didn't know where the information came from, but she wasn't going to waste time trying to discover the source of a, quote, verifiable fact."

He nodded.

"Well, as long as she's sorry and they'll correct it."

"I don't like that woman. I didn't like her as soon as she told me where to put my cold cereals and my staples. In fact," Kristin said, "I'm changing everything around."

"Huh?"

Teddy grimaced with surprise as Kristin lunged into the kitchen and began pulling things out of the cabinets. He shook his head, not knowing whether to laugh or be concerned.

"Don't you think you're overreacting, honey? I mean, why spite yourself just to spite them?"

"So we won't be as well organized as everyone else in Emerald Lakes, Teddy. You have a problem with that?" she challenged, turning on him, her hands on her hips.

He smiled and put up his hands.

"No, ma'am. No problem. Put the salt and pepper in the stove if you want," he said.

"Maybe I will," she said and returned to her delightful disorganization. Strategically, he made a retreat. Conversation remained strained at dinner, after which Kristin cleaned up and retired to the bedroom to watch television. Her emotional outburst and anger had exhausted her and she was asleep by the time Teddy joined her. He turned off the television and went to sleep trying to recall if Kristin was this emotionally tense during her previous two pregnancies. He knew being with child sometimes played havoc with a woman's hormones and moods, and decided he would try to think of something to cheer her up tomorrow.

Early the next morning, even before Teddy left for work, the door buzzer rang. Day security was there.

"What's up?" Teddy asked.

"Just delivering these," the guard said. He handed Teddy the new directory pages. "Would you please substitute them in the directory and destroy the old pages?"

Teddy gazed at the papers for a moment and then shook his head.

"Sure, thanks." He noticed the guard had a number of these pages under his arm. "You're delivering this to everyone this morning?"

"Yes, sir."

"Right, thanks," Teddy said. He brought the pages to the kitchenette.

"Who was that?" Kristin asked, lowering her coffee cup.

"Security. Delivering this." He handed the pages to her. She perused them quickly and looked up.

"Just for spite, Teddy. They got this out and done so quickly just to annoy me."

"Oh, come on, Kristin. You were upset so they got on their pedals and pumped to eliminate what disturbed you."

"Me? Disturbed me? Don't you mean us?"

"Of course. Let's drop it. It's over and done with. Why make everyone feel bad?"

"I didn't write those words, Teddy."

He nodded.

"The guard said to simply destroy the old pages and substitute these in the booklet."

"I'm sure everyone will do that first thing," Kristin said.

"It's not like they wrote we committed a crime or committed adultery," he said softly. Her eyes widened.

"Oh, really? Why do you say *that*?"

He pressed his lips together hard to punish them for permitting the words to escape. It was as if he had stepped on a land mine. During the last trimester of Kristin's first pregnancy, one of her jealous girlfriends had suggested Teddy was a little too cozy with a receptionist in the office, who just happened to be a bit of a flirt. She didn't actually accuse him of anything, but the cloud of suspicion hung over them until Jennifer's birth.

"Just as an example of what else it could have been. Jeez, Kristin, maybe Nikki Stanley is right. Maybe you are a bit paranoid," he said, regretting it almost as quickly as the words escaped his lips. She slammed her coffee cup down so hard on the saucer, the saucer split in two. Jennifer, who had been feeding Mr. Sniffles, looked up sharply. Even the puppy paused.

Kristin rose quickly, scooped up the two pieces of her saucer and dumped them in the garbage disposal.

"Sorry," Teddy said. She didn't respond. She started to take out last night's dishes from the dishwasher and kept her back to him.

"Looks like I move into the doghouse with Mr. Sniffles," Teddy told Jennifer. She looked at her mother and then back at Teddy, but she didn't smile. She knew when smiles weren't appropriate. This was one of those times.

Teddy waited another moment and then got up and went to Kristin. When he put his arms around her, she pulled away.

"Come on, Kristin. I said I was sorry."

"All right," she said. "Let's drop it. I've got to get Jennifer ready for school."

"Right," Teddy said, retreating. Before he left for work, he tried to kiss her good-bye. She turned her face so he would have to kiss her cheek instead of her lips. He promised to call and left.

After she got Jennifer off, she decided to take a walk and followed the path behind the house to the lake, where she sat on a large boulder and gazed across the water. The breeze was cool and brisk, and the pine scent was refreshing. It really was a beautiful setting, pristine, with flocks of geese in their A-formation flying north, the rocks in the water glistening like diamonds, squirrels scurrying to and fro with an ecstatic frenzy, and here and there a rabbit tweaking its nose and then hopping into the brush. She watched the ripples in the water, occasionally catching the sight of a fish leaping out to feed on insects.

Across the lake where there weren't any houses developed yet, the woods were deeper and darker. She thought she saw what looked like a hawk swoop down over the water and then fly into the trees. With the deep blue sky and the lazy movement of puffy milk white clouds above her, the scene had a meditative effect. She felt the tension seep out of her body. The profound, pleasurable experience of being in nature replaced her depression and anger with hope and calmness.

Maybe she had overreacted. How small and insignificant it seemed now that she had time to put it in perspective. A couple of busybodies, women who had little or nothing to do with their lives but devote their time to the nitty-gritty of development life, invaded her privacy and then quickly retreated. Teddy was right: it was the only glitch in an otherwise smooth and easy transition. Jennifer had friends, the school was nice, life was comfortable and simple. Teddy liked his work and how could she ask for a bet-

ter environment in which to dabble in her own dream
of becoming a successful composer of songs?

She sighed. She shouldn't have jumped all over him
like that and sent him away in anger. If anything, they
had come here to avoid tension, to escape the urban
world and all the complications, stress, and pressure.
It was just that she had been so shocked to open that
pamphlet and confront the most unhappy, tragic
event of their lives. The miscarriage had put a terrible
strain on their relationship and they had done all
they could to put it behind them. Neither of them referred to it anymore. It had reached the point where
it seemed like it never really happened.

That's why she was so positive neither of them had
said anything that would lead anyone to suspect it.
There was really only one place for them to have gotten the information: Doctor Hoffman, the O.B. who
lived in their development. At Nikki's and Jean's suggestion, she had decided to use him. She recalled that
Hoffman's wife, Arlene, was his receptionist. Maybe
she had read her file or even discussed the file with
her husband and then mentioned it to Nikki or Jean.
How unprofessional. Kristin made up her mind she
would question her and him about it at her next visit.
If she didn't like what she heard from the Hoffmans,
she would seek another physician. Teddy didn't have
to know.

Poor Teddy, she thought, he really jumped in his
seat when she broke that saucer. She was surprised at
her vehemence herself. She never liked him going off
unhappy when he went to work. He was a doctor and
his mind should be clear and relaxed when he dealt
with people and their eye ailments. Now she felt as
guilty about her reaction this morning as she had felt
angry. She would make it up to him, she thought. She

would cook his favorite dinner, serve it by candlelight and afterward, curl up in his arms.

She stood up, gazed across the lake to take in the beautiful scene one more time, and then started back to her house. The woods were thin here so she could see well into the backyards of other homes. One had a nice redwood deck with steps that led to a pathway to the lake. The next one over had a Wedgwood blue gazebo. There was a swing set, too. Once again, she thought how peaceful it was, peaceful and safe, a perfect place to bring up children.

Then she turned to her right and looked at the homes that ran along at a right angle to her street.

The sight of someone scurrying quickly over the yard of the first house stopped her. It was one of the security guards, and it looked like he had his pistol drawn. He crouched down and moved up the steps to the patio door. Kristin held her breath. What was going on? She waited and watched. When he reached the landing of the rear deck, he slapped his back against the wall and inched toward the door. He reached over with his left hand and tried the handle. It was locked so he crouched down again and went to a window. He attempted to open it, found it, too, was locked and then, using his pistol handle as a hammer, broke the glass, reached in, unlocked the window, and pushed it up.

Kristin moved closer, keeping herself behind a large oak tree. She heard a woman's scream and then silence. Her own heart was pounding. This was the brown and white ranch-style house she and Jean had referred to when they met the other morning. She tried to recall who lived there and tried to envision the map in the directory that listed the residents.

Scurrying quickly now, she moved around her

house to the front and hurried down the walk to the street. There was a security patrol car in front of the house. She looked up and down the street. No one else had come out to see what was happening. She waited a moment and then continued slowly toward the house. Just before she arrived, one of the security guards came out the front door. A moment later he was followed by the security guard she had seen break the rear window.

They saw her approaching, but they didn't stop.

"What's going on?" she asked as they opened their car doors.

"False alarm," the driver said. She recognized him as the man who had come to their house that first night, Spier.

"Yeah, thank goodness," the other guard said as he got into the vehicle.

"Everything all right?" she asked Spier.

"Fine," he said, smiling. He got into the vehicle and they drove off.

Kristin hesitated, looked back, saw there still wasn't anyone else in the street, and then impulsively decided to march up to the front door. She pushed the buzzer and waited. No one came to the door. She thought about it a moment. Maybe there wasn't anyone home and that's why the security guards came running. But then, who did she hear scream? She looked down at the doormat and saw the residents' name: Del Marco. Del Marco . . . the ones Jean said had an oil leak in their car.

She considered pushing the door buzzer again and decided against it, but as she turned and started down the walk, the door was thrust open. Kristin turned to see a tall, dark-haired woman, her hair disheveled, wearing a robe but barefoot. She had what looked like a frying pan clutched in her raised right hand like a club.

"I'm sorry," Kristin said. "I didn't mean to disturb you. I was returning from a walk to the lake when the security guards came and I saw one break into the rear of the house. I just wanted to see if everyone was all right."

The woman's arm slumped to her side. She leaned out to be sure the security guards were gone and then gazed at Kristin.

"You're the new resident? Morris?"

"Yes. I'm Kristin."

"Welcome to Emerald Lakes," she said and slammed the door.

"What part didn't you understand, Teddy?" Kristin asked, annoyed. She shifted the receiver from her left to right ear and leaned against the counter.

"They broke into the house? Why didn't they just ring the doorbell?"

"Curious, isn't it?" she said, the sarcasm dripping. Teddy thought a moment. "Well? What do you think? Should I report it to Nikki and have it included in the monthly newsletter? It isn't as juicy as a miscarriage, I know, but . . ."

"Maybe they tried the doorbell, but Mrs. Del Marco didn't hear it. She could have been in the bathroom or something, and they were worried. I'd rather have a broken window than a dead wife," he said. "Besides, I'm sure the window will be replaced at the homeowners association's expense."

"I'm not worried about the cost of the window, Teddy. The woman, Mrs. Del Marco, she came to that door with a frying pan to strike someone. I think she thought the security guards had returned. Why would she do that?"

"Maybe she was upset with the way they had come tearing into the house. Maybe she was in the shower."

"Maybe," Kristin said, "but the way she said, 'Welcome to Emerald Lakes.' It was as if she had said 'Welcome to hell.' "

"Oh, come on, Kristin."

"You weren't there."

"She was upset so she was sarcastic. It's understandable. I'm sure she feels sorry about it by now."

"I don't know."

"Well, I do. Relax. You want to go out for dinner tonight? Hank was telling me about this Italian place in Middletown, just what you like, a hole in the wall, mom-and-pop operation, authentic."

She thought a moment. Maybe it was better they get out. She could cook his favorite meal another night.

"I think we both need a night out, honey. Alone."

"Alone?"

"Yeah, why don't you call one of the teenage girls listed in the directory under baby-sitters."

"I like Jennifer to meet and get to know whomever we leave with her, Teddy."

"So? Have the girl come over early and spend some time with her. Call . . . Jean and ask her who she recommends."

"I don't know if I care for her opinion about anything except laundry detergent," Kristin said. "I'll rely on my own instincts."

"Fine. Gotta go."

She cradled the phone, thought a moment and then went to the homeowners directory to study the names listed under approved baby-sitters. Who approved them? How were they approved? The doorbell interrupted her train of thought. She closed the directory and went to the foyer.

"Hi," Jeannette Levine said and thrust a box of candy into Kristin's hands. "Peace offering," she said and tilted her head.

"What?"

"To make up for what I included in your interview. I'm sorry. It was on the notepad so I just typed it in. I guess I won't make editor after all."

"Oh. You don't have to give me this," Kristin said handing it back.

"No, silly. Of course I do. Sweet things always drive away unhappiness."

Kristin shook her head.

"Come on in," she said.

"This house is so nice," Jean said stepping through the door. "I remember when the Feinbergs first moved in. I thought Elaine and I were going to become good friends."

"I thought you said you were good friends in the beginning."

"I did? Oh, well, only for a short time."

"What happened?"

"She just didn't fit in to development life. That's the way Nikki put it." Jean followed Kristin into the living room.

"Sit down," Kristin said. "Did you hear about the incident at the Del Marcos' this morning?" Kristin asked as Jean sat on the sofa.

"No. What?"

"Their alarm went off and the security guards went to the house. Either Mrs. Del Marco didn't hear them ring the door buzzer or . . . I don't know. They broke into the house through a back window."

"What happened?"

"It was a false alarm."

"Oh," Jean said pressing the palms of her hands to the base of her throat. "Thank God. We've never had a break-in or a mugging or any kind of theft."

"I saw Mrs. Del Marco."

"Angela? How was she?"

"Unhappy."

"Yes, she is very unhappy these days. We don't like to gossip about each other, but I think she's having some marital problems. Nikki said that Bill said her husband lost a few big accounts this past month. Financial problems can work like earthquakes and shake a family's foundation. I hope things straighten out for them," she added mournfully.

"You said you had that item about me in your notes," Kristin said.

"Uh-huh."

"How did it get into your notes?"

"Oh, they weren't my notes; they were Nikki's. I just wrote them up. Eileen McShane does some writing, too, but she was very busy this week."

"Well, how did Nikki get the information?"

"From you at our interview."

"But I didn't mention that."

Jean shrugged.

"Nikki is sort of Mr. Slater's right-hand man, the one who does all the nitty-gritty. Nothing much happens here without her knowing about it. She enjoys it."

"Do you think she spoke to Arlene Hoffman about me?" Kristin asked, fixing her eyes on Jean's. Jean shifted her gaze uncomfortably and then widened them with surprise.

"What's that?" she cried nodding toward the rear patio door. Kristin turned and smiled at the sight of the puppy waddling back and forth.

"A toy poodle Teddy bought for Jennifer yesterday."

"It's a dog," Jean said, her voice still thick with shock.

"Yes, it is a dog. A poodle is a dog," Kristin said slowly.

"But . . . you can't have a dog."

"Can't have a dog? Why can't I? I didn't imply I was allergic to animals during the interview, did I? And I know I didn't tell Doctor Hoffman anything like that," Kristin said.

"No, not because of an allergy. Because of the CC and R's. Didn't you read the page on pets? The only pets we're permitted are birds in cages and tropical fish. We have no need for watchdogs, not with our security system."

"People have dogs for other reasons, Jean. What are you talking about? This is a house, not an apartment. I can have a dog if I want."

Jean shook her head.

"It's very specifically forbidden. The committee decided. Other developments have so many problems with cats and dogs invading other residents' property, barking, screeching, not to mention poop control."

"Poop control? Oh. Well, we don't intend to let our dog poop on anyone else's property."

"It doesn't matter. You're going to have to get rid of it."

Kristin stared at her a moment.

"We just got this puppy. My daughter is ecstatic over it. I think it's adorable. There is no way in hell I am going to give it away. If you want, you can put that down as a direct quote and publish it in the next issue of the directory," Kristin said and stood up.

"It's not my decision," Jean said. "It's the committee's and I'm not on the committee." She stood up, too. "Please don't be angry at me."

"I'm not. I'm just a tiny bit fed up with rules and regulations at the moment. I think a few people have let this thing go to their heads." Kristin smiled.

"I have to tell Nikki about the dog," Jean said sadly.

"You have to do what?"

"If she finds out I knew and didn't tell her . . . we're all technically officers in the Neighborhood Watch, all homeowners. Not reporting a violation makes you part of the violation. That was in the last monthly newsletter."

"The last thing I want is for you to get into trouble, Jean. Please, go right to the telephone and report my puppy."

"I'm sorry. I don't make the rules."

"I'm just following orders," Kristin said.

"What?"

"It was one of the famous refrains at Nuremberg."

"Where?"

"Doesn't matter now. It happened a long time ago," Kristin said. She looked at the box of candy and then seized it, tearing off the cellophane and ripping off the cover to pluck a chocolate out of the box. Jean shook her head when Kristin offered her one, and then Kristin put one into her mouth and smiled.

"You're right. Sweetness takes away sadness," Kristin said.

6

◆

THE FIRST THING TEDDY NOTICED when he arrived at home was how dark the house was. It was an overcast day and the gloom seemed to drape from the trees like Spanish moss in the Louisiana bayous. He pulled into the garage and entered the house through the kitchen. The lights were off there, as well as in the dining room and the kitchenette. When he stopped at the living room, he saw that all the lamps were unlit. At first he didn't notice Kristin sitting in the wing chair. She was so still and so quiet in the shadows. So he started down the hallway to the bedrooms.

"I'm right here, Teddy," she said. He turned, squinted, and grimaced.

"What are you doing sitting in the dark? Why aren't there any lights on? Where's Jennifer?"

"Those are easy questions," she said. "I'm sitting in the dark because there aren't any lights on and there aren't any lights on because I didn't turn them on. Jennifer's playing in her room. Next?"

"What's going on now, Kristin?" he asked stepping into the living room.

"Nothing," she said. "Actually, I should amend my response. I did turn on this lamp, and I sat here reading this fascinating book." She held up the two-inch-thick Emerald Lakes homeowners Covenants, Conditions, and Restrictions, but in the shadows Teddy didn't recognize it.

"What's that?"

"Here they would call it the Bible, the covenants, the commandments. Let me illustrate," she said as she snapped on the lamp. She opened the book, smiled at him, and began.

"Drapes: All drapes and curtains visible from the street or common areas shall be either the color and pattern of the original drapes and curtains or a color and pattern approved by the board and its authorized committee."

"Huh?"

"Wait. This gets better," she said. "Power equipment and car maintenance. No power equipment, hobby shops, or car maintenance (other than emergency work) shall be permitted on the property except with written approval of the board. The board will consider the effects of noise, air pollution, dirt or grease, fire hazard, interference with radio or television reception and similar objections."

"I don't understand why you're reading this stuff, Kristin."

"You don't? You should have read it more closely, Teddy. The board is not going to like finding out you've been here all this time and haven't."

"C'mon, Kristin, every homeowners association has that stuff and you heard that it's all just basic common courtesy and things that help maintain our property value."

"Not much of an excuse, Teddy. Sorry. In fact," she said, flipping a page and reading, "it is expected that each and every adult resident of Emerald Lakes will be line by line familiar . . . how do you like that expression? Line by line familiar? Line by line familiar with all the covenants, conditions, and restrictions for Emerald Lakes. Ignorance of these covenants, conditions, and restrictions will not be a justification for violating any. Nicely put, don't you think?"

"All right," Teddy said. "What did we do?"

"I should get to that, shouldn't I? Okay." She flipped the pages and held up the book. "Pets. Except for caged birds and tropical fish in aquariums no bigger than six feet in length, three feet in width and three feet in height, no animals, reptiles or insects of any kind shall be kept in any residence. This specifically refers to dogs of any breed and cats of any breed."

"No dogs?"

"Uh, uh, uh, Theodore Morris," she said, wagging her right forefinger at him. "Ignorance is no justification for violation."

"Let me see that," he said stepping across the room. She handed him the document and he read. After a moment he looked up. "Jesus. Who would ever think—"

"That you couldn't keep a pet in your own home? There's a lot more in there, Teddy, a lot more." She took the book back and turned the page. "Did you know, for example, that when and if you want to sell your Emerald Lakes home, you must use the Emerald Lakes real estate office and have your prospective buyer approved by the association?" She gazed up. "You look like you didn't know."

"Hey, Michele Lancaster told us the CC and R's were not much different from any homeowners', so I didn't go over it with a fine-tooth comb."

"You don't need a fine-tooth comb for this, Teddy. The restrictions are in bold, black and white letters. Yes, our garage door can't be kept open because it's unsightly, and yes, we can't have vehicles, especially trucks with advertising parked in our driveway for a prolonged period, and yes, no motor coach, trailer or camper can be driven on our development streets, but did you know we can't change a bush, plant a new tree, rearrange the sidewalk, add exterior lights or change the exterior lights without prior committee approval? We can't even increase the wattage in the bulbs!"

"Wattage in the bulbs?"

"It's called a uniform lighting code. All the approved wattage for the light fixtures is listed here." She flipped a page. "Here's one I especially love. Any gathering consisting of more than twenty persons must be approved by permit. So, if you want to have a house party, you'd better think hard about who you want to invite."

He shook his head.

"No dogs?"

"Yes, no dogs. Jean was here today to apologize for what she had included about me in the directory. She more or less confirmed that Nikki Stanley got the information from Arlene Hoffman, my doctor's wife. I'll see about that during my doctor's visit tomorrow. Anyway, then Jean saw Mr. Sniffles and nearly passed out with shock. She told me . . . no, apologized, I suppose would be the more accurate way of putting it, that she would have to turn us in."

"You're kidding. She turned us in?"

"Yes. The way it works is this . . . she's a member of the community and all members of the community are technically members of the Neighborhood Watch, so if you or I or Jean sees some violation and don't report it, we're conspirators."

"Well, I can understand their point. We should all care, but . . ."

"I know, kind of reminds you of children turning in their parents in a faraway land called Nazi Germany."

"Really, Kristin . . . Nazi Germany?" He started to smile.

"They had Eileen McShane call. She, too, apologized, but said she was calling officially as a member of the Neighborhood Watch because she had been informed we had a dog in the house. She asked if that were true.

" 'I cannot tell a lie,' I said. 'It's true.'

"She read me the restriction word for word and told me where to find it. I told her where to put it."

"You didn't?"

"More or less. I think my exact words were we were going to use the book of CC and R's for poop paper for our dog. She thought that was an unfortunate thing for me to say and told me she didn't like to be the one who enforces the laws, but someone has to do it. I told her I felt sorry for her and ended the conversation."

Kristin sat back.

"Mr. Sniffles is in Jennifer's room with her. Why don't you go in and tell her she has to give the puppy up? Read her the CC and R's."

"You think I wanted something like this to happen?" he cried, his arms out.

"No, Teddy, but I think you had better figure out a way out of it."

"This is unreasonable," he said. "I'm sure they have some sort of appeal procedure." He thumbed through the book until he found what he wanted and nodded.

"You can appeal to the board of directors for a variance. I'll call Phil Slater."

He turned and went to the phone in the kitchen, hesitating only when he lifted the receiver.

"Where's the directory?"

"It's in the stove."

"Stove?"

"Yes. I like keeping it in the stove," she said. He stared at her a moment and then opened the stove door. It was there.

"You are really cracking up, Kristin. You know that."

"You can't crack up in Emerald Lakes, Teddy. It's expressly forbidden in the CC and R's."

"Very funny." He looked up Slater's number and called. Kristin sat back in her chair to listen and watch. "Philip, Teddy Morris. You have a minute or is this an inconvenient time?"

"No, it's fine," Philip Slater said. "How can I help you, Teddy?"

"Well, I just found out that I violated a rule by buying my daughter a toy poodle puppy."

"I see. Yes, that's something specifically restricted."

"I realize that now, but I think this dog is so innocuous, a true house pet, it couldn't possibly annoy or bother anyone."

"Nevertheless, Teddy, it's one of our rules. You had the CC and R's before you even completed escrow."

"I know. I just . . . missed that section for some reason. Anyhow, I read where we can appeal to the board for a variance."

"Yes, you can submit a request and attend the next meeting which happens to be tomorrow night, but I can't guarantee anything. I have only one vote myself," Philip said.

"Right. Well, we'd like to do just that."

"Fine. Why don't you give your written request to Nikki Stanley before eight tomorrow. The board will meet in closed session at seven and then you can appear at eight."

"Thank you."

"No problem. How do you like working with Hank Porter and his medical group?"

"Oh, that's been great."

"I've already heard good things about you, Teddy. Matter of fact, Ben Stuart over at the laundry told me he's asked his medical insurance company to consider including you as a participating physician."

"Really? That's very nice."

"If your group picks up a half dozen or so of these small companies, it will be very, very nice," Philip emphasized. "I'm sure you will. Anyway, sorry about your problem, but we're proud of our homeowners association and the way it handles every possible issue."

"Right. Okay. Thanks," Teddy said and hung up. He stared ahead for a moment.

"Well?" Kristin asked.

"We have to submit our request in writing to Nikki Stanley and then attend the board meeting at eight tomorrow night in Slater's house."

"Do we need a lawyer to attend with us?"

"Very funny. I'm sure they'll see how innocuous this is and grant us a variance," Teddy said. "I feel like such a jerk for not reading the rules closely. This is all my fault. I created the situation."

"By wanting to buy your daughter a puppy?"

He gazed at her a moment and then shook his head.

"I'll go into the office and jot down a quick letter.

We'll give it to Nikki Stanley on the way out to the restaurant. We're still going out for dinner, aren't we?"

"Yes. I was too upset to cook."

"What about the baby-sitter?"

"I was too upset to deal with it. We'll take Jennifer along this time," she said.

"Okay. I'll just work up a quick letter and change."

He hurried down the hallway, pausing at the doorway to Jennifer's room. The scene brought a wide smile to his face. His daughter was sitting on the floor, her back against the wall, with one of her pop-up books in her lap, pretending to read. Beside her, sitting on its small haunches, was the puppy listening and staring as if he could actually understand. His little tail wagged when he turned to notice Teddy. Jennifer looked up.

"Hi, Daddy."

"Hey, Jen. What are you doing?"

"Reading to Mr. Sniffles. He likes this one the best. It's about Snooker the dog."

"Oh. I see. Great. Well, we're going out to eat soon."

"I know. Mommy told me."

"All right, honey." He hurried on, filled with determination to write a simple, sensible letter of request no one could reasonably deny.

A little over half an hour later, they left the house and drove toward the front gate. He slowed and stopped in front of the Stanley residence.

"I'll just be a minute," he said. He hopped out and jogged up the walk to the front door where he pushed the door button and then turned and smiled back at Kristin and Jennifer, who had her face up against the rear window.

The door was opened by Graham Stanley. The

eight-year-old wore a shirt and tie and had his hair slicked back, with a perfect part on the left side. He was a light brown-haired boy with dull hazel eyes and a somewhat chubby, soft face.

"Is your mother here?" Teddy asked.

"We're eating dinner now," Graham said sharply.

"Oh. I don't want to bother anyone. Could you give her this letter?" Teddy said. He handed the envelope to Graham who looked like he wouldn't take it at first. Then he snatched it quickly and closed the door. Teddy felt a cold stream of anger slide up his spine and stiffen his neck.

"Little bastard," he muttered, but when he turned to walk back to the car, he forced a smile.

"What happened?" Kristin asked when he got in.

"Nothing. Their son answered the door. I gave him the letter." He shrugged.

"She knew you were coming," Kristin said as they approached the gate. "She could have greeted you."

Teddy pressed his lips together. He was angry, too, but it seemed Kristin was jumping at every opportunity to be upset with Emerald Lakes and the residents. At the gate the security guard scrutinized them for a moment and then stepped out of the booth without opening the gate. He carried his clipboard.

"What's up?" Teddy asked.

"Just wanted to know if you would be gone long."

"Why?" Kristin demanded before Teddy could respond.

"Just a precaution, ma'am. If you're going to be gone long, we'll sweep by your house more often."

"Jesus. You people make me feel like I'm living in the middle of a war zone," she snapped. The guard didn't change his expression. He held his clipboard and his pen steady.

"I'm only doing my job, ma'am. It's what the residents of Emerald Lakes pay us to do," he said.

"We're just going to dinner," Teddy said. "A few hours at the most."

"Thank you, sir." He made a note, returned to the booth and opened the gate. Teddy drove out without comment, but the silence was too thick and heavy to keep long.

"There's no sense in our taking it out on the employees. If we don't like a procedure, we should attend a homeowners meeting and bring up the problem," he said.

"You like all this Big Brother stuff, Teddy?"

"I didn't say I like it exactly. Unfortunately, because of the world we live in, it's necessary."

"So's roughage in your diet."

"What?"

"Nothing. What's the difference? Let's just have a good dinner," she said and closed her eyes. Was it her condition? Was she being unreasonable? Ungrateful? Why wasn't Teddy as annoyed? A thought came to her. "I think we should ask a few more questions, Teddy."

"What do you mean?"

"All this security. Something terrible must have happened here to make it necessary. Something no one is telling us."

He was quiet. If he disagreed, she would say he was accusing her of the paranoia again. They drove on, the thick silence enveloping them once more.

Their dinner turned out to be spectacular. The atmosphere in the small, homey Italian restaurant was authentic. Everything was homemade, even the wine, which Kristin drank like water. By the time they arrived at dessert, she was giggling like a teenager. Teddy, relieved the tension had lifted, drank a little too much himself, and every time Jennifer asked them why they were laughing, they laughed again.

The good food, the nice time with the owners and the waitress, and especially the wine, made the ride back to Emerald Lakes different. The two of them sang old fifties songs. They no sooner finished one line when the other would think of some other melody and they would sing a chorus to Jennifer who sat back amused by the way her parents were acting. When they pulled up to the security booth, they both clammed up and tried to appear sober and respectable.

"Good evening," Teddy said to the guard, but Kristin couldn't subdue her giggle any longer.

"Remember us?" she called. "We didn't lie. We only went to dinner."

"Yes, ma'am," he said and hit the button to open the gate.

"Did you sweep by our house?" she demanded.

"Yes, ma'am."

"Is it still there?"

"Ma'am?"

She sat back and laughed. Teddy winked at the guard, but he didn't smile. Teddy drove into the complex. When he looked into his rearview mirror, he saw the guard was on the telephone. Kristin continued to sing and giggle, even as they pulled up to their driveway. As they did so, Teddy noticed the Emerald Lakes patrol car come around the opposite turn and slow down. The guard watched them drive into the garage. Teddy didn't say anything about it and hit the button to close the garage door as quickly as he could.

"Let's go see the stowaway!" Kristin cried when they entered the house.

Kristin took Jennifer's hand and they went into Jennifer's room where Kristin hugged and cuddled the puppy, who couldn't stop licking her face. Jennifer's melodic laughter filled Teddy with a cold ache that wrapped itself around his heart. How could something like this be undesirable? he wondered and vowed to convince the board to grant them their variance.

Neither he nor Kristin talked about the appeal in the morning, but when Jennifer kissed Mr. Sniffles good-bye before heading off to catch the school bus, they looked at each other nervously.

"Teddy, it's going to break her heart if we have to give up that puppy."

"I know," he said. "We won't have to. I'm sure."

She shook her head skeptically and kissed him good-bye. As she moved through her day, Kristin's exasperation with the situation grew into a small rage. By the time she was ready to go to her doctor's appointment, she was tense and irritable. She backed out of their driveway in her Ford Escort, and then shot off. She forgot about the speed bump and the jolt nearly drove her head into the car roof. It slowed her down, but it didn't calm her down. Before the security guard at the gate could ask a question, she fired her answer at him.

"I'm going to see my doctor. I'll be gone about an hour or so."

"Yes, ma'am," he said. She recognized him as one of the security men who had gone to the Del Marcos' house the day before.

"Wait a minute."

"Ma'am?"

"You were one of the guards who checked on the Del Marco false alarm yesterday, weren't you?"

"Yes, ma'am."

"Well, why did you have to break in through a window?"

"A full report is being given to the board of trustees, ma'am. You can make your inquiries to them," he said firmly.

"Thanks," she said and drove out. They treated everything around here like a world crisis. What would happen if something really serious occurred, like a murder or a suicide? She thought about Elaine Feinberg. It gave her the chills.

There were no patients before her at Doctor Hoffman's office. His wife, Arlene, looked up from her paperwork and smiled.

"Perfect timing," she said. "The doctor can see you right away." She opened the door.

"Good," Kristin said and followed her through the corridor. Arlene showed her into the examination room.

"I'll tell him you've arrived," she said. "How are you feeling?"

"Physically, fine, but I have other problems," she said sharply, her eyes narrowed and her implications clear.

"Oh. Oh," Arlene added and bit down on her lower lip. She was a stout woman who had lost her good looks to a weight problem. Her attractive dark eyes looked misplaced in the chubby face, and her bleached blond hair was cut too sharply under her ears, the trim emphasizing her plumpness. She shifted her eyes away quickly. "I'll get the doctor."

Kristin remained standing. A moment later Doctor Hoffman appeared. Only an inch or so taller than his wife, he was slim to the point of being thin. His face was lean, but not hard, and a bit bony in the nose and cheeks. Kristin had been satisfied with him during her first visit. He had kind, considerate eyes, a gentle touch and a soft, friendly manner of speaking. He projected a professional, experienced demeanor, one that would win over his patient's confidence.

"How are you doing?" he asked as soon as he entered. Kristin turned on him sharply, her face all business.

"I'm feeling fine, but I'm a little upset."

"Oh. Please, have a seat," Doctor Hoffman said indicating the chair by the examination table. He remained standing by the door, his arms folded under his chest. "What's the problem?"

"The problem is information I gave you is all over the housing development," Kristin said. Hoffman's eyes narrowed and his lips tightened.

"What do you mean, Mrs. Morris? What sort of information?"

"My miscarriage. It appeared in that . . . that directory of residents. You must have seen it," she said.

"I didn't read it, although I recall a new issue being delivered. Who told you the information came out of this office?"

"No one told me specifically. I figured it out," she said. "We're new here, Doctor, as you know. We haven't told anyone about our intimate problems in the past. This is the only place where it was mentioned and only because it's part of my medical history. Next thing I know, it's part of 'Introduction to Our Newest Residents, the Morrises.' I complained, of course, and they've already retracted it, printed new pages, but I can't tell you how terrible I felt reading it."

He stared at her for a few seconds and then nodded. "Excuse me a moment," he said.

She sat back. After a good five minutes, Doctor Hoffman returned with his wife at his side. Her eyes were bloodshot and her face a bit white. Her lips trembled.

"I think we owe you an apology, Mrs. Morris," Doctor Hoffman began. He looked at his wife.

"I'm so sorry. I might have said something to Nikki Stanley the other day. She has a way of asking questions and picking up on every word. I'm not making any excuses, but I might very well have made a comment and she remembered it. I'm so sorry."

"It's not something that's happened often, but that doesn't excuse it," Doctor Hoffman said. "We're a small community. People talk about each other, and my wife"—he gazed down at her with a look of reproach—"unfortunately forgets our professional responsibilities." She cowered and he looked at Kristin again. "You have every right to be upset."

Arlene Hoffman dabbed her eyes with her handkerchief and pressed her upper lip over her lower. Kristin felt sorry for her. She realized she was no match for the likes of a Nikki Stanley.

"Mrs. Stanley had no right to include it, even if she did hear about it," Kristin said.

"I agree," Doctor Hoffman said. "But that doesn't mitigate our guilt in the matter. All I can say is I'm sorry and I will personally see that nothing like that happens again. Of course, if you want to see another physician, I understand and will recommend someone nearby."

Kristin looked at Arlene Hoffman who looked so devastated, she appeared to be shrinking by the moment.

"No, I'm comfortable with you, Doctor Hoffman."

"Well, you're very generous and understanding, Mrs. Morris."

"I'm sorry," Arlene said again and then left quickly.

"She really isn't a mean-spirited person," Doctor Hoffman said as soon as his wife was gone. "I'm sure she had no idea the information would be spread."

"Who would?" Kristin quipped. Doctor Hoffman smiled and shook his head.

"Exactly. Who would?"

"I'm glad I'm not the only one who thinks it was bizarre."

"Life in suburbia has its problems too, I guess. Anyway, let's concentrate on the future," he said and then he narrowed his eyes with determination. "There'll be no miscarriage this time."

"I hope not," Kristin said softly. "I hope not."

Later as Kristin served dinner, Teddy listened to her description of the office visit and her discovery.

"I actually felt more sorry for his wife," she said sitting at the table. Teddy nodded and then shook his head. Kristin leaned forward, her eyes wide with fury. "Nikki Stanley lied to me, you know. She knew very well where she had gotten the information."

"She probably didn't want to implicate Doctor Hoffman's wife."

"But why put the information in then?"

"Overly enthusiastic, I guess. They get so excited about what they're doing and they're so proud of this development and how it's being run," Teddy offered. Kristin sat back, disappointed. Maybe it came from his being a doctor, but Teddy always had such control of his emotions.

"That's no defense," she insisted.

"No. It's just an explanation, but she did apologize

and they did retract the pages. What else can we ask for, Kristin? Blood?"

She glared ahead for a moment, her ire diminishing because of Teddy's calmness.

"How was your examination?" he asked. "That's far more important."

"He said everything looks good and I haven't gained too much weight."

"Great. You like him as a doctor?"

"Yes."

Teddy shrugged.

"So let's drop the other matter," he suggested and started to describe his work. "At the end of the day, Hank Porter came over to my office to tell me one of my patients had recommended me to Ben Stuart, who owns and operates a laundry with about a hundred employees. As a result Stuart called to get into our group. I mentioned that Phil Slater had said something about it when I called him yesterday. Hank wasn't surprised. You know what he said?"

She shook her head.

"He said it wasn't the first time someone from Emerald Lakes helped someone else from Emerald Lakes. He was envious of our family loyalty and support for each other."

"Family?"

"That's the way he put it. Made me feel . . . I don't know . . . part of something bigger. Know what I mean?"

"No," she said, but then added, "but maybe that's because you're in contact with so many more people than I am these days."

He nodded. After dinner he helped clean up, both of them eyeing the clock.

"Maybe we should bring Mr. Sniffles with us,

Teddy. If they see how small the dog is and how cute . . ."

"I don't know if Marilyn Slater would appreciate our bringing a dog into her home. Some people have allergies to animals, too."

When they were finished in the kitchen, Kristin went to the bedroom to fix her hair and put on some lipstick. She was surprised at how her hand trembled when she gazed at herself in the mirror. She was disturbed about her own nervousness. The telephone's ringing startled her and she pressed her hand to her heart. Teddy was in the bathroom, so she picked up the receiver.

"Hello."

"This Kristin Morris?"

"Yes?"

"Angela Del Marco. We met briefly the other day."

"Oh, yes."

"I'm sorry about my abruptness, but I was in a rather bad mood considering what had happened."

"I understand. Is everything all right now?"

"No. That's why I'm calling. How much did you see?"

"How much did I see? I saw the security guard go around to the rear of your house. I was in the rear of mine so I saw him try your patio door and then break the window and go into your house. I ran to the front but by the time I reached your house, the security guards were coming out."

"So you didn't see the other one open the front door? I was hoping you had."

"Open the front door? No. Was it unlocked?"

"He said it was, but I know it was locked. They have keys to our homes. I've always suspected that and I was hoping you saw him unlock the front door."

"No, I'm sorry. But if they had a key to your house, why would they break in?"

"That's the point," Angela said dryly.

"Didn't you hear them ring the doorbell?"

"They never did, although they said they did. They just came busting in on me. I was in the tub."

"Oh . . . I'm sorry. That's very disturbing."

"You're sure you didn't see any of this? You were in the front of the house when I came out," she said with some accusation in her tone.

"No. I'm sorry."

"If you did see it, would you tell me?"

"Of course."

"Maybe you would," Angela said after a moment's thought. "You're still new here. After a while you wouldn't," she added dryly.

"That's not true," Kristin retorted sharply. "Anyway, why don't you complain about this to the board? There's a meeting tonight. My husband and I are just about to go to ask for a variance."

"For your poodle. I know."

"You do?"

"Honey, you don't so much as get constipated here without someone coming over with a laxative. You'll see. Anyway, take some advice from someone who's learning. Whatever the committee decides about your dog, accept it gracefully. Thank them for their time and go home with your tail between your legs. That is, if you want to live and play at Emerald Lakes," she added. "Thanks. Good luck."

She hung up before Kristin could say anything. She stood there holding the receiver.

"Who was that?" Teddy asked.

"Angela Del Marco. She said she thinks the security force has keys to our homes. She thinks they lied about trying the door buzzer and deliberately busted in on her."

"Why would they do that?" Teddy asked smiling.

"Because she complained about something, I think."

"Oh, come on, Kristin. The woman's a bit of a troublemaker. I already heard something about her today."

"From who?"

"Larry Sommers. He's one of the trustees."

"When did you speak with him?"

Teddy smiled.

"When I went to see him about a new car. He sells Lexuses," he said. "I was told he gives Emerald Lakes residents a good deal and he does. We talked about the development a bit and the situation over at the Del Marcos' house came up."

"You used to tell me before you would go out and do something like buy a new car, Teddy."

"I wanted to surprise you. Because of the deal we got here and the money I'm making, we can afford it."

"And he told you Angela Del Marco was a troublemaker?"

"Well, there have been complaints about some of the things they've done around their house and when she's been approached, she's been very uncooperative. They don't fine people that often, but they had to fine the Del Marcos."

"For what?"

"Dangling cans off the roof for the kids to use as a basketball net. Unsightly and noisy," he added.

She thought a moment.

"Funny," she said. "For people who discourage gossiping about each other, it's amazing how much of it is done."

"Long as it's with each other and not the outside world," Teddy said.

"The outside world? Jean Levine referred to it that way when I asked her if she had heard about Elaine Feinberg. I wonder how long before I do, too."

"Not long," Teddy said smiling. He meant it as something good, but she didn't smile.

She wasn't sure.

7

◆

MARILYN SLATER SAT IN HER ROCKER and watched them walking up the street, their little girl between them, holding their hands, adorable in her flamingo pink dress with a matching bow ribbon in her hair. She knew why the Morrises were coming.

Philip sounded so sweet and reasonable on the phone the night before, but the moment he had hung up that receiver and turned, Marilyn had seen the rage in his eyes.

"Supposed grown-ups," he said through his clenched teeth, "mature, even professionals. First, they don't read what they're supposed to read, and then, when they do, they're like children thinking they're somehow special. The rules apply to someone else, but not to them.

"And the rules . . . they're written so clearly, precisely, carefully, no one could possibly misunderstand. We didn't create this whole thing overnight. It came from painstaking, careful research, days and hours of learning what works and what doesn't in other communities like ours. We evolved into the best, and yet, someone always wants a variance. Someone always wants to be treated special.

Someone's always trying to weaken the security we've walled around ourselves and our property."

"Why didn't you tell him all that on the phone, Philip?" she asked innocently. He looked at her as if he just realized she was alive and living with him.

"What? What are you talking about, Marilyn? That's not the way these things are handled. We have a specific, detailed, well thought out procedure for this sort of thing. My committee handles it and has handled it in the past."

"You're the committee, Philip."

"Stop that," he said, his face becoming even more crimson. "I guide them, I lead them, but I don't—"

"Control them?"

"Right. They each have a mind of their own."

"Who has ever voted against something you wanted or didn't want, Philip? Tell me," she challenged. "Nikki Stanley? I can't even imagine it. Vincent McShane? He trembles when you look at him. Sid Levine? Larry Sommers? They're all dependent upon you in some business way."

"Just because our decisions are reported as unanimous, that doesn't mean no one disagreed with me, Marilyn. We like to present ourselves to the development as united. Anyway, why are you suddenly so concerned? You rarely comment on development affairs," he said.

She turned away, but he pursued her.

"What is it? What's bothering you?"

She didn't want him to know just how much and how long she had been watching the Morrises. She was always at the window when the children returned from school and saw Kristin Morris greet her little girl. The love she witnessed filled her heart with joy and made it possible for her to close her eyes and remember Bradley running up the drive after he returned from school. The Morrises, unlike any other family in the development, appeared to be the family she wished she and Philip had been.

"I'd like to see some happy people for a change," she said softly, almost too softly for him to hear, but he did.

"What? Who's not happy living here? Just tell me one person. Go on. Who?"

"I'm not," she said.

"Don't be ridiculous. Besides," he said, "I told you I was building us a bigger and nicer house on the lake. I'm bringing the plans home tomorrow and I want you to start thinking about the decor. I want something different. I'm sure you do, too."

"If I don't, can I disagree?"

"It's our house, Marilyn. We have to agree."

"And appear unanimous?" She laughed. "All right, Philip. Bring home the plans," she said. Maybe, she thought, if she got involved in something as big as a new house, she would revive some dead emotions and feel alive again.

However, today, when he had brought the plans home and had spread them out on the table in his office, she had looked up with surprise.

"It's a two story, Philip."

"Right," he said. "You always wanted a spiral staircase. Now you'll have it."

"But two-story homes are prohibited at Emerald Lakes. You said they inhibit other people's views."

"We'll get the committee to grant a variance in this case," he said.

"You mean ask for special treatment like the Morrises are asking?" she responded.

His smile faded quickly and he rolled up the plans.

"This is different," he said sharply. "It's located where it won't block anyone's view and it's something that will enhance our property values here, not detract from them. It's in everyone's best interest.

"A dog," he said firmly, "is not."

Why isn't a dog in everyone's best interest? she wondered now as she watched the Morrises turn up the driveway toward the front door. What's wrong with someone having a nice pet? She would be terrible if she had to sit on Philip's committee and make decisions. She would grant everyone's little variances.

The doorbell sounded. Marilyn rose to answer it because the committee was already meeting in Philip's office and Philip hated to be interrupted.

"Hello," she said.

"Good evening," Teddy said. "I'm Teddy Morris and this is my wife, Kristin, and our daughter, Jennifer."

"I know. Come in. Please," Marilyn said stepping back.

Kristin, who was so tense she thought she clicked when she walked, unfroze her face and smiled. Marilyn Slater was much prettier and even much younger than she had anticipated. Her eyes were soft and warm, but they were set in a face framed with lacquered hair, not a strand out of place. This plastic-perfect demeanor was continued by her model's correct posture. She wore a stylish iridescent green dress with a bronze silk blazer and a flat, gold necklace with teardrop gold earrings.

"Please," Marilyn said indicating the living room. "Make yourselves comfortable while I go tell the committee you've arrived."

"Thank you," Teddy said.

Marilyn flashed a smile and then went down the corridor to the office. Teddy and Kristin looked around, Jennifer not letting go of either of their hands.

"Pretty house," Kristin said. "Expensive things."

Teddy nodded, half looking, his concentration on the presentation he expected to make to the committee.

"They'll be just a few more minutes," Marilyn said returning. "Can I get anyone anything?"

"No, thank you," Teddy said. Kristin shook her head.

"How about you, Jennifer? I have chocolate covered frozen vanilla yogurt on a stick."

Jennifer looked up at Kristin.

"If you want one, honey, say 'Yes, thank you.' "

"Yes, thank you," Jennifer parroted. Marilyn's smile widened and softened.

"I love your decor," Kristin said. "I favor traditional, too."

"Do you? Good. Sometimes I feel like I'm holding up the cause alone," Marilyn said. "I'll be right back." She went to the kitchen and Kristin turned to the picture window. She saw the rocker and gazed out at the street.

"They have a clear view of our street and the one adjacent from here," Kristin commented. "Almost as if they look down on everyone."

"So?" Teddy remained standing near the doorway, anxious to make his presentation.

"I wonder if she saw anything."

"What? What are you talking about? Saw what?"

"What happened to Angela Del Marco."

"Oh. Don't bring it up," he warned as Marilyn returned with the yogurt on a stick.

"Say 'Thank you,' honey," Kristin prompted.

"Thank you."

"Take the napkin and don't let it drip," Kristin ordered.

"It's all right," Marilyn said quickly. It had been so long since she'd had to worry about anything like that, she almost welcomed a little smudge. "Let her enjoy."

"I would have chosen furnishings like yours," Kristin continued, "if our home hadn't come already furnished."

"Would you? Well, you'll change it to your own liking over time, I'm sure," Marilyn said.

They all turned at the sound of footsteps and then Philip Slater's appearance. He smiled.

"Evening, folks."

"Hi," Teddy said. He shook Philip's hand.

"We're ready for you now. Hi there, Jennifer," he said. Jennifer backed up a few steps and brushed against Marilyn who instinctively put her hand on the little girl's shoulder.

"Why doesn't Jennifer stay with me while you two go in," Marilyn suggested. She smiled down at her. "Would you like to stay with me? I'll show you my collection of dolls."

Jennifer's eyes widened with interest.

"Will you wait with Mrs. Slater, honey?" Kristin asked. Jennifer gazed at Philip and then nodded. "Thank you," Kristin said to Marilyn.

"Oh, we'll have fun. Come on, Jennifer." She extended her hand. "The dolls are all in the sewing room."

"Right this way," Philip indicated. "Beautiful evening, isn't it? How I pity those poor souls trapped in some urban cage where the buildings block out the stars."

He opened the office door. The seats had been re-arranged for a hearing with the committee seated on both sides of Philip's desk. Nikki Stanley sat on the right end with Sid Levine beside her. She looked irri-tated, her lips pencil thin, her eyes picking up the dull, yellow illumination from the side lamp. Sid Levine appeared businesslike in his jacket and tie, but on the other side of the desk, Vincent McShane slouched, his lower shirt button undone with some of his stomach flowing over the belt buckle. His thick lips were twisted in an uneven smile resembling the grin of someone who had been on a drunken bender. Larry Sommers, tall and lean with thin dark hair, looked bored and impatient.

Two chairs had been set up just inside the door, fac-ing the committee.

"Have a seat," Philip said indicating them. He walked around to the back of his desk and sat. "I think you know everyone, don't you, Ted?"

"I don't," Kristin said sharply.

"Of course. Sorry. Nikki, you know. Sid Levine, Jean's husband, Vincent McShane, Eileen's husband, and Larry Sommers, Charlotte's husband." All of the men nodded.

"I have yet to meet Eileen and Charlotte," Kristin said. "Of course, I've spoken to Eileen," she added. "She was the one who first called us, officially."

Philip nodded, sympathetically and then raised his eyebrows.

"You know, it really is time for us to arrange a get-together," he said.

"Yes, it is," Vincent McShane said emphatically.

"We're all workaholics around here, I'm afraid," Philip added with a tight smile. "Don't know how to relax."

"I suggested something like that as a way to get to know everyone," Kristin said. She turned toward Nikki. "But I was told that was inefficient."

"Yes, well, that's a whole other issue," Philip said. "Let's get down to the point at hand. Nikki," he said shifting in his seat so he faced her. She raised her clipboard and read.

"This is an official hearing of the Emerald Lakes Board of Trustees, called to consider the formal appeal of Theodore and Kristin Morris of Emerald Lakes. The Morrises are asking for a variance concerning article seven point five, use restrictions applying to animals. To wit, pets." She looked up.

"I quote: Except for caged birds and tropical fish in aquariums no bigger than six feet in length, three feet in width and three feet in height, no animals, reptiles, or insects shall be kept in any residence. This specifically refers to dogs of any breed and cats of any breed."

She sat back, a ripple of satisfaction flowing through her face.

"All right," Philip Slater said. "Now, Nikki, you received a letter as head of the Neighborhood Watch, correct?"

"Yes."

"Maybe you better read it into the record. Sid?"

"Yes, she should," Sid Levine replied.

Nikki began, not looking down at the letter on her clipboard:

"Dear Mrs. Stanley,
We would like to appeal to the board of trustees
for a variance concerning the restriction on pets.
We have a nine-week-old toy poodle puppy we
have purchased for our daughter. It is a full breed

> *poodle with papers and it will be kept on our grounds. If taken off our grounds, it will be on a leash. We guarantee that our dog will not invade anyone else's property or create any annoying noise. This is a small dog, a house pet. Please give us consideration.*
>
> > *Sincerely yours,*
> > *Theodore and Kristin Morris"*

"You memorized our letter?" Kristin asked, amazed. Nikki smirked.

"It wasn't all that difficult to do," she said.

"Is that your letter?" Philip asked Ted.

"Yes, it is."

"Did you want to add anything to your letter, Ted?"

"Not really. It says it all. I know I should have read that restriction, but even if I had, I would have appealed to the committee. We have more than enough space in our yard for so small a pet. The truth is no one will even know he's there."

He smiled and shifted in his chair to look at everyone on the committee.

"There is something I want to add," he said after a dramatic pause. "Moving into a new community, a new home, is a traumatic experience for everyone, especially a child. The puppy has done wonders for my daughter in just the short time we've had him," he concluded, anticipating, hoping for a nod of understanding from at least one member. Not a head moved; not an eye blinked.

"You should know that you're not the first resident who has asked for a variance concerning this restriction," Larry Sommers said. "Matter of fact, I think we've had at least four or five, haven't we, Nikki?"

"Five," she said sharply, her eyes fixed on Teddy and Kristin.

"Well, that suggests to me that the restriction is not popular here," Teddy said quickly.

"Five over five years," Nikki said with a condescending smile. "That's less than fifteen percent of our community. Hardly an indication of anything significant."

"The thing is," Philip said softly, "we've turned down these other five applications for a variance concerning pets."

"Maybe you shouldn't have," Kristin said.

"Well, we did. It puts us in something of a bind. We all recognize your arguments and we're sympathetic, but we just don't think it would be fair to grant you a variance and not the others."

"So. Grant the others, too," Kristin said. "It won't bring down the development."

"It will chip away at one of the things that makes our property more valuable and more desirable," Sid Levine said softly. "When most prospective buyers discover they won't have problems with neighbors' pets, they're happy."

"Look, we're guaranteeing no one will have problems with ours. If there's one justified complaint, we'll get rid of the dog ourselves," Teddy pleaded. "That's reasonable, isn't it?"

"It's reasonable, but it's not fair, nor is it wise. We've got to protect our CC and R's," Philip Slater said in a firmer and more formal tone. "They are the fabric, the glue that holds our development together and makes it stand out from all the others in the state, in fact, in the country."

"But it is fair," Kristin insisted. "We won't be violating any of the reasons for having the restriction. No one will be bothered."

"You didn't read the restrictions and you went ahead and bought a pet that violates the article," Nikki said. "Now you want us to cover up your mistake. That is most definitely unfair. To tell you the truth, I was upset that you put the committee in this position. Not to mention the effect it's already had on other Emerald Lakes children, who have heard your daughter bragging about her poodle. Now they want to know why they can't have a dog or a cat."

"I think she has a valid point," Philip said.

"A toy poodle is going to bring down this development? Is that what you're telling us?" Kristin asked in a shrill voice, her eyes wide with fury and frustration. No one spoke for a long moment. Then Philip sat forward.

"One hole in the dike eventually widens and leads to a flood," he said. "Unfortunately, we've seen this happen time after time in other developments. Take Whispering Pines, for example. They've granted so many variances, their CC and R's are a joke. If you compare our property value with theirs, however, you will see a sharp difference. A comparable home in Whispering Pines sells for fifty to sixty thousand less. We might seem unreasonable and hard to you, but when, if ever, you decide to sell your home, you will appreciate all this and thank us," he said. He sat back. Everyone relaxed. Nikki put the clipboard on her lap and Sid Levine closed his notebook.

"So that's it? You read our request and gave us this hearing even though you already had made up your minds?" Kristin asked.

"We granted you the hearing because it's procedure

and we gave you the opportunity to add something to your arguments and request. We will discuss the things you've said and take another vote on the matter."

"Thank you," Teddy said, quickly jumping in ahead of Kristin, who looked like she was about to tell them all where and how to get off. "As I said at the start, I admit fault in not reading about the restriction, but I hope you will consider the particular circumstances."

Philip nodded.

"Anyone have any other questions for the Morrises?"

One by one they looked down. Philip stood. Teddy followed, but Kristin didn't move.

"I don't believe this," she said. "I really don't believe this."

"Kristin."

She rose quickly and spun around, pulling the door open before Teddy could get to it. He followed her down the corridor.

"Kristin."

"Let's just get out of here, Teddy." She looked in the living room. "Where's Jennifer?" She marched through the living room. "Mrs. Slater!"

"In here," Marilyn called from the sewing room. Kristin stepped through the doorway and stopped. The room was inundated with dolls—rag dolls, antique dolls, dolls from other countries—doll clothing, doll houses, little carriages.

"Wow," she said.

"It's my hobby," Marilyn said, smiling.

Kristin shook her head.

"Look, Mommy!"

Jennifer was on the floor with two dolls in her lap.

"I see, Jen. This must be a very valuable collection," Kristin said, gazing around.

"I don't know. I really don't do it for the money. It started when I realized I hadn't thrown out a single doll in my life. My parents and my relatives bought me dolls for every occasion. Philip started me on the dolls from other countries after . . . sometime ago."

"It's great. Come on, Jennifer. We're going home. Thank Mrs. Slater."

Jennifer stood up and handed the dolls to Marilyn.

"Thank you," she said.

"You're welcome, honey. And you can come up and play with the dolls any time you want," Marilyn added. Jennifer's eyes brightened with expectation. "How was your meeting?" Marilyn asked.

"Futile, I think," Kristin said.

"I'm sorry."

"So am I." She reached out for Jennifer's hand and they started toward the front door with Marilyn Slater following. Teddy was waiting at the door.

"Daddy, you should see all the dolls!" Jennifer exclaimed.

"Oh?"

"She has a remarkable collection, Ted."

"Oh. Thank you for keeping your eye on the little princess," he said.

"It was nothing. She's delightful. Come see me again, Jennifer."

"Okay," Jennifer said. Teddy opened the door and the three of them walked out. Marilyn watched them go down the driveway and then closed the door and went into the living room to sit in her rocker. She continued to watch them walk down the street until they reached their home and disappeared within. Shortly afterward, she heard the committee meeting break up and rose to say good night. After they had all gone, she turned to Philip.

"What did you decide, Philip?"

"What could we decide?" he responded defensively and returned to his office.

All the way home and even while Kristin was getting her ready for bed, Jennifer went on and on about Mrs. Slater's dolls. Some of them had names, and there were boy dolls, too!

Then, after Jennifer had brushed her teeth, she stood in the bathroom with a puzzled look on her face.

"Mommy," she asked, "where is Mrs. Slater's little boy?"

"They don't have a little boy, honey. Not everyone has children."

"She has a little boy somewhere. She said so."

"What did she say?"

"She said . . . she said Bradley likes the big puppet doll, the one that looks like a pirate. She said he always wants to play with it."

"You mean Mrs. Slater said he used to want to play with it, right? Not wants."

Jennifer shrugged.

"Where's Mr. Sniffles?"

"Outside, doing his tinkle, honey."

"Don't forget to bring him in to sleep, too."

"I won't."

Jennifer crawled into bed and Kristin pulled the blanket up to her chin and tucked her in. She stroked her hair and smiled at her and kissed her on the cheek.

"Mommy?"

"What, honey?"

"Mrs. Slater is a nice lady."

"I'm glad you like her, honey."

"Can I really go see her again? Can I?"

"I suppose so. She said so."

"I'll bring Mr. Sniffles next time," Jennifer suggested.

"I don't think so, honey." She sighed, put out the light and went to the living room to join Ted. He was sitting on the sofa, thumbing through the booklet of CC and R's.

"Think it'll make a good movie?" she asked. He looked up quickly.

"Most of this is good, you know. They're not completely off the wall."

"Did you see that woman? She's memorized that whole book, and then she memorized your letter, Ted. She memorized it!"

"I know." He smiled and shook his head. "She's a piece of work. I'll admit that, but the others are just doing what they think is right to do. You never know what you would do until you're in their seat," he added.

"I know what I would do, Ted. I would remember that there are people living in the houses, not marionettes."

Before he could reply, the phone rang. He reached for the receiver on the side table.

"Hello."

"Ted, Philip. I'm afraid the committee feels it can't grant the variance. What we did agree to do is reevaluate the restriction at our next monthly board meeting. The residents will be so informed and they can give their trustees input or even attend the session. You're welcome to attend, of course; but for now, you'll have to get rid of the dog."

"That's too bad," Teddy said.

"It's just a little glitch, Ted. Don't let this discolor your view of the development and the value it has. You're living in the best place and you got it at a more than reasonable price. Most people would jump at the opportunity."

"I realize that."

"Just put that up against this little problem and you'll see how insignificant all this is."

"Right," Teddy said.

"I'm sure you and Kristin will turn out to be some of our most highly respected and treasured residents," Philip concluded.

"You don't have to tell me what he said," Kristin said as soon as Teddy hung up. "I'm going to sleep."

"Kristin."

She spun around.

"What if we defied them, Ted? What if we refused to give up Mr. Sniffles?"

"They can fine us first and then they can go to court and get a judgment against us. The court would have the police remove the dog, if necessary. It's all here," he said indicating the booklet. "Besides, that would make us look so bad to everyone else."

She nodded.

"You mean, as bad as Angela Del Marco?"

"I guess," he said. Kristin thought a moment.

"You know what I think you should do? I think you should get rid of the dog tonight. I don't want to have to watch Jennifer play with Mr. Sniffles in the morning. Do that, will you, Ted."

He looked at his watch.

"Pet store will be closed."

"Just give it away. Give it to the animal shelter. Just get it out!"

"All right," he said. "This is all my fault, Kristin. I should have read the restrictions and known."

"You can believe that if you want," she said. "As far as I'm concerned, they're all a bunch of bastards."

She walked away before he could respond. He sat thinking for a few moments and then rose and went out to get the puppy. It had curled up by the patio door and fallen asleep. It whimpered a bit and its body jerked with what Ted imagined were dog nightmares. Probably misses its mother, Teddy thought and considered that to be a good explanation for Jennifer in the morning.

Teddy lifted the dog gently. It woke and immediately started to lick his hand. He laughed, put it in the box bed, and carried the dog in the bed out to the garage. He placed the dog on the passenger seat and started the car. Then he raised the garage door and backed out.

He lowered his window at the security gate and Spier, who was on duty, approached.

"There's an animal shelter about two miles or so off Route Seventeen, right?" Teddy asked.

"Yes, sir. I can call and tell them you're coming. An older couple runs it and they don't hear people come up to the shelter this time of night sometimes. They live in the rear."

"Thank you."

Spier nodded at the puppy.

"Didn't think you could keep a dog here, sir," he said.

"I didn't realize the guard had noticed when I brought him in," Teddy said.

"We noticed during door rounds that you had a puppy."

"I see. You guys don't miss much, do you?"

"Try not to, sir. It's why we get paid so well," he added nearly smiling. Then he returned to the booth and opened the gate. "I'll call the shelter," he said as Teddy drove out.

At least they take good care of us, he thought. When he returned, Spier stepped out and asked if it all had gone well.

"Yes, thank you. How long have you been a security guard at Emerald Lakes, Harold?" Teddy asked him.

"I was the first, sir. There are five of us now, splitting shifts, with Chuck Ryan subbing now and then."

"And what's been the most serious breach of security since you've been here? Nothing more serious than a puppy, I hope."

"I don't know if I could say, Doctor Morris. All our monthly reports are on file with the board of trustees. Why don't you read them and decide," Spier replied.

"I might," Teddy said and drove in wondering why a security guard would be so cautious about the things he said to the residents.

The next morning Kristin realized there was no good time for getting rid of Mr. Sniffles. Jennifer was so devastated, Kristin almost kept her home from school. Teddy talked her out of it.

"It's better if she doesn't lay around and pout, Kristin."

"Why did Mr. Sniffles have to go back to his mother? Why, Daddy?" Jennifer pursued.

"Well, you would be sad if you were taken from Mommy, wouldn't you?"

Jennifer nodded.

"So, don't be selfish."

"Oh, Teddy. Blaming her?"

"I'm just using reverse psychology," he muttered.

"You're just trying to rationalize away something you know is an injustice," she said bitterly. "You're using reverse psychology on yourself."

"He was too little yet, Jennifer," he said, ignoring Kristin.

"Will he come back when he's older?" she asked quickly. Teddy looked at Kristin, who had a tight smile of satisfaction. She wasn't going to bail him out.

"We'll see," he said.

"That's giving her false hope," Kristin whispered.

"They're meeting on the restriction, Kristin. Maybe our appeal will get them to change it."

"Maybe it will snow in hell," she said.

"Jesus." He grabbed his jacket. "I'm going to work," he muttered and charged down the hall to the garage.

"I miss Mr. Sniffles," Jennifer said, sadly looking toward the patio.

"Me too, honey."

Kristin got her to go to school, believing Teddy was right. For most of the day at least, she would be occupied. Late in the morning when Kristin had just settled down to tinker at the piano, the door buzzer rang. She opened it to confront a young delivery man from Smith and Wilson's Pet Shop.

"What's this?" she asked.

"Delivery, ma'am."

"What is it?" He held a large box in his arms.

"Aquarium," he said. "I'm here to set it up for you."

"Aquarium? I didn't buy any aquarium."

"It's a gift, I guess. Card's in the box with the fish food, gravel, and greenery. Where would you like this? It would look real nice on that shelf there with the plants behind it," he said nodding at the flower box. "Kind of blends in. Ma'am?" he said when she didn't respond.

"What? Oh. Yes, I suppose so."

He smiled and entered the house. She stood back and watched him take the aquarium out of the box. It was a fairly good size.

"Got some nice fish for you, too," he said. "Guppies and goldfish, of course, and some angelfish and black Mollies. Oh. Here's the card," he said plucking it out of another box. "I'll just get the fish and start filling your tank."

"Thank you," she said, stepping back to take the card out of the envelope.

Dear Teddy and Kristin,
I know this doesn't compensate, but I thought it might help with Jennifer during the transition. Please accept it and my apologies for an unpleasant event. Let this be the last glitch.

                        Sincerely,
                        Phil Slater

Her first impulse was to send it all back and say something like, "Sorry, it doesn't fit our personal CC and R's," but she knew how Teddy would react to that. Then she thought about Marilyn Slater and how nice she had been to Jennifer. Her suspicion was Marilyn got Philip to do this. Jennifer would be amused by it and it might very well help ease the situation. Reluctantly, she admitted to herself that it was a nice gesture.

She went to the phone to call Teddy.

"You're kidding," he said. "That is really nice of him."

"Maybe it's his way of relieving his own guilt," Kristin said.

"Maybe we should just say thank you. He didn't have to do that."

"You say thank you."

"I will. Jeez, I can't wait to get home and see it. How big did you say it was?"

"One thing is for sure, Teddy," she replied smiling at the opportunity, "it's not more than six feet in length, three feet in width and three feet in height."

Even he had to laugh.

"Memorized it already? See. Nikki Stanley isn't so weird after all," he said.

"Oh, yes she is, Teddy. Yes, she is."

After she hung up, she went to look at the completely installed aquarium. She had to admit it was pretty, and interesting to watch the fish. When Jennifer returned from school, she was crying.

"What happened, honey?" Kristin asked as soon as she greeted her.

"They said Mr. Sniffles was dead. They said he had to be killed for coming here."

"Who said that? Who said such a horrible thing?"

"Graham and Heather."

"Nikki Stanley's two creatures. It fits. No, honey. Mr. Sniffles is not dead. He's back with his mother and his brothers and sisters."

"Will he come back, Mommy? Will he?"

She sighed. Sometimes, little white lies are better.

"Yes," she said. "Someday he will. But come inside. There's a surprise," she added and took her hand.

When Jennifer saw the aquarium and the fish, her eyes brightened and she stopped crying. She sat in front of the glass case and watched the fish for over an hour. Kristin told her she would be the one to feed them, too. She was no longer crying over Mr. Sniffles.

One way or another, Kristin thought as she watched her child change from a mourner to a happy little girl again, they get what they want here.

One way or another.

8

◆

By the end of the week, Kristin thought life at Emerald Lakes had finally settled down for Teddy, Jennifer, and her. The incident with Mr. Sniffles was over and done. Jennifer, occupied with her tropical fish and with her new playmates, stopped asking about the dog. On Friday, Teddy came home bursting with good news. His medical group had picked up the laundry employees and Hank Porter had been clearly informed that it was mainly because of the nice things the owners had heard about Doctor Morris. Now, a second business was knocking on the door.

"Hank's thinking about us buying out a neighboring group and he's been talking to some government people about us picking up government contracts. We made the right move, honey. Boy, did we make the right move," Teddy said. He suggested a celebration and once again asked her to look into the baby-sitting services recommended in the directory. She called Jean Levine.

"Oh, I'm so glad you phoned me. I thought you were angry about what happened with your dog and blamed me for it."

"I don't blame anyone in particular," Kristin said. "It's a matter of collective guilt."

"Huh?"

"It's not important. What I'm calling about are baby-sitters. I thought you would know."

"Oh, yes, I do. We use either Steffi Thomas or Laurie Porter. They're both very reliable and, if you look in the directory, both have four stars by their names."

"Yes, what does that mean exactly?"

"They've received the highest recommendations."

"Who does this, finds out all this stuff and assigns the stars?"

"Nikki, mostly. I'm supposed to help, but by the time I call someone for feedback, Nikki's already done it."

"Dedicated individual," Kristin said dryly.

"Oh, yes. Nikki's made the development her life."

"How . . . nice. Sorta like a woman becoming a nun." Jean trickled a laugh. "All right. I'll call one of those two. Thanks."

"We might lose a resident," Jean said quickly, anticipating Kristin's ending the conversation.

"Oh?"

"The Del Marcos." She lowered her voice. "It's just a rumor now, but I heard their marital troubles are more serious."

"How do you hear these things?"

"A little bird," Jean said laughing. She changed her tone of voice quickly to add, "Angela lodged a formal complaint against our security people, you know."

"Angela lodged? What about her husband?"

"He didn't join in the complaint. That might be one reason for their problems. Anyway, Nikki says the development has a way of weeding out those who don't belong."

"Sort of the survival of the conformist, natural selection?"

"What? Are you joking again? I can never tell with you."

"No, I'm not joking. Thanks for the help with baby-sitters."

"When am I going to hear one of your songs?"

"When I write one. I've been a bit distracted these last few weeks."

"Don't forget to call."

"I'll tell the little bird when I have one ready for you to hear," Kristin said and Jean laughed.

"You're such a kidder."

She sat thinking for a few moments, wondering about Angela Del Marco. It had to have been quite a traumatic experience for her—men breaking into her house while she was in the tub. Why wouldn't her husband be more sympathetic and just as angry about it?

"So?" Teddy said coming into the kitchen.

"I've got two names. Four-star reviews by . . . you guessed it, Nikki Stanley, who personally evaluates gardeners, pool maintenance people, house cleaners, plumbers, electricians, doctors, dentists, car mechanics, dry cleaners—"

"All right," Teddy said laughing. "I get the point."

"Jean says the Del Marcos might be selling."

"Oh?" He looked away quickly.

"Did you hear anything, Teddy?"

"Yeah, something like that. But from what I've been told, if it happens, it's best for the development."

"What do you mean, from what you've been told? Who told you?"

"Well, I was waiting to tell you at dinner," he said smiling.

"Tell me what, Teddy Morris?"

"Can't I tell you later, after we've both relaxed with a few drinks?"

She tilted her head.

"It's not like you, keeping secrets."

"I'm not keeping secrets. I'm just choosing a fun time to tell you something. But if you insist . . ."

"All right. I'll play along. Let's see about the baby-sitter."

She called the Thomas girl who politely informed her she was booked and got her bookings a full week in advance.

"Really?" Kristin said. "I'll keep that in mind next time. Thank you."

"Thank you, Mrs. Morris."

Polite little bitch, Kristin thought and dialed Laurie Porter's number only to hear the same story.

"I guess I'm going to have to drop a star," she muttered and returned to the directory. She had to drop two stars before she found a baby-sitter who was available on such short notice. Her name was Melissa Erickson. After Kristin booked her, she wondered if she had made a mistake. After all, Melissa had only two stars. She phoned Jean again.

"I couldn't get Steffi or Laurie. In fact, I had to go down the list until I got Melissa Erickson who has only two stars."

"Oh, sorry," Jean said.

"What does that mean? She's not the original bad seed or anything, is she?"

"Oh, no. She's younger, only fourteen, and has less experience, but she has no demerits as far as I know," Jean said. "She'll do fine. I'll call you tomorrow for an evaluation, all right?"

"You mean, my opinion might get her another star?"

"It might," Jean said laughing. Then she turned serious. "Or it might drop her a star."

"Oh, such responsibility. I don't know if I can handle it. Sure, call me," she said. "Thanks."

What am I doing? she asked herself sharply as soon as she hung up the phone. Relying on the opinions of that female Napoleon, Nikki Stanley? How easily we all fall into line, she thought.

The Erickson girl was a pretty blond with sweet, friendly, warm blue eyes and dimples in her cheeks. Jennifer liked her immediately, especially when she told her she, too, had an aquarium.

Teddy told her the name of the restaurant and said he would leave the number by the phone.

"You don't have to do that, Doctor Morris," she reminded him. "If we need any assistance of any kind, I simply have to call security. They usually know where you are or how to reach you. It's part of the Neighborhood Watch program. Before anyone can baby-sit in Emerald Lakes, he or she has to know the rules for baby-sitters. The homeowners association made us a little booklet."

"Right. Well, if you want to ask us a question, it's all right to call without going through the security people," Teddy said, eyeing Kristin.

They kissed Jennifer good-bye and left.

Kristin really hadn't gotten dressed up since their arrival at Emerald Lakes. Anticipating some special occasion soon, she had bought herself a new dress early in the week. She splurged and bought a scooped neck Donna Karan cashmere. She hadn't told Teddy, deciding to surprise him with it instead. He didn't comment, however, until they were in their car backing out of the garage.

"Might I say, you look spectacular tonight."

"You like my dress?"

"Love it." He smiled. "It's new, right?"

"Observant for an eye specialist, aren't you?" she said.

He turned to her and smiled with deliberate licentiousness.

"It's beautiful, but only because it's on you."

"Even though my tummy's starting to show?"

"Looks delectable," he said and leaned over to kiss her stomach before turning to go up the street. She laughed and he shot away, only to hit the brakes right before the speed bump. "Always forget these damn things."

"Careful, Teddy. These are four-star speed bumps."

He shook his head. When they reached the gate, Spier stepped out of the booth with his clipboard.

"Tell him we're going to see an X-rated movie. See what he does."

"He wouldn't care. We're going to Martino's in Goshen. Need the number?"

"No, sir. Have a good time," Spier said and returned to the booth to open the gate.

"I know it irks you to tell them where we're going, but just think how fast we could be reached should there be an emergency," Teddy said. "It's a tradeoff, but the result is well worth it, don't you think?"

"I suppose, but it will always irk me," she said.

After they were seated in the restaurant and after Teddy had ordered champagne and they had their first toast, Kristin finally demanded he reveal his secret.

Teddy smiled.

"Well, it seems Larry Sommers is overwhelmed with work and has to resign from the board of trustees of Emerald Lakes."

"Poor man," Kristin said. "And he looked like he was enjoying himself so much, too."

"Stop it," Teddy said, a little sharper than she expected. "He's got some personal financial problems and he has to devote more time to his work, but I'm sure he regrets not being able to sit on the board. It's a great honor and a big responsibility. This is expensive real estate we're protecting."

"You mean an honor in the same sense it's an honor to be a doctor, or a father, or a lover?" she replied undaunted.

"Everything has its own value and importance," Teddy said.

"What does this have to do with us, Teddy?"

He sat back.

"Philip Slater called me this morning. Before I saw my first patient, in fact."

"And . . ."

"Offered me the spot."

"Spot?"

"Trustee."

She stared nonplussed for a moment.

"I thought that was an elected position," she said softly.

"It is. Larry's resigning and Philip Slater can appoint someone to fill out his term, after which, I would run for the office. Assuming anyone runs against me, that is. Well?"

Kristin just sat there speechless.

"You don't look happy about it. You know what a tribute it is for a new resident to be asked to join the board of trustees?"

"Does this mean we get back Mr. Sniffles?" she asked sharply.

His smile faded.

"Why did you get asked, Teddy? Is it some sort of a reward for accepting the board's finding after our appeal?"

"No. I think Mr. Slater likes us and believes we will make ideal residents of Emerald Lakes. I think," he continued in a deliberate, reasonable, if not a bit condescending tone, "he is impressed with my success at the group and the way other doctors and patients have received me. Sometimes, people see my potential and are impressed," he concluded.

She softened.

"I didn't mean you don't deserve it. I'm sure you would be the best trustee they have. It just seemed strange for you to be asked. We don't even know all the residents yet and they don't know us except through the directory."

"Which is something I want to change immediately. It's too impersonal a method. Look," he said after sighing, "we're both upset with some of the things that have gone on in the development. We can bitch about them at home or we can try to do something to change things, and what better opportunity will we have to change things than my being a part of the governing board?"

"As long as they don't change you," she warned.

"Come on, Kristin. It's a bit disappointing to find strangers have more faith in your capabilities than your own wife."

"It's not your capabilities I'm doubting, Teddy. It's just that after my experience with the board, I feel like you're joining the enemy. I'm sorry."

"I know how you feel about that and that's why I want to do this. We can't live there and think of the board as our enemy. It has to be our board and we've got to become a part of everything."

She nodded. Then she looked up and smiled.

"To the success of Emerald Lakes' newest and best trustee," she said, raising her glass. They clicked glasses and drank. Then Kristin laughed. "I wonder what Nikki Stanley's going to say when she finds out."

"Don't you think she knows already?" Teddy asked. Kristin thought and then nodded.

"Yes, but she's holding back on assigning your stars until she gets a full evaluation."

Teddy shook his head and laughed.

"You're impossible."

"Which is why you love me," she said.

They ordered their food and Kristin talked about some of the things she wanted to do to change the house and make it feel more like their home.

"I see you've really been thinking it out," Teddy said, impressed.

"Every day. I just want to shake off the feeling I'm wearing someone else's clothes, especially after what happened to the Feinbergs."

"I understand. Sure. Let's go forward. We'll be living in this house for quite a while."

"Which reminds me. What does all this have to do with the Del Marcos, Teddy?"

"Philip was telling me about their problems. Steve Del Marco sells insurance and apparently, he's lost some big accounts recently. That, plus his wife's ongoing wars with the Neighborhood Watch have put strains on their relationship." Teddy leaned over to whisper. "There are no divorced people living in Emerald Lakes. Have you noticed that?"

"No, I didn't think about it."

"Well, it's true, and in this day and age when one out of two marriages ends in divorce, that's quite an accomplishment."

"How is it accomplished?" she asked.

"Simple," he said. "The board never approves a buyer who's single and the board has the right to reject buyers, as you know from reading the CC and R's."

"Isn't that unconstitutional?"

Teddy shrugged.

"No one's taken them to court or tried to except . . ."

"Except who, Teddy?" she asked. He looked like he regretted the way the champagne had loosened his tongue and had bitten down on his lip to stifle the words. "Except who?"

"Sol Feinberg," he said and it was as if the fetus in her womb had retreated from the very idea of entering the world that waited. Her stomach churned, just as the food was brought to their table.

"But let's not bring up anything unpleasant tonight, Kristin. Let's enjoy. Please," he cajoled.

She nodded, swallowed the myriad of questions that bubbled at the surface of her mind, and tried to regain her appetite.

"More champagne?"

"Yes," she said. "More champagne."

The next morning after Teddy had left for work and she had sent Jennifer off to school, Kristin sat finishing her second cup of coffee and thinking about some of the things Teddy had told her at dinner the night before. She put her coffee cup and saucer in the sink and then, impulsively spun around and marched out of her house and up the street to the Del Marco residence. She rang the doorbell and waited, gazing back to see if anyone was watching her.

Why do I feel so guilty about visiting one of my neighbors? she wondered.

It took so long for Angela Del Marco to answer the

door, Kristin nearly turned away and walked home. Angela was dressed in the same robe and slippers she had been dressed in when Kristin rang her doorbell after seeing the security man break into her house, but now, Angela's hair looked even more disheveled. This close to her, Kristin also noted the woman's bloodshot eyes and the deep tension lines in her face. She looked drugged, exhausted.

"I'm sorry," Kristin said. "I didn't mean to wake you."

"Wake me?" Angela laughed. "Who sleeps anymore?" She smirked. "Are you here to borrow a cup of sugar?"

"Look," Kristin said. "I'm sorry I didn't see what you wanted me to have seen that day. I didn't get from the rear to the front of our houses quickly enough, but . . ."

"But?"

"I'd like to be friends with you."

"Why?" Angela demanded.

And I thought I was becoming paranoid, Kristin thought.

"Because I understand you've challenged the homeowners association before and now you've made charges against the security people."

"And that makes you want to be friends with me?" Angela asked with an amused smile.

Kristin nodded.

"They wouldn't let you keep the dog," Angela said, concluding. "Did Phil Slater send you a bird in a cage?"

"No. Aquarium."

"Oh. Right. It was time for fish." She wiped her right hand through her straggly hair. "I don't always look like this," she added. "Sometimes, I look worse." Kristin laughed and Angela stepped back. "Come on in," she said, "but I have to warn you, you're associating with a malcontent, and malcontents in Emerald Lakes are like lepers."

"Somehow," Kristin said, "I think that makes you one of the more interesting people here."

Angela led her down the long entryway to the kitchen. It was twice the length of Kristin's, the paneling and tile done in Wedgwood blue.

"I love your house," Kristin said. Angela poured out the coffee remaining in the pot and started to make a fresh one.

"Maybe you'll be able to buy it soon," Angela said. She turned. "If you're a cooperative resident, the homeowners board of trustees might approve a transfer. Your house will be sold and you'll move into this one."

"Are you really thinking of selling?"

Angela laughed.

"It's not a matter of thinking about it. It's a matter of accepting it. To tell you the truth," she said gazing around, "I love this house and even love the development. You know what I mean," she said with a wide gesture, "the scenic beauty here. Who, in her right mind, wouldn't want to live here? It does have everything, and for the most part, if you don't piss off Nikki Stanley or Phil Slater, you can have about as nearly perfect a Norman Rockwell painting life as is possible.

"But . . ." She sighed. "To my husband's way of thinking, I fucked things up."

"What did you do?"

Angela finished fixing the coffee and sat at the table in the nook adjoining the kitchen. The windows gave a sweeping view of the northeast part of the lake. Kristin saw someone in a boat, fishing.

"I challenged one of their damn CC and R's and came into direct conflict with Nikki and the committee. And then I complained when we were fined. I had the audacity to go directly to Phil Slater in his company office. He complained to my husband, made veiled threats. Suddenly, we found we were violating other ordinances, we got another fine for dripping oil on the street and then, just to be sure I got the message clear and sharp, they put the dogs on me."

"Dogs?"

"The security guards. That whole phony thing with the alarm and breaking into my home. I've lodged a formal complaint, even though my husband didn't want us to. Our marriage is a bit strained at the moment. Seems he's lost some accounts and he's blaming it on me."

"Why?"

"Why? I lodged a formal complaint, even threatened a lawsuit. Phil Slater has a lot of clout with business interests in the community. My husband wants me to rescind the complaint and get back with the program. I'm . . . not of that mind at the moment, so at the moment, we're at war. Sorry. I didn't mean to unload it all on you during our first chat."

"No. It's all right. I appreciate your candor. What are you going to do?"

Angela shrugged and then rose to pour the coffee. Kristin gazed out the window again, watching the person fishing. It did seem like a Norman Rockwell painting. She looked up when Angela brought the coffee.

"Sugar?"

"No, just milk. Skim, if you have?"

"Watching your figure? Oh, right," Angela corrected herself. "You're pregnant. I forgot. You don't look like you're gaining a lot of weight."

"No, I'm fine."

"Doctor Hoffman?"

"Yes."

"I used him. He's good and one of those residents you hardly ever see or hear about here. I call them ghosts," Angela added, laughing.

"Ghosts?"

"There are people in this development I haven't seen more than . . . four or five times in three years. They keep to themselves; they obey the rules and they leave everything up to the homeowners board. The truth is most people in most developments, condo associations, co-ops, do the same thing. I've made a sort of independent study of it and concluded it's a particularly American thing . . . indifference as long as you leave me alone to eat my junk foods and watch my junk television."

Kristin smiled. She liked this woman.

"So, what are you going to do?" Kristin asked.

"I'll probably give in if I want to keep my marriage and family," she predicted. "And when I do, don't be too quick to condemn me for it," she added quickly.

"I'm not condemning anyone for anything quickly these days," Kristin said. She sipped the coffee.

"Steven asks, what do you want, Angela? Look what you have: a beautiful home in a beautiful place with expensive furnishings, nice cars, clothes, jewelry, vacations. You don't have to worry about the violence people on the outside live with daily. Your kids are safe; you're safe. Why make waves just to prove a point?

"I tried to explain how I'm not upset about all that, but I don't like being made to feel like someone's puppet."

Kristin widened her eyes. They were sisters of the same temperament.

"I've got a mind of my own. I want to have freedom of thought, too. He thinks I'm crazy. We've gone round and round about it. He believes the small compromises, as he puts it, are a small price to pay for all the rest. So, he wouldn't go along with my formal complaints.

"You're new here, so I know you think I'm nuts, too. Even though you had to give up your dog, right?"

"Wrong," Kristin said. "I mean, everything your husband says sounds logical on the surface, but I haven't been exactly in heaven. I'm not comfortable with all this Big Brother security. I think Nikki Stanley is growing a penis on the side, and the homeowners board is a group of people in love with their power."

"Jesus," Angela said. "How did you slip past the homeowners' new residents review?"

"How did you?" Kristin countered.

Angela laughed.

"Well," she said, "maybe you and I can form the nucleus of a mutiny and eventually perform a coup d'etat and take over the homeowners association."

"Maybe. My husband is being appointed to fill Larry Sommers's position," Kristin said and Angela's smile evaporated.

"Oh," she said changing her tone. "I see. Is that why you're here?"

"Pardon?"

"Are you supposed to talk me out of my actions, get me to be more reasonable?"

"No. Absolutely not."

"Your husband was appointed by Philip Slater after you people have been residents here for so short a time, and you want me to believe you're not making deals?"

"We've made no deals."

"Really," Angela said dryly.

"Really. In fact, Teddy's going to try to change some of these things. He's going to—"

"Sure," Angela said sharply.

"Look," Kristin said, fixing her eyes firmly on Angela. "After some of the things you've been through, I don't blame you for being distrustful. Under the circumstances, I might be the same way, especially after seeing how aggressive the security people were, but what I've told you I believe and I feel is the truth. I didn't come here to talk you out of doing anything. In fact, I hope you do pursue your complaint, and if you want me to come and testify to what I did see the security man do, I will."

Angela stared at her a moment and then nodded.

"Okay, I might just have you do that," she said. "There's a preliminary hearing about my complaint this coming Thursday at Phil Slater's."

"I'll be there," Kristin quickly vowed.

Angela sipped her coffee, keeping her eyes on Kristin.

"What did they tell you about Sol Feinberg before you bought his house?" she asked.

"That he committed suicide."

"Did anyone say why?"

"Marital problems, financial problems . . ."

"They didn't mention his actions opposing the homeowners association or his lawsuit?"

"No, but last night my husband told me he found out Sol Feinberg was going to take the homeowners association to court, and I recall Jean Levine telling me Elaine Feinberg was not the development type."

"Jean should know. She's the original Stepford Wife. I once pinched her to see if she would feel pain."

"I know what you mean," Kristin said and then, after a moment added, "I had a very strange encounter with Elaine Feinberg in the supermarket."

"Really? When?"

"Right after we moved into the house. She had suffered a miscarriage."

"I heard about that."

"She seemed very odd and she said I would be sorry I was living here unless . . ."

"Unless what?"

"I became one of them," Kristin replied.

"Which is what you think might happen now that your husband is on the board of trustees?"

Kristin didn't reply.

"Sol and Elaine became very bitter people here. I didn't befriend them when they needed it, but I was with the program then. I was just as guilty as everyone else." She sighed as if she carried the weight of that guilt on her bosom.

"But was that enough to drive him to suicide?" Kristin asked.

"They broke him financially. But you're right," Angela said, "to ask if that was enough. I did. He was a strong-willed man, a real challenge for the board and for Slater."

"Who found him?"

"His wife. And then our security guards were on the scene with miraculous speed," Angela said.

"You know," Kristin said, "maybe this job is too big for one or two people to handle, but that doesn't mean it can't be done. I'd like to challenge some of the things going on. Maybe you and I can go around to some of the ghosts and talk them into joining us. Then, when we have enough strength, we'll approach the board and get rid of some of these ridiculous restrictions and elect some more reasonable people. With my husband already there, it won't be impossible."

Angela nodded.

"Maybe. All right," she said after another moment of consideration. "I trust you. I'll keep up my defiance and risk Steven's ire a while longer. Who knows, maybe he'll see the light too. Say," she added, laughing, "is this the way revolutions begin . . . over a cup of coffee?"

"It is in Emerald Lakes," Kristin said. Angela's laugh was lighter, her smile warmer.

"I have to admit, I did read up on you in Nikki's little directory. It makes it easier to peep into someone's life. So you write music?"

"Yes. I've had a few entertainers try some in nightclubs. No one big or anything, but it was fun going to the lounges and listening to the songs I wrote being sung."

"What have you written since you've been here?"

"That's just it," Kristin said. "Nothing really. And the first time I saw this place, I thought it would be the perfect setting for creativity."

"It is. It's just some of what's being created by our residents we might find difficult accepting."

Kristin laughed and nodded.

"Say," Angela said. "I know this great place in Wurtsboro for lunch, and right beside it is this wonderful store selling antiques and housewares, furnishing, all country style. If you feel like it . . . I mean, I don't want to take you away from your work."

"No, that sounds great."

"Good. I have a reason to shower and dress today! Maybe, just maybe, we can do something about this place," Angela said buoyed. "I'll call the restaurant and make our reservation for about one, okay?"

"Sure."

"I didn't mean it when I told you that day the security people broke in," Angela said, lifting her coffee cup in a toast, "but welcome to Emerald Lakes."

They tapped their coffee cups and laughed like coconspirators.

Lunch was as wonderful as Angela promised, and afterward, they had a great time shopping and finding unique things. Kristin hadn't laughed and felt so light and happy since she and Teddy had moved into Emerald Lakes. They returned in time to be home for their children. Angela had two boys, Anthony, age seven, and Daniel, age nine.

"They're pretty independent for their age, already macho Italian young men," she said. "But God forbid I'm not home when they want me. They're still momma's boys and want me there the moment they need me."

They made a date to meet the next day and begin their own analysis of the coveted Emerald Lakes CC and R's. They planned out their strategy at lunch. They would begin slowly, challenging this rule and that, supporting their challenges with reason and logic, and they would try to build support with the unassuming residents, Angela's ghosts, getting them to at least endorse some of the requests for changes. Then they would ask for a hearing and present their suggestions, campaigning for them just the way they would campaign for any election. They would make phone calls, visit with residents, explain, cajole, and urge others to make phone calls to the board members. They thought if they broke some of the ironclad regulations, they could begin to tear down the domination the homeowners board had over the residents.

Later that evening at dinner, Kristin, who was energized by her day and her alliance with Angela, overwhelmed Teddy with her ideas and hopes. He barely had an opportunity to comment before they were finished eating. Finally, Kristin brought their coffee to the table and sat again, anticipating Teddy's reactions anxiously.

"Well?" she said. "What do you think? You haven't said a word."

"How could I? I never got an opening."

She laughed.

"So? I'm working within the system. Aren't you happy about that?"

"Sure," he said, but in a noncommittal tone. "It's only that . . ."

"Only what, Teddy?"

"Only I wish you were working with someone else. You just met Angela, and I'm glad you're making friends . . ."

"But?"

"But from what I've been told she's gotten on the wrong side of many residents here, not just a couple on the board. She's not the best one to go around the development with and solicit support for new ideas."

"Who told you this, Teddy?"

"Phil Slater, for one."

"Who else, Teddy?"

"Well, he's . . ."

"Did Doctor Hoffman tell you this?"

"No, but . . ."

"Did you speak to the Kimbles, the Mateos, the Dimases, the Meltzers?" she asked. He widened his eyes as she continued to rattle off the list of residents from memory.

"You memorized everyone?"

"Nikki Stanley isn't the only one with a mind here, Teddy. I think things are the way they are because people haven't bothered challenging them properly. We intend to and I thought you did, too. I thought that was the point of your becoming a trustee."

"Yes, it is."

"So?"

"I . . ." He shrugged. "Great," he said. "Let me know what I can do."

"Oh, we'll let you know, Teddy. You can be sure of that," she said. "In fact," she said, thinking, "why don't you speak to Steven Del Marco and see if you can get him to ease up on Angela."

"What?" He shook his head. "Not me. If there's one thing I don't ever want to do, it's get involved in someone's marital problems. No, thank you. I've got enough to do with my own."

"What's that supposed to mean, Teddy?"

"Nothing," he said quickly. He put up his hands. "Honest."

She stared at him suspiciously a moment.

"When are you taking your seat on the board, Teddy?"

"Immediately. I'll be at Thursday's meeting."

"Then you'll also be at the hearing concerning Angela's formal complaint against the security guards," she said.

"Yes. I will."

"Good. I'll be there, too. As a witness."

He smiled quizzically.

"A witness?"

"I saw the man break her window, Teddy. I saw him enter the house and I saw them come strolling out."

He nodded, a troubled expression on his face.

"Abuse of power is a serious thing. Don't let them belittle her complaint," Kristin said.

"I wouldn't do that," Teddy said. "I'll be fair and impartial."

"We'll see," Kristin said.

"Hey. She could be in the wrong here. You be fair and impartial too."

"Deal," Kristin said in the tone of a challenge. Teddy sipped his coffee pensively as did Kristin. Suddenly, neither of them was very talkative.

She rose, put the dishes in the dishwasher and then went into the living room and began her very close, critical analysis of the Emerald Lakes CC and R's.

9

◈

MARILYN KNEW PHILIP WAS IN A BAD MOOD when he slammed the front door behind him as he entered the house. She sucked in her breath, closed her eyes and pretended she was light as a cloud, gliding gracefully under a soft blue sky high above Emerald Lakes. While she was safely ensconced in this imaginary world, she could ignore Philip's rage and the ugly things he did with his eyes and mouth when he ranted. She could pretend to be listening without being uncomfortable.

Sometimes, if he paused in his tirade to look at her and really see her as someone to whom he was speaking and not just another place off which to bounce his frustrations, he would sense she wasn't there. Then he would rage about that and forget his topic for a while until he successfully pulled her down from her cloud. But usually, by then he was emotionally drained and disgusted with her. He would say she didn't deserve to hear his problems. Don't bother apologizing.

This evening he came charging into the kitchen with more anger and energy than usual, kicking a chair that was out from the table. His tie was loose and his collar unbuttoned. He looked like he had been running his fingers through his hair for hours and the creases in his forehead were deeper than usual.

"That woman called me at my office just before the end of the day today to tell me she was confirming she would be present at the special hearing and she would bring a witness. A witness!"

Marilyn opened the stove to check her roast turkey breast and basted it in its own juices.

"One of our own people is attacking our system and then finding an innocent bystander and involving her. Where is her husband in all this? You would think he would have learned on which side his bread is buttered by now, wouldn't you?"

He paused.

Marilyn turned and smiled softly. She and her cloud were over the lake.

"Don't get yourself so worked up before dinner, Philip," she advised softly. "You know what havoc that plays with your digestion."

"What? My digestion? Didn't you hear what I said? I've got to hold a formal hearing over a formal complaint concerning our security system. Our own security system, for crissakes!"

"I'm sure you'll handle it the way you want and get the result you want," she said, holding her smile. The calmer she remained, the more furious he grew, the crimson tint flowing up through his neck and cheeks like mercury up a warming thermometer. His eyes widened, the glint of madness blazing brighter.

"I said," he hammered, sharpening his consonants and vowels, "she's bringing a witness . . . that woman you like so much," he added and Marilyn winced. She felt some weight added and imagined herself sliding off her cloud and falling slowly to earth, dropping directly into her own house and this very kitchen.

"What woman?" she asked.

"Ted Morris's wife . . . the dog lady," he said twisting the corner of his mouth.

"Kristin?"

"Yeah, Kristin. And I have no idea what she's going to say."

"About what?" Marilyn asked.

Philip's face dropped into an expression of incredulity for a moment before returning to a mask of rage.

"Didn't you hear a word I said? You knew about the formal hearing. I told you about it yesterday, too."

Marilyn's eyelids flicked repeatedly as she searched the dark corners of her memory for the information. She had buried it in her mental vaults along with so many other unpleasant things. What hearing? Who? she wondered. Philip didn't have the patience to wait for her to recall.

"The damn Del Marco woman," he reminded her, and she located the information.

"Oh."

What had complicated it when Philip first told her was her own knowledge. She had seen the entire episode from her vantage point at the window, but she had never told Philip. Marilyn had also seen Kristin Morris come up the street just as the security guards were emerging from the Del Marcos' house.

"I never quite understood that, Philip," she said quietly. "Why did they break into her home and frighten her?"

"They didn't break into her home to frighten her," he said through clenched teeth. "They entered the house because they had an alarm indication that the home's security had been breached."

"Breached?"

"A burglar!" he roared.

She held her ground but kept her face nonplussed. "In the daytime?"

"Daytime, nighttime, what difference does it make to thieves?"

"They would be more afraid to break into our homes in the daytime, wouldn't they?" she asked.

"Normal ones would, but in this day and age, you can't be too careful."

"I didn't see anyone break into the home, Philip. I happened to be looking out the window when the security guards arrived. I saw one run around to the rear before they even tried the front door."

He stared at her and waited for her to continue.

"Then another guard went to the front door, but he didn't even seem to ring a bell. He seemed to have had a door key. Do they have keys to our homes, Philip?"

"NO!" He lifted his arms, his hands folded into tight fists. "That's what she's alleging. You didn't see any guard open any door with a key and don't you even think of telling someone in Emerald Lakes such a story, understand?"

"I don't gossip with the people here, Philip. You know that."

"I don't care where you gossip. Tell no one such a story," he ordered. Then, with painstaking emphasis, he stepped toward her and recited, "My security people were worried about Mrs. Del Marco so when they couldn't get her to open the front door, they broke into the house. That's the only story you are to know and confirm. Are you clear about that?"

She nodded.

"Okay, Philip," she said obediently. He simmered down, the crimson tint turning more pinkish than scarlet. "But Philip," she added when he started to turn away.

"What is it?" he asked, annoyed.

"How did they think the burglar had gotten in if all the doors and windows were locked?"

He stared at her.

"They didn't have the time to check each and every window, Marilyn. It was an emergency. Since when did you become a detective?"

"I just wondered," she said.

He scrutinized her face and then stepped toward her again.

"Why didn't you tell me about what you had seen that night?"

"Didn't I? I thought I had," she said shaking her head. He smirked. It wasn't the first time she had a memory lapse and it wouldn't be the last. It was his particular burden to bear as long as he lived with her.

"Just look after the dinner, will you, Marilyn, and I'll look after Emerald Lakes. Okay?"

"Okay, Philip."

"And remember what I said about telling anyone your story. I don't need my own wife undermining my efforts to make this a perfect place to live."

She nodded. Satisfied, he left her alone and went to his office to make some phone calls. By dinnertime, Philip was calmer. He didn't mention Angela Del Marco and the hearing again. Instead, he talked about the new house and some of the ideas he was developing for its interior design. She listened with enough vague interest to keep him talking. He complimented her on the meal and then went into the living room to catch the early evening news.

As she cleaned up in the kitchen, she wondered about Kristin Morris coming forward to be a witness for Angela Del Marco. What could she have seen that I hadn't? she wondered. More important, did she understand what it would mean to testify for Angela and against the development's security people? It was the same as testifying against Philip, for he took everything at Emerald Lakes personally. His imprint was on all of it.

Marilyn considered calling Kristin to talk to her about it. She didn't want to see anything unpleasant happen to Kristin's family. Their comings and goings had become such an enjoyable part of the world outside her window.

Marilyn had been sitting at the window the night Sol Feinberg died. Philip was working late in his office. She had been watching television, but she had turned away from the set and gazed at the streets of Emerald Lakes. In fact, she had been the one who first told Philip what was happening. She got up from her seat and hurried back to the office. Usually, she knocked and waited, but he didn't respond when she knocked this time, so she opened the door and found him talking softly on the phone. He raised his hand to say she should wait and then he said something so low she couldn't hear and hung up the phone.

"What's wrong, Marilyn?" he asked.

"I heard a commotion outside," she said, "and looked out the window. The security guards are at the Feinbergs'."

"Really?" Philip sat a moment and then stood up. He looked very concerned. "Maybe I should go down there," he said, but before he could step away from the desk, the phone rang and he lifted the receiver. "Hello," he said and listened. She watched his eyes widen. "I'll be right there," he said and hung up the phone. "You're right," he told her. "Something terrible has happened."

"What?"

"Sol Feinberg committed suicide. He shot himself," he said. "What a horrible blight on the reputation of Emerald Lakes," he added and hurried out, leaving her trembling in the office.

What a horrible blight on the reputation of Emerald Lakes? What about the blight on Elaine Feinberg?

Yes, she thought, she might speak to Kristin Morris without Philip knowing about it.

Teddy pushed back his dinner plate, some of the angel hair pasta with basil and tomato still left.

"I'm stuffed. That was a great salad. I ate too much," he said.

"That's all right. I'll serve the rest for lunch with Angela tomorrow. It's my turn," she added taking his plate. Teddy watched her move about the kitchen.

"You and Angela are really going gung-ho at this, huh?"

"Believe it or not, we're enjoying it. I really think some of this borders on violation of constitutional rights."

"So we're going to take the homeowners association to the supreme court, is that it?" he joked.

"You can laugh if you want to, but it's been done, Teddy. Angela and I were at the library yesterday. They have a pretty good one for a small town, you know."

"And?"

"We found stories about other homeowner disputes

with homeowners associations that went as high as the state court of appeals. A number of them resulted in the court deciding in the homeowners' favor."

Teddy played with his napkin for a moment. Jennifer, who had eaten earlier, was watching cartoons on the Disney channel with her life-size doll, Baby Walk-Along, beside her.

"Kristin, the whole idea of living in a community like this," Teddy said softly, "is to avoid the stress. The goal of the CC and R's is to prevent arguing and disputes, not stimulate them."

"Nikki Stanley couldn't have put it any better, Teddy," Kristin quipped. He reddened.

"I'm not Nikki Stanley, but I wanted us to move here and so did you," he reminded her sharply, "because I thought this was a wonderful place to live and raise our family."

"It is," she said. "Or rather, it can be. No place is perfect. All Angela and I are doing is pointing out the areas where the homeowners board went too far and, working within the system, asking them to reconsider. Is that so terrible? Well?" she demanded when he hesitated.

"No."

"But you're embarrassed by my activity, right, Teddy? Here you were given the honor of the appointment to the homeowners board and your wife is starting a revolution, right?"

"I didn't say that. I told you I would help rewrite and change anything that was unreasonable. Don't forget I argued for the variance with pets."

"And lost," she said dryly. "Don't forget that."

"The issue is one of the first orders of new business at the next board meeting. I'm going to insist the community have a chance to vote on it."

"Good," Kristin said. "So we're really on the same wavelength?"

"Yes, that's what I'm saying, only . . ."

"Only what, Teddy?"

"Don't go overboard in the other direction and become just as fanatical as Nikki Stanley."

"I'll keep a level head," she promised. "Okay?"

He nodded, but his smile quickly faded.

"What are you going to say at Angela's formal hearing?" he asked.

"Now, Teddy," she said with her hands on her hips, "you're on the board. You have to be objective. I can't tell you that beforehand."

"Stop it, Kristin. It isn't funny."

"You're not kidding. It isn't funny."

"So? What are you going to say?"

"Just what I told you I saw."

"Nothing more?"

"What else can I say?"

"I know how you feel about some of the security people. I just thought—"

The doorbell chimed.

"That's Angela," Kristin said.

"Jesus, we didn't even have our coffee yet and you two are back at it?"

"I invited her to join us for coffee, Ted. You can associate with a known complainant, can't you?"

"Known complainant? I don't think you two are going overboard. You are overboard, Kristin," he said.

"So? You'll rescue us."

"I only hope I can," he muttered as she went to the door.

"Hi. Am I too early?" Angela asked.

"No. Perfect timing actually. I was just putting up the coffee."

Angela, carrying a leather bound file under her arm, followed Kristin to the kitchen.

"Hi, Ted."

"Angela. How is it out? Did it start raining?"

"No, but you can feel the drops forming. It's that humid. Did you ever notice how dark it is out here when it's overcast, even with our state-of-the-art streetlights?"

"That's a tradeoff we make for rural living," Ted said.

"The lake always looks so inky and foreboding on nights like this," Angela said. "I keep expecting the creature from the dark lagoon or something to appear."

Kristin laughed.

"What creature?" Jennifer said, coming in from the den.

"Oh, no. Little pitchers have big ears. No creature, honey. I was just joking. Who's that?" Angela asked indicating Jennifer's doll.

"Baby Walk-Along," she said. "We're watching Mickey Mouse." She turned and ran back to the den.

Angela smiled.

"Isn't that doll too big? I thought I read something in the CC and R's . . ." She pretended to thumb through some papers. Kristin laughed, but Teddy shook his head.

"You two are too much. How's Steve handling all this?" he asked, which put a kink in the humor. Angela grew dark and serious quickly.

"Not too well. We're just grunting at each other these days."

"Are you sure it's worth it, Angela?" Teddy asked.

"Only if we want to stay here," she said. "To tell you the truth, Ted," she said, smiling at Kristin, "I was ready to give up until Kristin came over and we had a good talk."

"Really?" He looked at Kristin, but she wasn't sure if it was a look of admiration or a look of disappointment.

"Yes. It was refreshing to meet someone who had a mind of her own, and some intestinal fortitude, as my father used to say. You can be very proud of your wife." When Teddy didn't respond, she added, "I hope you are."

"Oh, I am. I just worry about the two of you getting into cat fights with some of the diehards, that's all."

"We can scratch and kick as well as the best of them, can't we, Kristin?"

"Better. Come on, spread the papers out on the table and I'll get us some coffee. You want to sit in, Ted?"

He shrugged.

"I'll sit in if you'll consider suggestions."

"Of course we will," Angela said and they all sat together, reviewing some of the research and analysis Angela and Kristin had already completed. Nearly an hour later, Teddy rose from his seat to go watch television with Jennifer.

"We've got to relax," he said. "If we get too intense about all this, we'll lose our perspective."

Angela waited for him to leave and then leaned over to ask in a low voice, "He's not too happy about our efforts, is he?"

"He is and he isn't. Teddy's a bit confused these days," Kristin said. "But," she said smiling, "he wants to make changes. He just worries about me."

"I wish that was the reason Steven is so cantankerous. He's worried about offending the wrong people." She thought a moment. "Maybe I oughta go home and try to talk things out with him."

"Sure. Once he understands we're only out to improve what we have . . ."

"I just resent the way he behaved after the incident with the security people, blaming it on me. He insists I must have screwed up the alarm in the house. I never touched the damn thing."

Kristin nodded. Angela folded the file and stood up.

"All right. I'll call you in the morning and let you know how things go on the home turf."

"Good luck."

Kristin walked her to the door. When she opened it, she saw the rain had begun, but it was only drizzling.

"I'll lend you an umbrella."

"Nonsense. I'll just put these papers under my jacket and trot home," Angela said. "See you at the Okay Corral, partner."

"Night."

Kristin watched her run down the walk and then wave and start for home. She closed the door, took a deep breath and went to join Teddy and Jennifer. For a while the three of them just sat together, watching a sitcom. Then Teddy turned to her and smiled.

"I'll call Steve Del Marco tomorrow and see what I can do," he offered.

"Thank you, Teddy. That will help."

"I hope so," he said.

About a half an hour after they put Jennifer to bed and started to watch a movie on one of the cable networks, the phone rang. They looked at each other. Neither anticipated a call this late.

"I'll get it," Kristin said, thinking it might be Angela reporting either some success with her husband or terrible failure. But it was Steve Del Marco himself.

"Hello, Kristin," he said. "I don't like to call anyone this late," he said emphasizing the word late, "but it is late. She could have at least come home to say good night to the boys. She promised them she would, and I'm—"

"What are you talking about, Steven?"

"I'm talking about my wife," he said disdainfully. "Can you please put her on the line."

"But Steven . . . Angela left hours ago."

Teddy turned sharply from the television set. Kristin checked her watch. "We're talking two hours at least."

"You're kidding," Steven said.

"Is there someone else she said she was going to see?" Kristin asked.

"As far as I know, you two are the only ones doing this," Steve replied bitterly.

"Steven, you're worrying me."

"How do you think I feel?" he snapped. "Jesus. What is she doing, trying to punish me?"

"Well, where could she be?"

"I don't know. I'll see if her car's here. She left it in the driveway today. I had the television up loud and maybe didn't hear her go."

"I'm coming right over," Kristin said. She hung up quickly.

"What?" Teddy asked.

"Angela's not home. Steven thought she was still here."

"Really? Where would she go?"

"Nowhere I know. When she left, she was heading home. I watched her jog away."

"So where are you going?"

"I'm just going to go up there and see if she took the car."

"Why don't you wait for him to call, Kristin? It's pouring out there," Teddy said, but she no longer heard him. She went to the hall closet and got out her raincoat and an umbrella. It was coming down pretty hard, the drops pelting the macadam and thumping her umbrella as she started down the walk. The wind forced her to grip the umbrella handle very tightly and swept the raindrops in and under the protection of her umbrella. It slowed her gait. Looking up the street, she saw Steven Del Marco standing in his doorway. She saw Angela's car in the driveway and shouted to him as she hurried her pace. He had no umbrella, but he stepped out into the rain anyway when she approached. He looked angry enough to strike her.

"The car's obviously here," he said. "I called the security gate. They haven't seen her. They're on the way."

"Well, where can she be?" Kristin cried, spinning around. "She must be visiting someone."

The raindrops soaked him, but he didn't move to protect himself. He was that enraged. She raised the umbrella to give him as well as herself some protection. The water streaked down the sides of his face. His dark eyes looked like two pieces of gray slate, catching a little of the diffused light from the street lamps and the lamps on his front lawn and driveway.

"Visiting someone?" He raised his arms. "What am I supposed to do, call every resident of Emerald Lakes at this hour and ask if my wife is there? See what she's doing to me? You had to encourage her," he said accusingly.

"I didn't encourage her, Steven. I agreed with her. She went through a very traumatic experience and—"

They both turned as the security guards pulled up in their car. Spier and Stark stepped out slowly as if they were immune to the rain. They swaggered arrogantly through the downpour, both draped in black rain capes, the water streaming over the brims of their caps. Both carried long flashlights.

"What's going on, Mr. Del Marco?" Spier asked.

"My wife's missing, I'm ashamed to say," Steven replied.

"Missing?" Stark said, a wry smile on his lips.

"Let's step under the roof here and talk," Spier said pointing to the portico with his flashlight. They all walked up to the patio.

"My wife went to visit with Mrs. Morris here about three, three and a half hours ago. Mrs. Morris claims she left about two and a half hours ago, only she didn't come home."

"Well, she's probably visiting someone else, don't you think, Mr. Del Marco?" Spier said. "I know she's been going around the development a great deal lately," he added and shifted his eyes to Kristin.

"I doubt it. She had no umbrella. When she left my house, she put her papers under her coat and ran toward home," Kristin said.

"Papers?" Stark said.

"Yes, papers. So she wouldn't be traipsing all over the development knocking on doors, Mr. Spier," Kristin snapped. Spier and Stark just stared at her.

"Did she have anything to drink?" Spier asked.

"Anything to drink? What do you mean?"

"Alcoholic?"

"Of course not. What are you suggesting? Angela got drunk and wandered off into the night?"

"Just asking. She didn't come home and your house is not that far away," Spier said gazing down the street.

"Well, what are you going to do about it?" Kristin demanded impatiently.

"She didn't come through any of the gates," Stark said to Spier. He nodded.

"Yeah. She should still be around here somewhere. Sure she didn't go visit anyone else, now?"

"I told you. When she left my house, she was going straight home. I watched her walk away!"

Spier nodded calmly.

"I guess we'll have to sweep the area. You go right and I'll go left, Carl."

"Sweep the area?" Kristin asked, the reality of what was happening finally settling in and making her heart pound.

"Maybe she fainted or something. We've got to check around, Mrs. Morris. You just asked us what we were going to do and there isn't much else to do except go house to house and knock on doors."

"Sorry," Steven Del Marco said when the two security guards stepped back into the downpour.

"This is what we're paying them to do for us, Steven. You don't have to apologize," Kristin said firmly. Their tight-ass attitudes and innuendos annoyed her. Steven didn't reply. "Are the boys still awake?"

"Yes," he said. "They know something's up."

"You want me to go inside and talk to them?"

"It's all right," he said and glared at her as if to say, "You've talked enough to members of my family."

She looked down the street and saw Teddy walking up quickly, holding an umbrella.

"What's happening?" he shouted.

"We don't know. They're looking over the area," Kristin said.

"She didn't say she was going to see anyone else?"

"No, Teddy. I saw her to the door and she started to run home in the drizzle," Kristin said, feeling like she had turned into a broken record.

"Jesus, this is weird," he said, walking up the drive.

"Tell me about it," Steven Del Marco said. "She's probably sitting under someone's back porch, just letting me stew."

"Oh, Steven, she wouldn't do that. She was going home to talk things over with you and—"

"You don't know her," Steven insisted. "She could do something like that."

They heard Spier shouting.

"What's that?" Teddy said turning. The beam of Spier's flashlight whipped through the raindrops as he waved at them.

"He's found something," Steven Del Marco muttered fearfully.

The three of them charged off the portico toward the security guard who waved them back toward the lake. He walked ahead and then turned to wait for them.

"What?" Steven asked as they approached.

"It ain't pretty," Spier said and turned.

Kristin's heart seemed to bob in her chest. Her legs felt light and wobbly.

"I would stay back," Spier said when Kristin stepped forward.

"No," Kristin insisted. She took a deep breath. "Show us what you've found."

She took Teddy's arm and the three of them followed the security guard back to a row of wild bushes. Stark was standing behind one, his flashlight directed down. They turned around the bushes and saw her.

Angela was face down on the grass, her skirt raised over her waist, her panties gone, her rear end sopping wet and gleaming. Her head was twisted to the left, her right cheek soaking in the mud. Behind her head, just under her scalp was a clear, red gash. The raindrops made the blood gleam like rubies.

Kristin screamed.

"Christ Almighty," Teddy said, going to his knees.

"Oh, my God," Steven said. "Oh, my God," he muttered. "What happened?"

Teddy checked her pulse.

"She's still alive," he reported. He took off his coat and put it over her. Then he looked up at Stark. "Call an ambulance, quick. And call the police!"

Stark turned to Spier who nodded and Stark shot off toward the car. Teddy held his umbrella out for Steven to take. "Hold this over her, Steven," he ordered.

"I'll do that, Mr. Morris," Spier said, seizing the umbrella.

"Let me have your flashlight," Teddy demanded. Spier handed it to him.

Steven Del Marco crumbled to his knees beside his wife, his eyes wide with disbelief, while Teddy carefully examined the wound. He checked Angela's eyes.

Kristin, who had turned away to catch her breath, looked back slowly.

"How is she, Teddy?"

"Unconscious. I don't know what sort of damage has been done by this blow to her head." He examined the rest of her body as best he could. "I don't see any other trauma, but I don't want us to move her until the paramedics arrive and we place her on the stretcher carefully," he said.

"What should I do?" Kristin asked.

"Go get some blankets and a hot, wet towel," he said. "Steven, are you all right?" he asked the gaping man who had taken his wife's hand into his. He was swaying and gasping audibly, but he nodded, his eyes fixed on his wife.

Kristin hesitated for a moment, deciding whether to go into the Del Marco house or her own. The rain continued to fall around them relentlessly. However, she concluded it was better not to alarm Angela's children and hurried to her own house. When she returned with the blankets and towel, she saw Stark was back, holding an additional umbrella over the fallen woman and the two men and directing the beam of his flashlight down.

"What did they do to her, Teddy?" Kristin asked as he draped the blanket over her and began to carefully wipe away the blood from the wound. He shook his head. Steven Del Marco had broken into a chanting of her name.

"Angela . . . Angela . . ."

"Check around here," Spier told Stark and gestured toward the woods and bushes behind them. He then looked at Kristin. "Someone obviously struck her and did God knows what else," he replied coolly.

"Who? How?" Kristin wondered aloud.

"They didn't get in through the gate, so my guess is through these woods or . . . I told the board this was a concern of mine," he added, gazing toward the water.

"What?" Kristin asked. Talking kept her calm.

"Someone coming over the water," he said. "Like some covert operation," he added. "We can do just so much," he muttered. "Just so much."

Stark shouted for him and he moved into the darkness.

"She's been out here like this for more than two hours," Steven Del Marco said as the realization struck him. "I waited so long to call. I waited . . ."

"Where's the ambulance, Teddy?" Kristin asked, looking back. She understood that every passing moment was precious.

As if on cue, the sirens could be heard in the distance.

"There's no one at the front gate to let them in," Kristin cried. "Mr. Stark!" She stepped through the bushes toward the lake. "Mr. Spier!" Where were they? She stumbled on some rocks and caught herself on a tree trunk. It was too dark. "Mr. Spier!"

Kristin stepped forward again, the inky lake just discernible in the darkness. She recalled Angela's joke about a creature from the dark lagoon. Some creature got to her, all right.

"Mr. ———"

"Right here, Mrs. Morris," Stark said. He was literally inches away. She gasped as he stepped out of the shadows. He could have been here earlier, she thought. He could have been the one.

He had something in his hands.

"The ambulance," Kristin said breathlessly. "I hear it, but you two are here. No one is there to let them in," she said.

"We left the gate open in anticipation of that, Mrs. Morris. We have procedures to handle any sort of emergency," he said. "Found this down by the water," he said directing his light to what was in his hand. He held it inches from her face. It was Angela Del Marco's panties.

Kristin tried to swallow, but couldn't. She glanced at his dark face and thought she saw a tight smile on his lips. Without comment, she turned away, terrified, and fled through the darkness, back to Teddy just as an ambulance and a police patrol car pulled up.

10

THE RAIN NEVER LET UP. The paramedics worked swiftly, loading Angela onto the stretcher and into the ambulance. Two detectives from the sheriff's office joined the state highway patrolman who had initially responded to the dispatcher. By now the bubble lights and noise had drawn many of the residents of Emerald Lakes out of their homes. Some gathered with umbrellas and looked on from across the street, adding to the funeral atmosphere that had fallen over the housing development.

Phil Slater and his board members were clumped together in front of the ambulance, Phil remaining in his car, the others standing by with umbrellas. Everyone watched and waited as the paramedics shut the ambulance door and started away.

Teddy put his arm around Steven Del Marco.

"I'll take you to the hospital, Steven," Teddy said. Steven nodded.

"We'll use my car. Let me just check on the boys."

"I'll wake Jennifer and take her over here and stay with the boys," Kristin told him. "Unless there's someone else you want."

Steven just shook his head.

"You just take it easy, Kristin," Teddy warned as softly as he could. "Remember, you're pregnant."

"One of us can stay with them, Mrs. Morris," Spier said. He had been standing close enough to overhear the conversation.

"I'll do it," Kristin said sharply. "They're going to be very frightened."

"Suit yourself. Just trying to make things easier for everyone," he said.

Phil Slater got out of his car and joined Teddy and Steven. They spoke for a moment and then, when Teddy backed out of Steven's driveway, driving Steven's car, Philip Slater followed. The groups of residents continued to mill about until the highway patrolman pulled away. The sheriff's detectives remained to interview Spier and Stark and do what they could with the crime scene in this rainstorm.

Meanwhile, Kristin hurried back to the house to wake Jennifer. Nikki Stanley and Jean Levine met her in front of her house.

"What happened?" Jean asked first.

"Angela was attacked going home from my house tonight. Attacked and . . ." She shook her head.

"Attacked! How could someone be attacked here!" Jean exclaimed as if she were challenging Kristin's veracity.

"You're right. It's against the CC and R's," Kristin muttered, tears streaming down her cheeks.

"What?"

"Nothing. I've got to get Jennifer and go back to stay with the boys."

"Can't we do anything to help?" Jean asked.

"I don't know. Nothing right now, I guess," she said. "But . . ."

"Obviously Kristin has things under control," Nikki said.

"Under control? Right, under control." Kristin shook her head and hurried inside to wake Jennifer.

"We've got to stay with Anthony and Daniel, honey. Their mommy had to go to the hospital and Daddy had to go with Mr. Del Marco."

Jennifer groaned. She remained half asleep and Kristin had to carry her to the car. Nikki and Jean and all of the residents had gone back to their homes, but Kristin saw the sheriff's detectives were still at the scene, running a bright yellow tape around the area. Jennifer woke up when they pulled into the Del Marco driveway.

"Why are we here, Mommy?"

"I told you, honey. We've got to stay with Anthony and Daniel until their daddy comes home from visiting their mommy at the hospital," she said.

"Where's Daddy?"

"He had to go with Mr. Del Marco."

The boys were awake, but still in their beds, both too frightened to get up and wander about the house. They had heard the sirens and seen the lights and Steven had told them to just wait for Mrs. Morris.

"Where's Mommy?" Daniel asked as soon as Kristin appeared.

"She's had a little accident," Kristin said. "She had to go to the doctor in the hospital, but she's going to be all right."

"I want Mommy," Anthony complained.

"She'll be here as soon as she can, honey. You guys want to watch television with Jennifer and me? We can wrap ourselves in blankets and spread out in the living room."

The two boys looked at each other and considered the offer. It was very late, even late for adults, and watching television at this hour was like forbidden fruit. They both nodded.

"Come on, sweetheart," Kristin said lifting Daniel. "Jennifer's already on the sofa waiting."

They found Jennifer had fallen back to sleep. Kristin was grateful for that. She got the two boys comfortable and put on a movie. Ten minutes later, all the children were asleep. She stared at the glowing screen, mesmerized by the light. Now that she had a quiet moment, she felt the full impact of what had occurred. It left her chilled. She had to wrap a blanket around herself, too. Suddenly, she was feeling her pregnancy. Her lower back ached.

This has to be a bad dream, she thought. It has to. I'll close my eyes and count to ten and then . . .

She heard the door chimes and rose slowly.

"Evening, ma'am. I'm Lieutenant Kurosaka with the sheriff's department and this is my partner, Detective Martin."

Kristin nodded at the five-foot-nine-inch stout Japanese man with coal black hair now wet and shiny. He wiped his face dry with his handkerchief. Both he and his partner were soaked, but his partner looked a great deal unhappier about it. He was a much younger looking man, at least six feet tall, with strawberry red hair and a face peppered with freckles along the ridges of his cheeks and over his forehead. He had the kind of face that would look young until he was well into his sixties.

"Come on in," she said, "but, please be as quiet as possible. I have all the children sleeping on the living room floor."

"Thank you."

They shook their clothes off in the entryway. Kristin led them to the kitchen.

"I'll put up some water for tea," she said.

"Thank you. That's very kind of you," Kurosaka said.

"Yeah, thanks," Martin parroted.

"We just have a few questions for you tonight. We know it's late, but I figured while things were still fresh in your mind . . ."

"No, it's all right," Kristin said. "I'm glad you're here. I won't sleep. I need something to keep me occupied."

"I understand," Kurosaka said. He looked at the chair, but was too polite to just take a seat.

"Please, sit down," Kristin said and searched the cabinets for Angela's cups and saucers.

"We spoke at length with the development's security people. You told them Mrs. Del Marco was at your home earlier?"

"Yes. We were meeting to discuss the CC and R's."

"CC and R's?"

"Covenants, Conditions, and Restrictions," Kristin replied. "Our development's constitution," she added.

Kurosaka flipped open his notepad.

"Can you pinpoint the time for us, Mrs. Morris?"

"Yes." She turned and thought a moment. "Teddy and I had just finished dinner. I was making coffee when Angela arrived. We had agreed to meet about seven. She was ten minutes or so early. She stayed until eight-fifteen. I remember it was eight-fifteen," she said nodding.

"And then what?"

"Steven called looking for her about ten-thirty."

"So, this happened sometime between eight-fifteen and ten-thirty?" Martin commented. Kurosaka turned to him.

"No. It had to happen in a more narrow range of

time, Carey. The woman was on her way home. She didn't linger in the streets for an hour and then get attacked. She had to have been attacked shortly after she left. It's only a few minutes at the most between the two houses, so she was attacked about eight-seventeen, -eighteen," Kurosaka pointed out.

Detective Martin glanced at Kristin and then shrugged, his face somewhat crimson with anger and embarrassment at the way Kurosaka had corrected him in front of Kristin. Kurosaka either didn't notice or didn't care.

"Did you find anything else out there?" Kristin asked.

"Else?"

"Besides Angela's . . . panties?"

"Well, it's too dark for a thorough investigation. We'll be back early in the morning. Who found the panties?"

"I don't know who actually found them. Mr. Stark showed them to me.

"I went looking for the two security guards because I thought they had left the front gate locked and the ambulance wouldn't be able to get in when it arrived at the gate. Mr. Stark appeared with the panties in his hand."

"Did he say where he found them?"

"Not exactly."

"So as far as you saw, only those two handled the undergarment?"

"I only saw Stark with it," she emphasized. Kurosaka smiled, appreciating her exactness.

She thought a moment and then, just as the tea kettle whistled, widened her eyes. "The papers!"

"Papers?" Kurosaka asked. Kristin turned off the range and then spun around to face him.

"When Angela left my house, she had our file. She put it under her jacket so it wouldn't get wet. But I didn't see the papers anywhere. Did you find them?"

"No, Mrs. Morris. We haven't found any papers yet, but it's really dark and hard to search out there now," Kurosaka emphasized. "What were these papers exactly?"

Kristin poured the hot water into the cups.

"Our work revising the CC and R's. Our suggestions, research, all of it," she said shaking her head. "You'd think the wind would have scattered everything all over the place."

She served the tea.

"Thank you."

"Thanks," Martin said.

"We'll look for them in the morning," Kurosaka said. "We've got the area roped off."

"Do you think you'll find who did this?" Kristin asked.

"We're going to try, Mrs. Morris. We'll canvas the street tomorrow and see if anyone else might have heard or seen anything."

"It had just started to rain," Kristin said. "I went to the door with her and watched her start for home." Her lips trembled so she brought the teacup to her mouth and sipped.

"You didn't see a car go by or anyone else out there?" Kurosaka asked.

"No. But Mr. Stark said he thought the attacker came from the lake. He called it a covert operation," she said. Everything that happened around Angela's fallen, wounded body remained vivid in her mind: words, images. The scene was in a continuous replay every time she closed her eyes.

"Covert?" Martin said, curling the corners of his

lips up. She nodded. He looked at Kurosaka, but Kurosaka remained stone-faced.

"Are you sure she started right for home?" Lieutenant Kurosaka asked.

"Yes. I'm sure."

The three sipped their teas.

"Because those security guards seem to think she was going around the development trying to get signatures for some sort of petition," he added.

"No, we weren't ready for that yet," Kristin said. "I'm afraid our security personnel are not . . ."

"What?" Kurosaka asked, sensing her hesitation.

"The most reliable source of information concerning Angela right now. In my opinion," she added quickly.

"Why not? They're your own security people," Martin said.

"We were making a formal complaint against them this coming Thursday at a special hearing," Kristin said, and explained the circumstances.

"I see," Kurosaka said. "And it was these two?"

"Yes. Do you think they're right: someone came over the lake?"

"I just recently moved here," Kurosaka said. "I'm not that familiar with the territory. Carey?"

"Sure it's possible," Detective Martin said. "It's a good fishing spot," he added. "Fished there myself. Always envied the people who lived here," he added.

"Not tonight, I bet," Kristin said. He shrugged.

"Bad things happen to people everywhere, Mrs. Morris."

"All right. You've been very helpful," Kurosaka quickly said, gazing reproachfully at Detective Martin. "We'll stop by tomorrow morning." He looked at Martin again. "We'd better head over to the hospital."

"Right." Martin gulped the rest of his tea and stood up.

"Thank you for your kindness," Kurosaka said with a slight nod after he rose.

"You're welcome," Kristin said. She walked them to the door.

"Is this sort of thing happening more often around here now?" she asked, still uncomfortable with Detective Martin's comment.

"Detective Martin is right. It's happening everywhere, Mrs. Morris," Kurosaka said. "Only . . ." He paused and eyed Martin again.

"Yes?"

"Not as much in developments as secured as this," he added.

As soon as she closed the door behind them, the phone rang. She hurried to answer it before it woke the children.

"Hello."

"How's it going?" Teddy asked.

"The children are all asleep. The police just left."

"Oh, they came to talk to you now?"

"They were very nice and wanted me to tell them what I could while my memory was still fresh. I'm not sleeping anyway. Teddy, how is she?"

"She's in a coma, honey. She was hit really hard. It's too early to tell how bad it's going to be."

"Oh, God, Ted."

"Steven's pretty bad. The doctor wants to give him a sedative, but he's refusing. What about the kids?"

"They're all asleep on the living room floor."

"I'll be here a while yet, honey. The specialist has just arrived."

"How could this have happened, Teddy?" She recalled Kurosaka's last words. "And in Emerald Lakes?"

"I don't know."

"Teddy," she said, swallowing hard, "besides hitting her, what else did they . . ."

"She was raped, honey. But it probably happened after she was unconscious," he added quickly.

"My God, Teddy. What animals." She thought a moment. "He's blaming me, isn't he, Teddy? Steven's blaming me."

"He hasn't said anything like that, honey. If he's blaming anyone, he's blaming himself."

"But . . ."

"Look," Teddy said sharply, "if we can't walk safely through the streets of Emerald Lakes at night, where can we walk safely? There's no one to blame but the freak who did this. Hopefully, the police will get this guy. I'll call you again in about a half hour if we're staying much longer. I'm going to try to talk Steven into going home after the specialist examines her so he can get some rest for the long haul ahead."

"She's going to be all right, isn't she, Teddy? Isn't she?" she asked when he didn't respond.

"I don't know," he said and for the moment she hated that he was a doctor and that he was truthful. If there was a time she needed fantasy, it was now, she thought. "Hang in there," he added and hung up.

Kristin knew she wouldn't sleep until she passed out from exhaustion and she feared it; she feared the images that would be free to return, images like the smirks on Stark's and Spier's faces.

Was this a case of the fox guarding the henhouse? If so, what good was all this faith in security?

Security for whom? For those who obey, who make no waves only?

She wanted to drive out these thoughts, drive out these fears, drive out the picture of poor Angela on the ground in the rain. There was so much to fear after all, but most of all, she feared the sound of her own scream in the night.

Teddy and Steven didn't return until a little after 3 A.M. However, Teddy hadn't called to let her know they would be staying that long. She fell asleep waiting and was asleep when they pulled into the driveway; but she woke up the moment she heard the front door open. She ground the sleep out of her eyes and stood up just as the two of them entered the living room.

Steven Del Marco was washed out, his face pale, his shoulders slumped. Teddy glanced at Kristin and shook his head. She felt her heart stop and then start with long, deep beats. She bit down on her lower lip. He, too, had the look of a man who had experienced a face-to-face confrontation with the Grim Reaper.

"Teddy?" she said in a tiny, broken voice. Steven Del Marco raised his eyes slowly to look at her. They were so bloodshot they looked lined with rouge.

"The blow created too much internal pressure," Teddy said softly. "Before they could operate . . . she never regained consciousness," he concluded quickly.

Kristin felt her legs give out, so she leaned toward the sofa and folded her torso into it. It seemed as if all the oxygen in the air immediately around her had been sucked away and replaced with an intense heat. Her lungs filled with it to the point where she thought her chest would explode. She gasped and clutched her stomach, her face flushing with panic as well as sorrow. She was terrified she would have a miscarriage on the spot. Teddy came to her side and embraced her as quickly as he could.

"Easy, honey. Easy. Take some deep breaths."

"Oh, God," she said burying her face against his

shoulder. The pain in her back whipped around and tightened over her kidneys. She took the deep breaths and it eased, but the throbbing in her head and in her lower spine remained.

Steven Del Marco moved like a zombie. He came into the living room, gazed down at his two little boys and then fell to his knees beside them. Danny woke first, rubbed his eyes and started to sit up, the confusion moving through his face in waves. He gazed about, saw his father and, frightened by his kneeling and his expression, started to cry. Anthony's eyes opened. He sat up more quickly when he saw his father and his brother crying.

"Where's Mommy?" he moaned.

Steven put his arms around both his boys and drew them to him, holding them as he shuddered with his deep sobs. Kristin, unable to watch the scene unfolding before her, dropped her head back on the sofa and closed her eyes. Jennifer heard the commotion and woke. Teddy went to her and lifted her into his arms quickly.

"I want Mommy," Danny cried. He tried to break out of Steven's hold, but Steven clung to his children tightly, holding them like a shield between himself and the agony.

Kristin took another deep breath and sat up. She had to find the strength.

"Mommy?" Jennifer asked, confronting the agonizing scene unfolding before her.

"It's all right, honey. It's all right," Teddy comforted.

Kristin rose like an arthritic old woman, but with renewed strength went to Steven and the boys.

"Steven. Let me help with the boys," she said. "I'll put them to sleep in their own beds."

He rocked with the boys in his arms, the tears

streaming down his cheeks, oblivious to their moans and cries. Kristin looked at Teddy helplessly.

"Steve," Teddy said. "Let's get the boys to sleep. Everyone's going to need some sleep."

Kristin went to lift Danny out of Steven's arms and Danny screamed so shrilly, it stung; but it snapped Steven Del Marco out of his daze. Realizing what he was doing and what was happening, he loosened his grip and the boys sat back.

"We've got to put them back to bed," Kristin said softly. Steven gazed up at her, finally comprehending. He took a deep breath and nodded.

"Come on, Anthony," he said standing. "You and your brother have to go back to bed."

"Where's Mommy?"

"Mommy's . . . sleeping," he said. "In the hospital. Come on, Daniel." He got them to stand and put his hands behind their heads to direct them back to their bedroom. Teddy turned to Kristin.

"You all right?"

"I'm okay. Let me help Steven," she said, and followed.

After she helped Steven get the boys into bed, she joined Teddy.

"We gotta take Jennifer home now," he said. "And I want you to rest, too."

"I'm okay."

"Never mind. No one's okay," he insisted in his best stern doctor's voice. Steven came out of the bedroom and Teddy turned to him. "You going to be all right, Steve?"

"Yeah. I'll call my sister first thing in the morning. She'll get here by late afternoon. Angela's family's all in Paramus, New Jersey."

"I'll come over first thing in the morning and help

with the boys," Kristin offered. "Until some of your family arrives." He nodded, his chin quivering.

"I told her," he said with a jerky laugh, "I told her she should be grateful we were living in such a secure community, a place where we could raise our family without the fear haunting everyone else. I told her she was being unappreciative; she was a spoiled—"

"Steven, don't," Kristin urged. She reached out for his hand, and he closed his eyes and nodded.

"It's all right. I'll be all right," he said.

"You better get a little sleep, Steven," Teddy advised.

"Yeah, sure." He went into the living room to the bar and poured himself half a glass of bourbon. "Thanks for your help, Ted."

"I'm sorry," Teddy said. "We'll be here for you. The whole complex will be."

"I know."

Teddy put his free arm around Kristin and led her to the door. She looked back once to see Steven gulp his drink and pour himself more. Then they left.

It had stopped raining, but the mist hung heavy in the late evening air. The clean, macadam streets of Emerald Lakes glittered under the streetlights Angela Del Marco had earlier called state of the art. Kristin gazed up the street and saw the lights were on in the Slater's house. Teddy saw where she was looking.

"Philip was at the hospital the whole time," he said. "He got the specialist out of bed and down there in minutes. He looked like he was taking it worse than Steven. All he kept saying was he couldn't believe such a thing could happen in Emerald Lakes."

"Yes, I know," Kristin said with a sigh. "It's going to hurt our real estate values."

"That's not fair, Kristin. He was really very upset

about it and felt terrible for Steven. He's taking care of everything for him, the funeral arrangements, everything," Teddy said with obvious admiration.

"Funeral arrangements," Kristin whispered and shook her head. She gazed at the taped-off crime scene quickly and then closed her eyes. She loaded Jennifer into the car and they all drove home in silence.

After Kristin put Jennifer to bed, she came out to the kitchen. Teddy was making some tea.

"You want a cup?"

"Yes, please," she said and sat slowly, her hands against her lower back. She groaned. Teddy watched her, concerned. The miscarriage before had started with sharp back pain and then the hemorrhaging. "I can't believe this, Teddy."

"It does seem like a bad dream."

She sat back. "Did you know she was going to die when you called me from the hospital?"

"I was afraid. Her pulse was so weak and that gash went so deep."

"Oh, God," Kristin moaned, embracing herself and rocking in her chair. "This is my fault. If I hadn't encouraged her and she wasn't here tonight . . ."

"That's stupid, Kristin. Whoever did this was lingering out there looking for an opportunity to pounce on someone. If he didn't do it tonight, he might have done it tomorrow night to someone else, maybe even you," Teddy said and Kristin looked up sharply, that realization crystallizing.

"It had to be someone familiar with the development and the area, right?" she asked. Teddy shrugged.

"We'll have to wait for the police to finish their investigation, honey."

He poured them their tea and they sat sipping the hot liquid and staring blankly at the table.

"Are you going to go to work tomorrow, Ted?"

"Yeah, I've got to. I have appointments I have to keep. Some were made weeks ago."

"Can you work?"

"I'll be all right. This place is going to be crazy in the morning as more of the residents find out what's happened. How about you?"

"I'll be okay. I'll keep busy helping Steven."

"I don't want you doing too much tomorrow, Kristin," he said. "Don't go lifting and carrying those boys. They're big and—"

"I won't. Teddy, Steven didn't say anything about me after . . . I mean . . ."

"He's not blaming you if that's what you mean, Kristin. He's not stupid. What's bothering him, in fact, was the feud between them before she was killed. He kept saying they never got to kiss and make up."

"Oh, Teddy," she moaned. "Poor Angela."

He put his hand over hers and then they embraced and held each other. Finally feeling the exhaustion, they crept into bed and fell asleep in each other's arms.

But Kristin woke abruptly just before the first light of morning. She thought she heard the front door open and close. She waited and listened with her heart pounding. Teddy's eyes were shut tight and his breathing was slow and regular. Apparently, he hadn't heard anything.

Was it just her imagination? She listened hard, heard nothing, and lay back again. She closed her eyes and didn't open them until the sunlight invaded the darkness and drove it back into the corners until its time to return.

*   *   *

Marilyn Slater didn't get up to make Philip his breakfast. When he stepped out of the bathroom after taking his wake-up shower and saw she was still in bed, he shook the footboard so she would open her eyes.

"What are you, sick?" he demanded. She stared at him, but didn't respond. "What the hell's going on with you?"

"I'm . . ."

"What?"

"Tired," she said, and closed her eyes again.

"Tired? From what? Watching television? Organizing your doll collection? Cooking dinner? What?"

"Maybe I'm sick," she offered.

He relaxed.

"You have a headache? A stomachache? What?" He sounded like a lawyer in a cross-examination driving for an exact response.

"Just an overall fatigue. I feel too weak to get out of bed right now," she said. She kept her eyes closed.

"You want me to arrange for you to see Doctor Pauling?"

"No."

"You want some aspirins or something?"

"No. I'll be all right," she said.

"This has nothing to do with what happened last night, does it?" he suddenly asked. She opened her eyes, but didn't answer. "Because I have some ideas about how we're going to prevent it from ever happening again. You don't have to worry about that," he assured her. "I mean, I understand why you would be nervous and upset, just as I'm sure most everyone in Emerald Lakes is, but I have some ideas, a contingency plan.

"I'm disappointed in my security people, of course," Philip continued, "but I recognize they can do just so much. No one is absolutely, beyond a doubt, safe from harm in this day and age." He paused. "Is that what's bothering you?"

Instead of replying, she asked, "Is she really dead, Philip?"

"Of course, she's really dead," he said. "I wouldn't say she was if she wasn't." He softened a bit. "They couldn't do much; it was too late."

Marilyn closed her eyes again.

"You can't sleep your way out of a crisis, Marilyn. You have to face up to it and defeat it," he insisted. "Ignoring and putting your head in the sand doesn't solve anything," he added with his characteristic relentlessness.

Then why do we pretend Bradley never existed? she wondered and was even about to ask, but he turned abruptly to get a tie. He babbled on about the way to handle disappointments and correct errors. He guaranteed her that he would make Emerald Lakes safe again.

"And if anyone calls today to talk about this, you can reassure them I'm on it, Marilyn."

"Who will call?" she asked.

"I don't know. Some nervous Nelly will call, I'm sure." He stared at her a moment. She hadn't behaved like this since Bradley's death, and then he practically had to turn the bed upside down to get her up and at it again. "You going to try to get up and about in a while or what?"

"I'll get up. I just need a little more rest this morning," she said.

"I'll go to the diner for breakfast. I'm sure there's going to be a lot of chatter about Emerald Lakes because of this and I better start putting out the fires before they get too big. But I'm not worried," he said. "I have a solution." He thought about telling her but decided she was not the sort of audience he wanted at the moment.

"I'll call you later," he muttered and left her. When she heard the front door open and close, she released a breath and felt a sense of relief.

She had sat by the window last night and watched the rain get heavier and heavier until the downpour sounded like a pack of rats running back and forth on the roof of the house. The glimmering streets, wet under the lights, were mesmerizing, as was the hypnotic rhythm of the rain. She had seen Angela Del Marco emerge from the Morris residence. She knew from Philip's ranting and raving why the two women were meeting. Marilyn had seen them together a number of times now and she had looked at them with envy, wishing she could be with them, a part of something, a friendship. She could be out with them, shopping, having coffee, going to a matinee. They could giggle and laugh with each other and tell each other some personal things because they understood each other's problems.

But she couldn't join them, not the conspirators. Philip would consider it an act of treason. As he most certainly would if she stepped forward to volunteer her witnessing the attack on Angela. It was hard to see what actually happened, of course. So much of it had occurred in the shadows, but the rain hadn't gotten as heavy yet, so she did see Angela trotting up the street. Then she had seen the shadow take the form of a man and come up behind her and another shadow step in front of her. She had seen them envelop Angela and swallow her up between them. It had looked like she had been absorbed into the darkness. A moment later she was gone.

It all happened so fast Marilyn questioned what she had seen herself. She had actually stood up and brought her face to the window, straining to see anything else, but there was nothing, no one.

"What was that?" she had wondered aloud and had gone to the front door and had stepped out on her patio to look down the street. The rain had started to fall harder. Marilyn had waited, listened, and watched, but she saw nothing, heard no one.

Then she had gone back inside and had thought about it.

I'll tell Philip, she had decided and had gone back to his office. She had knocked, waited, and when she heard nothing, opened the door. His lamp was on, but he wasn't behind his desk; he wasn't in his office. She had gone through the house, checking all the rooms. She even opened the basement door. Of course, it was pitch dark. Marilyn had looked in the garage and had seen his car was still there and so was hers.

Now, more confused than ever, she had returned to her chair and waited. It seemed like an hour or more before she had heard footsteps in the hallway and had looked up in shock.

"What's wrong with you?" he had asked. "You look like you've seen a ghost."

"Where were you?"

"Where was I? Working."

"But I went looking for you and you weren't there," she had said.

"Maybe I was in the bathroom then."

"I looked in the bathroom."

"Maybe I was in the closet, hiding," he had replied and had smirked. "Jesus, Marilyn, you see things, you don't see things. What you ought to do is make an appointment to have our new resident, Doctor Morris, give you an eye examine," he had said. He had started to turn away from her and then had stopped. "Why were you looking for me anyway?"

"I thought I saw something terrible happen," she had said. "I was looking outside at the rain when I saw . . ."

"Saw what?"

She thought about it a moment and then had shaken her head. He wouldn't believe her. He might even get angry she would suggest such a thing occurred in his precious development.

"Nothing," she had said.

"You know what, Marilyn," he had said, "I know you hit the vodka now and then. Don't deny it. You thought I didn't know or didn't care, but I do. I don't like it," he had said. "You had better get hold of yourself before you become a basket case."

She had stared up at him. He must have just found out, she had thought, or he would have said something earlier.

"I'm tired. I'm going to sleep," he had said.

Marilyn had watched him leave and then she looked out the window again. The rain was really coming down now, in torrents. She had seen no one in the streets. After a while she had risen and finished putting away some dishes that were still in the drier. Then she had thought a moment and had gone to the garage again. She had opened the door and had snapped on the lights. There was still some water just inside the side entrance and Philip's raincoat and a pair of boots were wet. He had been outside. Why had he said he was in the office or in the bathroom?

She thought that it was suspicious. Why lie? If she

questioned him about it, he would surely become outraged. She was not in the mood to have him bawl her out for snooping. She had put out the light and had gone to bed, too. Philip was dozing with the television on. He didn't open his eyes when she had crawled under the covers. Then the phone had rung.

He groaned, lifted the receiver, listened and then said, "I'll be right there." He nearly broke the receiver when he slammed it down.

"What is it, Philip?"

"That Del Marco woman got herself in trouble."

"How?"

"She got attacked," he had said. Philip put on his pants and stood up to put on his shirt.

"Oh, my God," she had said sitting up. "I told you I saw something."

"No, you didn't," he had said sharply. He pointed his finger at her. "No, you didn't. And don't go saying you did. I don't want my wife involved in any of this stupidity."

"Is she all right? Philip," she had asked. He buttoned his shirt and went to his closet to grab his jacket. "Philip. Is she all right?" she had called after him.

He had never replied; not until he had come home at nearly three o'clock in the morning.

"Philip?" she had asked when he got back into bed.

"She's dead," he had said. "Let's get some sleep. I'll tell you about it in the morning and what I'm going to do."

He hadn't really told her much about it, of course. She didn't want him to; she didn't want to hear his ideas about preventing such terrible things in Emerald Lakes either.

That was the way she remembered it all.

Marilyn reached over to the night table and opened the drawer. Fumbling, she found Philip's pistol again. She brought it out and sat back against his pillow. Then she brought the gun to her temple and started the count.

This time she reached nine before she put the gun back.

"Only one more number," she whispered. "Only one more."

11

◈

TEDDY ROSE FIRST, actually showering by the time Kristin's eyes fluttered open. The pain in her back had subsided and was just a dull ache now. Kristin looked in on Jennifer, but decided to let her sleep longer. She wanted her to go to school, of course. She wanted her away from the development today.

She fixed the coffee and prepared some breakfast.

"How are you?" Teddy asked with concern. "Your back still hurt?"

"No, it's much better."

"You sure?" he asked skeptically.

"Yes, I'm sure, Teddy. I'm all right. Stop worrying."

"I was thinking," Teddy said, pouring himself some coffee. "I can take Jen to school so you could get over to Steven's earlier, if you want."

"That's a good idea, Teddy. She went to bed so late, I let her sleep longer, but I'd better get her up."

Later, just as they were finishing breakfast, the doorbell chimed. Teddy answered it and greeted Lieutenant Kurosaka.

"I hope I'm not calling on you too early, Doctor Morris," he said, showing his identification. "I was hoping to catch the two of you for a moment."

"No, but I was just getting ready to leave for work. I'm dropping my daughter off at school first."

Kristin came around to greet the policeman. He nodded and smiled.

"I'm sorry to bother you so early, Mrs. Morris," he said.

"It's all right, Lieutenant."

"Come on in," Teddy said, stepping back. Kurosaka entered. Jennifer had come around and stood by Kristin, gazing at him. He smiled at her.

"Say hello to Lieutenant Kurosaka, Jennifer," Kristin urged.

"Hello."

"Good morning," Kurosaka said with a small bow. "Mr. Morris, were you present last night when your wife and Mrs. Del Marco had their meeting?"

"Yes, I was."

"And did you see Mrs. Del Marco leave with a packet of papers, too?"

"I guess," he said gazing at Kristin. "I didn't really see her leave, but I imagine she took her papers with her."

"You're both sure those papers are not here?"

"You couldn't find them?" Kristin asked quickly.

"No, Mrs. Morris. We've been at the scene for about an hour already and we have found no papers of any kind."

"She took them with her. I saw her leave with them. I'm positive," she added in a strained voice.

"I understand," he said.

"Did you ask Stark and Spier?" she demanded quickly. Kurosaka nodded.

"Neither claim to have seen any papers last night. I know," he said looking at Teddy, "that it seems like a minor point at this time, but . . ."

"I'm an ophthalmologist, Lieutenant. No symptom, no evidence of any kind is to be neglected."

"Precisely," Lieutenant Kurosaka said, his eyes brightening with appreciation. He turned back to Kristin. "Can you give me a more detailed description of those papers, the file, whatever?"

She thought a moment.

"She was carrying the papers and a copy of what we call our CC and R's in a tan folder. There was a yellow lined notepad, the long type."

"Eight and a half by fourteen," Kurosaka said.

"I guess."

"Did the folder have anything written on the outside?"

Kristin smiled.

"Yes. She wrote 'Declaration of Independence.' It was just a joke. We . . ."

"I understand," Kurosaka said.

"I bet they found them and destroyed them, those bastards," Kristin muttered.

Teddy glared at Kristin before turning to Kurosaka.

"Kristin! Have you found anything useful at all?"

"We did find evidence of some sort of landing on the lakeshore. There were some footprints protected from being washed out because they were under some heavy tree foliage, but they might have been made by the security personnel. We'll see. We're going to drive to the other side of the lake now and see if we can find evidence of an approach made from the highway or if anyone over there has seen anything suspicious."

"So you think someone did invade the complex from the lake?" Teddy asked.

"It would appear so."

"But you're not convinced?" Kristin asked quickly.

"Honey, they've just begun. You can't expect them

to reach conclusions so quickly," Teddy said. "Take it easy."

"We always question the obvious, Mrs. Morris," Kurosaka said. He nodded. "I'm sure you'll agree that's a good quality for a detective. Thank you. I'll speak with you again," he said and left.

"How do you like that," Teddy said, "an inscrutable Oriental detective working for our police? This place is more cosmopolitan than we thought." He tried a smile, but Kristin just stood thinking.

"Why would some psychotic row across the lake to invade our complex and attack and rape one of our residents, and then steal Angela's papers with our CC and R's, Teddy?"

"When you're dealing with such a disturbed person, honey, logic and reason don't apply. Let's leave the police work to our criminologists," he said. "Come on. Let's get started and do what we have to do."

"I saw her leave with the papers, Teddy. And you see they're not here!"

"Okay. I believe you," he said. "I'm sure they'll turn up somewhere." She didn't move. "Kristin?"

"What? Oh."

Kristin snapped out of her deep thoughts and hurried to get Teddy and Jennifer off, and go over to the Del Marcos'. When she arrived, she was surprised to find Jean and Nikki already there. Jean opened the door for her.

"Hi. We came over early. I baked some cupcakes for the boys," Jean said.

Nikki emerged from the kitchen.

"We've already seen to their breakfast," she declared.

"I got here as soon as I could. I—"

"That's all right. You were right in the thick of it last night. You must be a mess yourself," Jean said. "And you're pregnant."

"We didn't want anything to happen to you, too," Nikki added.

"What do you mean?"

"Your pregnancy, what else?" Nikki replied.

"I'm all right," Kristin said quickly.

"Nikki and I felt we just had to do something, too. The poor dears."

"Where's Steven?"

"He's resting. He finally took something to help himself rest," Jean whispered.

"Well, now that you're here and you appear all right," Nikki said, wiping her hands on a dish towel, "I'll be going."

"There's going to be an emergency meeting of the homeowners tonight," Jean revealed.

"Teddy didn't say anything about it," Kristin said, turning to Nikki.

"Philip will call him at work," Nikki replied. "He wasn't sure of the time yet. The boys are still in their pajamas. I thought it was best we get them to eat something first." She opened the door. "If you should need me, I'll be working at home most of the day," she added, directing herself more to Jean. Then she left.

"Nikki's taking this very badly," Jean said, looking after her. "She wants the security people raked over the coals. She says we should even think about finding another company."

"Really?"

"Nikki thinks they've become lackadaisical because we haven't had a single real problem since the development was started. She says they've even skipped her house for door checks. She had an unlocked door a few days ago and the night security never told her."

"Somehow," Kristin said, "I can't imagine Nikki leaving a door unlocked."

"Oh, it was done deliberately. Just to check on the security," Jean explained and smiled. "Nikki's always checking up on them. She takes her position as the head of the Neighborhood Watch very seriously. She says you can never be too safe," Jean recited.

"I guess not. Let's see about the boys."

The two of them remained until Steven and Angela Del Marco's family began to arrive. Steven's sister took charge of the boys and Steven's brother got him up and dressed. He thanked Jean and Kristin for their help and they left, both glad to leave the house of heavy mourning.

"The sun is out and it's a beautiful day," Jean said as they walked toward their own homes, "but I feel like there's a dark, heavy cloud over us. Don't you?"

"Yes."

"What are you going to do today?"

"I don't know. Rest for a while, I guess."

"You want to have lunch with me? I just don't feel much like being alone and Nikki is terrible company right now."

"Sure," Kristin said, smiling.

Actually, she was grateful for the distraction. Her flighty friend talked nonstop from the beginning of lunch into the mid-afternoon, her nervous tension giving her the fuel to take Kristin on a journey through her biography, the history of her marriage, and the latest in fashions and recipes. The interruption came when Nikki called with a request.

"She wants me to call my people," Jean revealed after she hung up.

"Your people?"

"The phone chain. I've got ten. You're one of them, so I don't have to call you. The emergency meeting is tonight at eight at Phil Slater's house. Development baby-sitters are available free of charge to anyone who needs one. It's part of the emergency procedure."

"There's an emergency procedure?"

"Oh, yes," Jean said with a thin laugh. "It's a supplement to the directory. Didn't you notice?"

"Somehow I must have missed it."

"Nikki designed it herself. With the board's approval, of course. You can reserve one of the four-star girls if you want. We'll call right now."

"That's all right. I'll use the girl I had. She was four star as far as I was concerned."

"Oh, that's right. I promised Nikki I'd have you fill out one of these evaluation forms." Jean went to the den and returned with a paper.

"Was she on time? How was she dressed, including every aspect of her appearance? Did she leave the house as she found it? Was there any evidence of anyone else being there?"

"All right. I get the idea," Kristin said. She filled it out quickly and then went home. Minutes afterward, Teddy called to tell her about the meeting at eight.

"I already know. I was with Jean when Nikki told her to call her people on the phone chain. I have a baby-sitter lined up, too."

"Very efficient."

"It's part of the emergency procedure. As a member of the homeowners board, you should know that, Teddy," she said. She couldn't help being cranky. Her back had started aching again, but she wouldn't dare mention it.

"Right. How are things at the Del Marcos'?"

"Thankfully there is a crowd of relatives, with more arriving every moment. The boys are in a daze."

"My last appointment is at three. I'll come right home afterward. You better rest a little, honey."

"I will," she promised and she did go to lie down. Moments after her head hit the pillow, she was asleep and she slept so deeply, she never heard Jennifer return from school. She felt her shaking her shoulder and woke with a start.

"Jen!" She sat up quickly and wiped her eyes. "What time is it?"

"Mommy."

"What's the matter, honey?" she asked swinging her legs off the bed. Jennifer looked terrified.

"Graham said we can't go out after dark anymore. He said there's a monster in the woods who grabs you."

"Oh, there's no monster here, honey. At least, not in the woods," she added.

"He said his mother said so. Heather says so, too."

"They're wrong, honey. They're just being . . . stupid. Besides, you don't go out alone at night anyway, do you? So you don't have to be afraid. Okay, sweetheart?"

Jennifer nodded, but Kristin could see her daughter was well on the road to Nightmare, U.S.A.

"Damn that Nikki Stanley. She'll have us living like cavemen," Kristin muttered. When Teddy arrived, she told him how the Stanley children were terrifying all the other kids in the development. He didn't seem very upset. "Doesn't it bother you?" she demanded.

"I don't like Jennifer having nightmares about where we live, of course, but a little fear is a good thing, honey. It makes us more careful, don't you think?"

"No," Kristin responded sharply. "And I'm surprised you do. Fear doesn't make us more careful; it makes us weaker, more vulnerable. People like Nikki Stanley feed off it," she added. He could see how close Kristin was to becoming hysterical.

"Take it easy, honey. Don't get yourself so upset."

"Don't get so upset?"

"You know what I mean."

She stared at him.

"You still think somehow the miscarriage was my fault, don't you, Teddy?"

"Of course not. I never said that."

"You thought I was too active, too arrogant about my capabilities while I was pregnant, right?"

"Kristin, don't."

"Don't what? Have an opinion? You want me to sit in our house like some bird in a nest?"

"I've got to be at Phil Slater's at seven for our executive session," he said. "I need a hot shower." He retreated quickly, leaving her fuming. After a few minutes, however, she was no longer sure why, and guiltily ascribed it to her condition. It was unfair to take it out on Teddy, she thought. But at dinner that night she was fighting with Teddy again.

Whatever was gnawing away inside her, reared its ugly head once more.

"You don't have to come to this meeting, Kristin. Everyone will understand. You and I were the last to see Angela alive. It's pretty traumatic."

"I'm not an invalid, Teddy."

"I didn't say you were, honey."

"I'm all right. Besides, I wouldn't miss it for the world. I can't wait to see what new ideas Nikki Stanley and Phil Slater have developed."

"Just give them a chance," he said. She understood what his real fears were.

"Don't worry, Teddy. I'll keep my mouth shut and I won't embarrass you."

"I didn't mean that," he said defensively, but she got up from the table and drowned out his protest with clanking dishes and pans until he finally got up and left.

The emergency meeting was held in the Slater's finished basement. Phil and his committee sat at a table facing the residents who had been provided with metal folding chairs. The few general assembly meetings held since the development homeowners association had begun had been held here. After it was clear that everyone who was attending had come, Marilyn Slater closed the basement door, came down the stairs and took a seat in the rear.

Kristin sat up front next to Arlene Hoffman. Doctor Hoffman was at the hospital delivering a baby.

"He was disappointed when he got the call right in the middle of our dinner. He wanted to be here tonight," she told Kristin.

Phil Slater tapped a gavel and Nikki read off the list of residents. The turnout for the emergency meeting was heavy. Only two residents besides Steven Del Marco were missing, and that was because they had airplane flights they had to make. Even so, Nikki Stanley made a point of pausing after each of their names and letting the silence linger until someone shouted the reason for their absence, even though she knew.

When she was finished, Philip Slater sat forward. Everyone looked very somber. Even Vincent McShane was sitting up straight.

"I'm sure most of us would give a great deal not to have to be here tonight under these circumstances," he began. "As you all know, the security of the residents and their homes at Emerald Lakes has been a top priority. When I originally envisioned a luxury housing development situated on this prime property with this beautiful lake, I concentrated on ways to make it as safe as possible because in our day and age, safety and security are in direct proportion to real estate value. The exact house in an ungated area without security guards would be worth fifty percent less these days.

"However, an old truth has reared its ugly head," he said. "Willie Sutton, the famous bank robber, was once asked, 'Why do you rob banks?' He replied, 'Because that's where the money is.'

"Why would someone invade our development and attack one of our residents? Well, of course the police are still investigating, but my guess is he was here because, in the minds of most people in our area, this is the most desirable place to live and therefore attracts the more affluent. It's where the money is. Angela Del Marco unfortunately was out there last night just as a would-be burglar or mugger made an entrance onto our property from the one direction we could not secure—the lake. Angela Del Marco confronted him and you all know the rest.

"Your executive board has met in executive session, and has some recommendations to make and a solution to propose. By the way, I'd like to introduce Doctor Theodore Morris, our newest resident, who has accepted appointment to the board to complete the term of Larry Sommers. Doctor Morris."

Teddy nodded as the residents clapped. He gazed at Kristin who offered him a tight smile.

"I will turn the meeting over to the chairman of the Neighborhood Watch committee, Nikki Stanley," Philip Slater said and sat back.

"Thank you, Philip," Nikki began. She pulled her shoulders back and fixed her eyes intently on the audience. "It's most natural to ask, where were our expensive security guards while all this was taking place? Concerned about that, I met with the company and discussed their activities here. As you know, we pay for one guard to man the north gate and another to man the south gate, which is the gate used for deliveries. Since deliveries end at six, that gate is unmanned but locked. There is a guard on duty twenty-four hours at the north gate. The security company provides us with car patrols four times a day, once in the daylight hours and three times from six o'clock to dawn. The patrols vary so that anyone watching our development wouldn't be able to predict when they would appear and anticipate them.

"At eleven-thirty every night, the security guard at the gate is relieved for about an hour so he can make door checks. There have been some problems with them forgetting door checks occasionally, and I have spoken with the security company and been assured they will be corrected," she added.

"Now, this is a very expensive service for us. It does serve its purpose and I would be the last to suggest we end it, but what last night illustrates painfully to us is that we don't have enough protection. I believe we have to supplement what we do have, so would-be thieves and other criminals will know we're more difficult to invade.

"Therefore, we propose to establish a Neighborhood Watch patrol manned by all of us," she said and paused. There was a quiet murmur in the audience.

"Wait a minute," Frank Mateo said rising. "Are you suggesting we become security guards? I'm not trained to be a security guard. I'm an accountant. As

I look around here, I don't see too many people who could qualify to serve as night policemen."

"We're not asking you to be a policeman," Nikki retorted. "None of us are expected to confront a thief."

"I'm glad of that," Frank said, nodding. There was a murmur of approval.

"But what we are capable of doing is showing a presence," Nikki came back quickly. "We'll all carry flashlights and whistles. The leader of the patrol, who will be one of the members of the executive board, will also carry a beeper and will be able to alert the security guard at the gate should the patrol come upon anyone or anything suspicious."

"Still sounds dangerous to me," Frank said. "Why don't we just hire more security?"

"Some of you have already expressed dissatisfaction with the rising cost of our homeowner's fee as it is," Philip replied. "How many are willing to raise their homeowner's fee another thirty to fifty percent?" Only a few hands went up.

"Well, why can't we get the sheriff to patrol our development more?" Paul Meltzer suggested. There was a chorus of agreement.

"I've already been in discussion with the sheriff," Nikki said. "He says there have been some serious cutbacks in his budget and he's had to reduce his staff by three. The county sheriff's office can't expand its patrols."

The room was still.

"Well, maybe we oughta look into investing in some television cameras," Bill Kimble said.

"Do you know how expensive that could be, Bill? Also, anyone can get around a camera, especially at night," Nikki replied, shooting him down quickly.

"What I'm suggesting," she continued after a pause,

"is not a big deal. The patrols won't be much longer than forty-five minutes to an hour at most. My committee and I will construct a roster of three people, two of you and one of us to do a single night patrol each and every night. If you or your husband or wife can't make your patrol, it will be your responsibility to arrange for someone to substitute. You may trade your own patrol with someone else in the development."

"You want women on these patrols, too?" Susan Lester asked.

"Why not? We're not asking you to physically attack someone. We're asking you to be part of a presence to ward off would-be thieves and to warn us if something is happening." She waited a moment and then panned the audience. "Any other comments?"

"Do we need special uniforms?" Frank Mateo asked.

"Of course not. This is a citizen patrol. One thing I want everyone to understand, however, is that we will not keep to the streets only. Wear old shoes or boots because we're going to wander through yards and on the perimeter, especially near the lakeshore since that's where the police suspect our intruder made his entry. Is there anyone here who has a problem with the patrol moving through his or her property?"

No one responded.

"Good," Philip said. "Thank you, Nikki. Nikki will have the roster out tomorrow and we'll begin with our first patrol tomorrow night. I have already spoken to Dan Spiro at the *Herald* and he will have a reporter and a photographer here to get the story and take pictures. I want to publicize the fact that our little community is doing something about a breach of security. I believe this will discourage other potential criminals and also will reinforce the belief that Emerald Lakes is a special place to live, despite what occurred here last night."

"Do the police know anything yet?" Barry Lester asked.

"I spoke with the detective in charge just before I came home from work today," Philip replied. "He and his partner did find evidence supporting the theory that someone rowed himself across the lake and rowed himself back. They believe it was one man. From the shoe size and imprint, they're estimating him to be about one hundred and seventy pounds, probably around six feet tall."

"That's not much of a description," Lester complained.

"They're working on it.

"Did anyone see anything suspicious last night between eight and ten? I told him I would ask just in case he might have missed someone."

"The way it was raining, who could see anything?" Kay Meltzer said. People nodded. No one raised his or her hand.

"Okay. Are there any other questions?"

"The streetlight is out on my corner," Bill Kimble said.

"That's something our Neighborhood Watch patrol would pick up," Nikki underscored. "Thank you."

"Anyone else?" After a moment of silence, Philip said, "Okay, thanks for coming." The meeting broke up.

"I don't know if I should have said something or not," Arlene Hoffman whispered to Kristin as they both stood.

"What?"

"We came home last night about eight-thirty."

"And?"

"The gate was open when Gary and I returned. Gary thought the guard had just stepped off somewhere to go to the bathroom."

"Did you tell the police?"

"Police? No, no one asked me anything. Why, do you think I should?"

"Absolutely," Kristin said. "That means the killer could have come through the front gate. Was it close to eight-thirty?"

"Yes. But anyway, Philip Slater just said the police were positive the killer came from the lake. Gary was probably right, and I hate to get someone in trouble for something like that," she said with a grimace.

"But why was the gate left open?"

"In case someone came while he was indisposed, don't you think?"

Kristin shrugged.

"I don't know. I think the police should be told anyway," she said.

"I'll tell Gary to call them," Arlene said, but Kristin didn't have much faith that she would. "How are you feeling? I know how these things can affect someone in your condition."

"I'm okay. I'm not letting it get too deeply into me, if you know what I mean."

Arlene smiled and patted her hand.

"You call the doctor anytime you want," she said.

"Thank you."

Teddy stepped up to her as Arlene Hoffman walked away. "So? What do you think?"

"I think we should have uniforms and ranks. Then Nikki could have more stripes and finally be happy," Kristin replied. He smirked and took her arm to lead her along.

"You don't have to like her, Kristin. I'm not saying I do. But she did do a lot of good work today and this idea is a good one. Even if it only serves to help people breathe easier."

When they reached the upstairs, Marilyn Slater tapped Kristin on the arm.

"How's Jennifer?" she asked. "I'm sure it was a terrible time for her."

"Horrible. She's probably going to ask to sleep in our bed tonight."

Marilyn nodded and then smiled.

"Let me give you one of my dolls for her. Maybe it will bring her some comfort."

"Oh, really, I—"

"No. I insist, please."

Kristin looked at Teddy who smiled and nodded.

"Thank you."

Kristin followed Marilyn back to the doll room.

"Let me give her one of my nicer dolls," Marilyn thought aloud. "Oh, I know, this one," she said and plucked the Dutch girl off the shelf.

"That looks like an expensive one."

"It doesn't matter. Please, take it for her."

"This is very nice of you," Kristin said, accepting the doll.

"It's so horrible and so frightening for everyone, not just children," Marilyn said, shaking her head. "To be plucked off the street by shadows. Horrible."

"Shadows?"

Marilyn stared at her a moment.

"I mean men."

"Why do you say men?" Kristin recalled Marilyn had a penchant for sitting in front of her window, watching. "Did you see something?"

Marilyn's face reddened.

"No . . . I just thought . . ."

Kristin studied her for a moment.

"You did see something, didn't you, Marilyn?"

"Oh, no. And don't tell anyone I did. Philip would . . ."

"Philip would what?"

"He'd be angry if such rumors were spread. Please," she cajoled.

Kristin shook her head.

"Marilyn, it's up to you to come forward if you saw something, not for me to force you. Thanks again for the doll." She turned and walked out quickly, pausing in the living room to gaze at the rocking chair that was turned so the person sitting in it could gaze out the window. From her previous visit Kristin knew the view Marilyn would have of the street, her home, and Angela's. She turned as Marilyn followed. Their eyes met and Marilyn Slater bit softly on her lower lip. Then Kristin hurried to join Teddy at the door.

She didn't say anything until they were down the street, away from the Slaters' residence.

"She saw something last night, but she's too frightened to tell."

"Who did?"

"Marilyn Slater."

"What are you talking about, Kristin?"

"She said something to me that suggested two men attacked Angela, but when I followed up, she said she saw nothing and then she asked, no, practically begged that I say nothing about it for fear Philip would find out."

"You're kidding. She said that?"

"Yes. She acts like she's living in abject terror. Well?" Kristin demanded. Teddy shook his head.

"From what I've been told, she hasn't been right

since she lost her child. That's why she's such an introvert and dwells on her dolls, even though she gets up and dresses like she's going places every day. The Slaters don't socialize, are rarely seen in restaurants, shows, or movies. You can't give credence to anything she tells you, honey."

"How do you know all this?"

"I was the first to arrive tonight. Phil opened up about her while we waited for the others to arrive."

"I still think she saw something, Teddy. She has a good view from that bay window."

"If she had, why wouldn't Phil want her to tell the police? You see how hard he's taking this breach of security. It's like a personal affront. You saw how proud he was of his security system here."

"Which reminds me. Arlene Hoffman told me she and Doctor Hoffman returned to the development about eight-thirty last night and the gate was wide open and no guard was there."

"Really?" Teddy paused. "I wonder why."

"She said the doctor thought the guard went off to take a leak and left the gate open in case someone arrived while he was watering the flowers," Kristin offered.

"Sounds logical. It's not something these security guards would like to be caught doing."

"I told her to tell the police anyway, but I don't think she will."

He nodded, but still didn't look as concerned as she would have liked.

"They took the papers, Teddy," she offered quickly. "Maybe they did more."

"Huh? You mean our own security guards?"

"Exactly."

"Why?"

"I don't like them. I never did. They scare me more than they give me a feeling of security," she said.

"Kristin, the police have already concluded the intruder came over the lake. They even have an idea about the man's height and weight."

He thought a moment and shook his head before starting toward the house again.

"I think everyone's seeing monsters in the shadows now. We've got to get hold of ourselves and restore our sense of proportion. This Neighborhood Watch patrol is a good idea. It gets everyone involved and helps heal the psychological wounds."

Kristin walked along quietly, pausing once to gaze back at the Slater house and the window from which Marilyn Slater could have easily witnessed the attack on Angela Del Marco. There's something more going on here, she thought, there has to be.

12

◆

IN THE MORNING, after Teddy and Jennifer had left the house, Kristin got into her car. The guard at the gate started out of his booth when she approached.

"I'm just going shopping. Let me out," she demanded sharply. He backed up immediately and opened the gate. She drove out quickly, not so much as glancing at him. About twenty minutes later, she pulled into the parking lot for the sheriff's department and went in to ask for Lieutenant Kurosaka. He came out quickly to greet her.

"Mrs. Morris. How can we help you?"

"Actually, Lieutenant, I think I can help you," she said. He nodded and led her back to his office where his partner, Detective Martin, sat reading a newspaper. He looked up with surprise and folded the paper.

"You remember my partner," Kurosaka said.

"Of course." She nodded at Martin who smiled and nodded back.

"Please, have a seat," Kurosaka said indicating the free chair. Unlike detective offices and desks depicted in movies, Kurosaka's office and desk were neat and well organized. The papers on his desk were stacked in distinct piles, the furniture clean and polished. After she sat, he went behind his desk.

"We're all ears," he said.

"We had a residents meeting last night, during which I spoke to Arlene Hoffman, Doctor Gary Hoffman's wife. He happens to be my doctor."

"An O.B. Yes. How many months are you?"

"Five and change," she said quickly. She gazed at Martin who just stared with a deep look of boredom on his face. "Anyway, she told me that the night of Angela's murder, she and the doctor returned to the development about eight-thirty and found the gate open, the guard missing." Kurosaka nodded.

"He claims he was indisposed and left the gate open so no one would be inconvenienced," he said.

"Oh, you know about that?"

"Yes. Spier told me himself when we were back there yesterday," Martin said.

Kristin thought a moment.

"He probably thought you would find out anyway," she said. Kurosaka was silent, but he did shift his gaze toward Martin who sat back and folded his arms across his chest as he shook his head.

"Look, I know these guys," Martin muttered, "from other jobs. I started as a security guard myself. You're way off suspecting them of anything. They've got impeccable records and references," he added. "Otherwise, Mr. Slater wouldn't have hired them."

After a moment's thought, Kristin straightened up and with determination said, "I think Philip Slater's wife saw something from her window, but she's too frightened to say."

"Oh?" Kurosaka's eyebrows lifted. "Why do you say that?"

"She mentioned something about men attacking

Angela and when I pursued, she denied she meant anything or saw anything, but I stood by her living-room window that looks out on the street and she would have had a view. No matter what she says, she definitely said *men*, not *man*," Kristin hammered with unrestrained excitement.

Kurosaka stared a moment and then sat forward calmly.

"We did find a rubber boat on the north shore of the lake," he revealed. "It had been punctured, slit, and left under a bush as a way of hiding it. There were some clear footprints which match the prints we found on the development shore, the footprints of only one man. Close by, we found a tire iron with the bloodstains that match Mrs. Del Marco's blood. He probably brought it along to use as a means of getting through locked doors, windows, whatever. It looks like he either used gloves or wiped it clean of prints," Kurosaka added.

"But why would he take Angela's papers?" She looked at Martin, too, but he just shook his head.

"I don't know the answer to that, Mrs. Morris," Kurosaka said. "Maybe he thought he had something valuable. She didn't have a purse with her, but he did take her watch and a ring."

"Oh. I didn't know that."

"Well, we hope he tries to fence the items quickly, so we don't advertise the information. All of the area hock shops and jewelers are aware, of course. And we're trying to track the rubber boat. It's a common type, sold in camping stores." He paused and then leaned forward. "I'm sorry. I know how much you want us to catch the man who did this to your friend, but believe me, we have a full investigation under way with assistance from the state police and—"

"No, I realize you're doing your best. I just thought . . ."

"Yes?"

"We should concentrate a little more on our own . . ." She looked up at him. "Neighborhood."

"These things are usually a lot simpler than you think," Detective Martin offered. "Everyone's stuck in the conspiracy mentality these days," he added, looking at Kurosaka.

"I'm not stuck in any mentality," Kristin snapped, but Martin didn't look apologetic.

"It was probably just some transient thief who saw all those fancy houses," he said.

"Why are you so confident of that? Perhaps you're stuck thinking of simplistic solutions," she retorted. His smug smile evaporated instantly and his eyes brightened with the fury of one who had just been slapped across the cheek.

"Mrs. Morris, we've run checks on the security guards. Detective Martin is correct. They all have clean records, not so much as a speeding ticket. Two are former military police," Kurosaka said softly.

"Spier and Stark?" she asked. He nodded. "I thought so."

"The company they work for is well respected in the area and services a number of other developments," Detective Martin said. "You don't seriously think they would rape and murder a woman because she was complaining about their procedure after a routine alarm check, do you?" he added, the corner of his mouth lifting with ridicule.

Kristin ignored him and turned to Kurosaka.

"Mrs. Morris," he began softly, "I'm from a more urban environment than my partner here, but I've seen what happens when someone in the neighborhood is attacked or murdered. It's the same everywhere. Everyone becomes . . . overly suspicious."

"Don't patronize me, Lieutenant. I'm not a kook. It was dark out there; it was raining. What did this rapist-thief do: stop to read the file and decide he could sell the CC and R's to other developments?"

Kurosaka reddened. Detective Martin laughed, seemingly enjoying his discomfort. Kurosaka flashed a look of reproach at him and then turned his eyes on Kristin.

"No," he said calmly. "It was precisely because of those conditions that he might have taken the file. He didn't have the time or the capability to see whether or not they were valuable. When he did, I'm sure he discarded them."

"They why didn't you find them on the other side when you found the remains of the raft and the tire iron? He threw that away, but he didn't throw away papers that would be worthless to him?"

"Papers are much easier to transport than a boat or a tire iron, Mrs. Morris, and frankly, we're not convinced they hold the key to the discovery of who did this unless they can reveal some fingerprints. Maybe after he realized they were worthless to him, he threw them in the lake. Maybe the papers are washed up on shore some place. Maybe they're in his car. Give us a chance to complete the investigation, Mrs. Morris."

"Okay," she said. "I just thought I had some information that would help."

"And we appreciate it. You can call me whenever you like."

"Even if I'm overly suspicious?"

"Yes," he said smiling. She stood up and he rose to walk her out of the office. At the doorway, she turned to Detective Martin who had reached for his newspaper again and then she looked at Kurosaka, her eyes firm, determined.

"Marilyn Slater saw something the other night. I'm certain," she insisted.

"I did speak to her when I canvassed the neighbors, but I promise you, we'll stop by to speak to her again. Try to relax, Mrs. Morris. I know it's hard. Your safe and secure world has been invaded. Your concern is understandable," Kurosaka offered.

"Thank you," Kristin said.

She left them, feeling as if she had just walked into an oven, the heat trailing behind her as she departed the sheriff's station.

After she returned home, she saw she had a message on the answering machine.

"Hi, it's Jean. I was hoping you would agree to be on my Neighborhood Watch patrol team, if Teddy will let you in your condition, of course. Vincent McShane will be our patrol leader, but Nikki and maybe Philip will accompany all the patrols for the first week or so. Nikki let me pick my teammates. Call me when you get in. She's whipping up the schedule and the patrols as I speak, but that's Nikki for you."

Kristin shook her head. Madness, she thought, but maybe Teddy was right. Maybe it had some value, if even only to calm the residents and give them a renewed sense of security. She called Teddy at the office and told him about Jean's message.

"Absolutely not," he snapped.

"Why not, Teddy? I thought you said it was a good idea."

"It is, but not for you right now."

"I'm not going to arrest anyone. You heard Nikki at the meeting. All we do is—"

"No," he insisted.

"But—"

"You were in your fifth month last time, Kristin," he reminded her. It sent a chill down her spine. "Let's get past it, okay?" he pleaded. "Let me do the patrol duty for our family. Everyone will understand."

"Why shouldn't they? Thanks to Nikki Stanley, they all know about my miscarriage."

"Kristin!"

"All right, all right. I'll tell Jean you'll serve in my place, Teddy. Enjoy yourself," she said and hung up. She stood there seething for a moment and then she lifted the receiver and punched out Jean's number.

"Hi," Kristin said in a deliberately saccharine voice. "I got your message. I'm afraid Teddy wants me to stay safely in the nest for now, but he would be happy to be part of your team."

"Oh. Well, I'm sure he's right," Jean said. "We're going to be the first patrol."

"Ginger peachy," Kristin cooed. "Catch the bad guys!"

Jean laughed.

"It's so nice that you can have a sense of humor even at a time like this," she said.

"Isn't it? Talk to you later," she said and hung up. She went to the French doors and gazed out at the lake a moment. Then she had an idea. She changed into a pair of jeans, an old, light cotton sweater and some old shoes.

It was a rather muggy, but relatively clear May day with a line of clouds hemming the horizon and fore-shadowing the next overcast sky and rain. The May flies were out for blood, but she drudged relentlessly up to the spot where Angela had been found. Drops of dried blood were still visible on some rocks. It turned her stomach, but she took deep breaths and continued down to the lakeshore where she began her long, arduous journey around Emerald Lake, searching for the elusive papers that Kurosaka suspected might have been dumped in the water. She tried to keep as close to the shore as she could, stumbling a few times and nearly falling into the water.

When she reached a relatively undeveloped area, she hesitated. Here the woods were thicker, the bushes heavier. She pondered turning back, but decided she would go all the way to the road that ran by the lake. Just as she stepped into the forest, she heard a branch crack and spun around to see Harold Spier approaching quickly. He had his pistol out and held it up as he plodded along persistently.

Her heart began to pound. Spier didn't appear to see her and she didn't move. Then he stopped and dropped his arm, pointing the gun at her. She screamed.

"Oh," he said raising the gun. "It's you, Mrs. Morris. I thought for sure I had caught me a prowler." He drew closer, still not putting the pistol back into his holster.

"You nearly frightened me to death," she said.

"Sorry, but I was up there behind the Lesters' house and I heard you walking through the woods. I couldn't imagine a resident down in here. What are you doing?"

"I'm taking a nature hike," she said. "Would you put your gun in your holster?"

"Oh. Sure. Sorry. Can't be too careful around here after what happened to Mrs. Del Marco. You sure you want to be walking alone in the woods?"

"I'm fine," she said.

"You're pregnant, too, Mrs. Morris. This isn't an easy stroll."

"I think I'm capable of deciding what I can and can't do right now, Mr. Spier."

"Just trying to be helpful, ma'am. It's what—"

"We pay you to do. I know," she said nodding. Their eyes met and for a moment, she felt in even more danger. Then he smiled coolly.

"Okay, if this is what you want to do. Just keep your eyes open, ma'am. We've had a rattlesnake or two around this lake," he added.

She felt her Adam's apple bounce in her throat, but she didn't change her expression.

"I've taken nature hikes before, Mr. Spier."

"Suit yourself. Forewarned is forearmed," he added, tipped his hat, and turned around. She watched him plod through the forest. Not until he was completely out of sight, did she feel her heartbeat slow and her breath come back. She couldn't hear his footsteps in the forest, but she knew that didn't necessarily mean he was gone, so she decided she would go until she reached the roadside of the lake and return to the development that way.

Nearly a half hour later, she spotted a sheet of paper floating near the shore and then, a few feet away, she found another. When she knelt down and plucked them out of the water, she saw they were Angela's and her notes on the revisions for the CC and R's.

It filled her with a terrific chill. She looked around to see if she was being watched and then she pressed the papers against herself and hurried away.

Spier was back in the security booth when she came down the road to the front entrance.

"That's quite a walk you took, Mrs. Morris," he said.

"Invigorating," she said, and started through the gate.

"What's that you found?" he asked. She paused.

"Part of what Angela had on her the night she was attacked." She studied his reaction. He looked impressed, not frightened.

"No kidding. You should give that to the police."

"I intend to," she said.

She hurried back to call Kurosaka and confirm his suspicion. He wasn't in the office, but he phoned her from the road.

"I should put you on the payroll," he said. "Hold on to the papers. I'll stop by later. Maybe we'll take off some fingerprints besides yours and Angela Del Marco's. I'll get Angela's from the coroner and when I stop by, I'll take a sample of yours, if that's all right."

"Fine," she said. Emotionally and physically exhausted, she went to lie down and fell asleep with Angela's pages beside her on the bed, this time waking up before Jennifer had returned. When Teddy returned, she hesitated to tell him about the papers. She was afraid he would bawl her out for taking such a dangerous trek through the woods.

That night the Neighborhood Watch patrol began. The ever efficient Nikki Stanley had the security guard deliver an instruction sheet to all the residents, outlining how everyone should dress, what he or she should bring, and what the patrol would be expected to do.

"They recommend we dress completely in black," Teddy read. "The whistle will be provided by the patrol leader, but we're to bring our own flashlight. The patrol time will vary between eight-thirty and nine P.M."

Kristin pretended not to be listening and then, impulsively, turned to him and said, "Lieutenant Kurosaka is stopping by any minute."

"Kurosaka? Why?"

"I took a walk earlier and I found some of the missing papers Angela had when she left. They were in the lake."

"The lake? You went all the way down to the lake?"

"I needed a good walk," she said.

He stood there staring at her. Before he could utter another comment the door chimed her tune.

"It's probably him," Kristin said, and got the papers together as Teddy went to the door.

"Good evening, Doctor Morris."

"Lieutenant."

Kristin came around him and held out the pages she had found at the lakeshore. She had placed them in a plastic bag.

"Thank you, Mrs. Morris," Kurosaka said, taking them. "Very professional," he added, indicating the bag. "No one but you has touched them since they were found?"

"No one," she said.

"I'm going to run the fingerprints as I explained, I'll need a copy of yours." He produced an ink pad. "Where would you like this done?"

"We can do it right here," she said, moving to the counter beside the aquarium. Teddy watched with his mouth open, shaking his head as Kurosaka took Kristin's prints. He put the sample into the envelope carefully. Kristin held her hands up.

"I better wash before I touch anything."

"Yes. Thank you. Oh. As to the other matter," Kurosaka said, "we stopped by to reinterview Mrs. Slater."

"And?" Kristin asked quickly.

"She wasn't feeling well. Her husband said she's somewhat confused by the excitement. From what he tells me, however, the time frame wouldn't be right anyway," he added.

"You've got to talk to her yourself. I'm sure that when you do—"

"Let's see what this turns up," Kurosaka said, indicating the papers. "I'll let you know. Thank you."

As soon as the door closed, Teddy spun on Kristin.

"You deliberately went walking through the woods, searching for papers, didn't you? It wasn't just some relaxing stroll, Kristin."

"The important thing is I found them, Teddy," she replied marching down the entryway steps and toward the bathroom. She wanted to tell him about Spier coming at her in the forest, but she was sure he would simply compliment the security guard for being alert.

"And you had them go see Mrs. Slater?"

"I'm sure she saw something," Kristin insisted. She ran the water and began to scrub the ink off her fingers.

"When did all this happen? I mean, when did you see Kurosaka?"

"Today," she said nonchalantly, "at his office."

"You went to the police station? Jesus. Everyone's going to think you've gone nuts."

Kristin spun around.

"Who's everyone, Teddy? Huh? Nikki? Philip? The other members of the politburo here? Anyway, you'll be happy to know it only reinforces the theory that it was one man who came here to rob and steal. Steven was too overwrought to mention it, I suppose, but Angela's ring and watch were taken. They found a raft, the weapon, a tire iron, and footprints on the roadside of the lake and they think the killer just threw the papers into the water."

"Good. At least maybe you'll stop suspecting our own people."

"They may be your people, Teddy, but they'll never be mine," Kristin said and closed the bathroom door.

The heavy curtain of silence fell between them until Teddy left for the Neighborhood Watch patrol. Jennifer was asleep, the doll Marilyn Slater had given her at her side. Kristin had tried to watch some television, but then turned it off and sat in the oversized chair by the front window staring out at the street. She saw Teddy returning and pretended to be reading a magazine when he entered.

"Well," he announced as he stepped down to the living room, "we did good."

She looked up.

"What do you mean?"

"We discovered a hole in the fence on the west side, two more blown streetlights, and a car in the driveway with the keys in the ignition."

"Whose car?"

"The Kimbles. Bill was embarrassed. It will all be in the report. Everyone's going to get a copy of each patrol report on a weekly basis."

"So if someone screws up, like leaving his keys in his car ignition, the whole development will know about it?"

"And he or she won't do it again," Teddy said.

"I wonder what they'll find we're doing wrong."

"My mother always says an ounce of prevention is worth a pound of cure." He smiled. "Come on, Kristin. Lighten up. You have to admit this is a good idea, even if it came from Nikki Stanley."

"Somehow, I think that woman could even make Christmas a bad experience," Kristin said, but she softened. "So? Did you enjoy your patrolling?"

"You know," he said coming closer, "as I was walking around the development, I suddenly got this amazing sense of accomplishment, of doing something substantial to protect my family and possessions, and there was something I realized."

"What?" she asked when he continued his pause too long for her curiosity.

"I will agree with you about our security force to this extent: we have become too dependent on others to provide our basic protection. It softens us and therefore makes us more vulnerable."

"We need more John Wayne in us, huh?" she said, half in jest.

"What? Yeah, I guess. I'm not saying we should all become Charlie Bronson in *Death Wish*, but we should take some charge of our own security and be more prepared, more fit. It's like muscles. If you don't use them, they atrophy.

"Ever since the caveman," he continued, "we've had a basic need to defend ourselves. Technology has made us too dependent on monitors and alarms. Affluence enables us to hire others to stand at the door. It deadens our instinct to survive."

Kristin started to smile.

"Where the hell did you come up with this theory?"

"We had a chance to talk a bit."

"Who's we?"

"The patrol and Philip."

"I see," Kristin said. "I still think there's something sick about all this. It's like a monster consuming us."

"It'll pass," Teddy said softly. "Things will calm down. You'll see."

"Maybe," she said.

They both went to bed without another word. She kept her eyes closed, even when the eleven-thirty door check occurred and the locks were gently rattled.

She couldn't help wondering: were they locking the enemy out or were they locking themselves in?

Surely, there was a difference.

Marilyn Slater retreated to the doll room early in the evening after dinner and remained there pretending to be sewing doll clothing when Philip looked in on her. After Lieutenant Kurosaka had come to question her for a second time because of a remark she had made to Kristin Morris, Philip became so enraged, she thought he was going to hit her. The whole time he ranted, he had his hands clenched.

"Until this whole thing blows over," he said in a very controlled voice, the veins and arteries in his neck pressing against his skin, "I don't want you speaking to that woman. You understand, Marilyn?"

She nodded. When Philip was like this, it was better to nod and look away, better to wait for the storm to subside. So as soon as they were finished with dinner and she had cleaned up, she went to the doll room. They had become her only companions anyway. Each of them had his or her own personality, something different in his or her eyes that suggested his or her temperament.

There was the French doll that she thought resembled her with its diminutive facial features and dainty clothes. It had real human hair, her own shade. Philip had bought her the doll a year after they were married on their anniversary trip to Paris. In those days all she had to do was gaze at something and he would lunge ahead to buy it for her. But even then, she recalled, he bought it as if he had to prove something, prove anything was within his reach. Still, she loved this doll, loved the way its eyes reflected her own moods.

Across the room sat the doll that reminded her of Philip. He had told her he had bought it because it was the first doll he had ever seen that had a real masculine feel to it. He bought it at an antique store in New Paltz when he was there for business. The doll had big features, emphatic shoulders, and a barrel chest. To Marilyn, it looked perpetually angry and distrustful. Whenever she entered the doll room and glanced at it, she saw how its eyes followed her every step. She rarely, if ever, touched it, and did so mainly when she dusted. When she did take it in her hand, she imagined it squirming like a rodent. Of course, she was afraid to give it away or throw it out. Philip would know.

Today, Philip's doll looked angrier than ever.

"Don't look at me that way," she muttered. "I didn't do anything wrong. Why shouldn't I tell people what I saw? I did see something. I did. I'm not imagining things and I didn't have anything to drink that night."

Philip's doll had thicker lips than all the other dolls. In her imagination, those lips undulated and looked like two worms. It turned her stomach.

"No one can ever say anything negative about your precious development," she added, dropping her gaze to the floor. The doll's eyes were too intimidating.

She didn't hear Philip come to the doorway, so when he spoke, it was as if his doll were speaking. It sent her heart on a wild tumble, the reverberation carrying down her spine and into her very soul.

"Who are you talking to, Marilyn?" he demanded.

She gasped and raised her eyes.

"No one. I'm not talking," she said.

He stared at her, the disgust etched along his lips and printed in his dark eyes.

"I made a mistake," he said. "I should have sent you for some professional help a while ago. Telling people you saw shadows swallow up Angela Del Marco." He shook his head. "How do you think this makes me look? A policeman has to come by to ask questions like that and mentions it to me? Why wouldn't I have told them what you thought you saw? Just lucky you were sleeping and I could get rid of him, but I'm warning you. You're going to end up in a loony bin yet if you keep this up, Marilyn."

"I'm all right," she insisted.

"Right," he said nodding. "It's the rest of us who are crazy." He straightened up like a soldier at attention. "I'm going out to join the first Neighborhood Watch patrol," he announced. "Stay in the house. You're liable to be mistaken for a prowler."

Occasionally she did take a short walk on a nice evening, but she had no intention of doing that tonight. She nodded. After he left, she looked at his doll. It was smiling. Furious, she got up and went to it to turn it around so she wouldn't have to look at the face, but when she reached toward it, her fingers hesitated as if there was an invisible wall between the doll and her. She couldn't touch it. It stared up at her, defiant.

She spun around and left the room and went to her chair by the window. She spotted the Neighborhood Watch patrol moving down the street, the beams of their flashlights slicing the darkness, illuminating areas under trees, beside houses and garages, and then the patrol disappeared around a corner. It reminded her of a group of children trick-or-treating on Halloween.

As soon as the patrol disappeared, she went to the liquor cabinet and got out her vodka. Despite Philip's warning, she poured herself a half glass and didn't even add a mixer. She returned to the window and sipped her vodka, enjoying the way it unlocked all the doors and allowed her to lift herself up and out of her body. She closed her eyes and saw herself floating gracefully. The sense of freedom was wonderful. She was gliding over the lake and moving so softly . . . She sipped more and more.

But the grating sound of the telephone brought her down to earth and returned her to her body. Marilyn thought about letting it ring, but whoever was calling wasn't going to give up. Finally, she rose from her chair and lifted the receiver on the phone next to the sofa.

"Hello," she said. There was such a long delay, she thought the caller might just have given up. But then she heard her name in a deep, hollow whisper.

"Marilyn."

"Who is this?"

"Marilyn."

"I said, who is this?"

"It's one of the shadows. You must not talk about me or I'll come for you next."

She released the phone as if it had turned into fire and backed away. She turned and charged toward the front door, but when she opened it, she froze. Was that a shadow moving up the street? She slammed the door and backed down the hallway until she was against the basement door, her eyes wide and blazing. Suddenly, she heard the sound of a child laughing. It was coming from behind her, from down in the basement.

"Bradley?" she muttered, turning slowly to open

the basement door. She gazed down the dark stairway and listened. There was silence, but when she
closed her eyes, she could hear him calling her just
the way he used to.

"Mommy. Mommy."

Marilyn wobbled a bit and took hold of the banis-
ter. Then she started down the stairway without turning on the light. She was more comfortable with the
darkness. She heard a trickle of childish laughter
again and she smiled. Her eyes did well in the darkness and she knew every inch of this basement. She
rounded the turn at the bottom of the stairway and
made her way to the storage room. There, she turned
on the light, half expecting to see Bradley sitting by
the box of memories. His absence broke her heart.

Marilyn crumbled slowly to her knees beside the
box and stroked it as if it were the coffin in which her
precious little baby had been placed. It felt hard and
smooth like the coffin. She closed her eyes and fum-
bled with the top of the carton until she opened it and
then, when she opened her eyes and looked in, she
saw him, just as he had been: his eyes sewn shut by
death, his little lips pale, his cheeks chalky white and
his hair dry like thin straw.

She embraced herself and rocked back and forth
on her knees, the tears streaming down her cheeks.
The ache in her heart traveled to her ribs and her
stomach and settled in her back. She curled up beside
the box, her right arm around it, holding it to her
bosom, just the way she used to hold her child when
he was sick or frightened. She closed her eyes and
muttered words of comfort until she fell asleep.

Marilyn didn't wake up until she heard, "Jesus
Christ! What the hell are you doing?"

Her eyes fluttered open and she looked up at Philip

standing over her, his hands on his hips, his face swollen with anger.

"What?" For a moment she forgot where she was. Then it all rushed back over her.

"The phone is off the cradle upstairs, and I see you hit the bottle again. Now I find you on the basement floor," he recited like a judge reading the charges.

"Guilty," she said, smiling.

"What?"

"I plead guilty, Philip."

"Get up, Marilyn. For crissakes."

She sat up and looked into the carton. Bradley was no longer there. She folded it closed and started to stand. Philip seized her arm at the elbow and helped her to her feet.

"He called before," she said.

"Who called?"

"One of the shadows. He told me to keep my mouth shut or he would come for me next. Let him come, Philip. Let him come."

"One of the shadows? He said 'shadows'?"

"Yes."

"Oh, man," Philip said. "Just go upstairs to bed, Marilyn. You're drunk again." He directed her toward the stairway. "Come on," he insisted. She walked, a smile on her face. Philip turned off the light in the storage room and closed the door. Then he followed behind, making sure she went up the stairs successfully.

He closed the basement door and turned her toward the bedroom.

"Go to sleep, Marilyn."

"He called, Philip. He really called."

"Okay. You can call those detectives tomorrow and tell them everything."

"You'll let me?" she asked, turning around.

"Why not?" Philip muttered. "Everyone should know what it's like receiving a phone call from a shadow," he said.

She thought a moment.

"Yes," she said. "Everyone should know. Then they would understand."

She turned and continued toward the bedroom without looking back.

So she didn't see the smile on Philip's face.

13

◆

BY THE END OF THE FOLLOWING WEEK, life at Emerald Lakes had finally settled back into the old picture-perfect residential splendor. Angela Del Marco's funeral had a sobering effect, of course. That day and the day following left a pall over the development. Parents kept their children in their homes more. People drove even slower through the development's streets, and when they met each other either in the development or at the gate, they simply nodded, or if they spoke, spoke so softly they were nearly inaudible.

Steven Del Marco put the house up for sale. As soon as he had the sign on the lawn, Michele Lancaster began bringing prospective buyers to see the home. The boys were sent to stay with Steven's sister and the talk was that Philip Slater had arranged for Steven to find a new position with a different insurance company closer to her.

All week the Neighborhood Watch patrols paraded through the development at night. Either Nikki or Philip, most often both, still accompanied each team, as well as going on their own tour. The first Neighborhood Watch patrol report was issued at the end of the week and delivered to each resident by the security guard. It listed problems spotted on the property of five residents, ranging from Bill Kimble's keys in his car ignition to Claude Simmons's portable television set on a picnic table in his backyard, which, it was not so subtly mentioned, faced the lake and thus could tempt potential thieves. The patrol cited two residents for forgetting to lock screen windows as well. Every violator's name was printed in bold type.

Teddy was still upset with Kristin for trekking through the woods and around the lake and for sending the police to the Slaters, but he didn't bring up the topic anymore. In fact, he tried to change the subject every time Kristin mentioned Angela Del Marco's death.

On Thursday, he drove home in their new Lexus and took Kristin and Jennifer for their first ride. They went to dinner and the truce that had fallen again between them expanded into a warmer exchange. Teddy encouraged Kristin to elaborate on the changes she wanted to make in the house and then announced that their income was going to take another jump.

"We picked up the new accounts," he said, "and the partners all feel I had a lot to do with it."

"That's wonderful, Teddy. You're really very happy where you are now, aren't you?" Kristin asked a little wistfully.

"Yes, I am," he said. "Once we get over the hump here and things go back to normal . . ."

"Over the hump," Kristin said and sighed, but she didn't obsess about it. She decided that from now on whatever thoughts she had about Angela's murder and the conduct of the homeowners association, she would keep to herself. This new attitude was reinforced when Lieutenant Kurosaka called her late

Wednesday afternoon to tell her they were unable to find any usable prints on the papers she fished out of the lake.

"The perpetrator most likely wore gloves," he said.

"Oh. Too bad. Are you going to try to speak with Mrs. Slater anyway?" she asked him. He was silent a moment.

"I received a phone call from her on Tuesday," he said. "I shouldn't be telling you this, but since you put me on her . . ."

"What did she say?" Kristin asked, excited.

"She told me she had received a phone call from one of the shadows."

"Shadows? I don't understand."

"One of the shadows she claimed she had seen attack Mrs. Del Marco. This shadow called and threatened her that if she didn't keep her mouth shut, she would be hurt, too."

"She said the shadow called?"

"Yes. Detective Martin, who has lived and worked in this area most of his life and has worked for Mr. Slater, explained to me why Mrs. Slater is a troubled woman these days. I suppose you know about it," he said softly. "She's a woman still in deep grief and pain," was all he added. She sensed his reluctance to gossip.

"Yes. I'm sorry I put you on a wild goose chase."

"Not at all. I meant what I said when you were here. Should you have anything you think is important, please call. I'll let you know if we get any break in the case soon."

"Thank you," Kristin said and retreated to her own thoughts, concluding Teddy was probably right: she should leave the police work to the police.

Her backache subsided, but didn't disappear so she

went to see Doctor Hoffman. After he examined her, he told her he was concerned.

"You seem emotionally strained to me, Mrs. Morris. I don't think you appreciate how traumatic an experience you had and what a toll it has taken on you. You're wearing yourself down at a time when you should be building your strength. Why don't you just concentrate on yourself for a while? Pamper yourself and don't worry so much about the outside world," he suggested.

He gave her a prescription to help her relax, but she didn't tell Teddy about it. It would revive his fear of her having another miscarriage.

She tried to go back to her music and found her melodies coming out even heavier than before. She took frequent walks and sat by the lake to watch the birds over the water. Occasionally, she saw someone fishing. People would back their boats up to the lakeshore from the roadside. She got so she recognized the regulars, older men who reminded her of her father and her Uncle Pete, two anglers who spent most of their time arguing over who had the right bait or the best fly for trout, neither very successful at it. It made her laugh.

Summer was stampeding its way in. The air was getting warmer and warmer every passing day. The bushes and trees, all the overgrowth, thickened, the leaves and vines turning a richer shade of green, which gave the surface of the lake its emerald sheen. It's like a grand deception, Kristin thought. Who could believe anything so horrible would happen in such a beautiful, peaceful setting?

Kristin considered continuing the work she and Angela had begun. However, she decided it was better to wait until after she gave birth. Doctor Hoffman was right; this was a time to pamper herself and certainly not a time to be in conflict with her neighbors.

She liked the Kimbles and the Simmonses, and twice she had stopped to talk with Kay Meltzer about the schools and raising children. They had a good conversation and promised to do something together in the near future. Most of the people here were not unlike the rest of middle-class America, she decided. They wanted the same things for themselves and their families. It was just a few like Nikki Stanley who were over the top. If she could just ignore them . . .

But, of course, she knew that was going to be impossible. That fact was hammered home early in the evening the following Monday when the door chime rang her tune. She was at the dining-room table reading a story to Jennifer. Teddy had gone back to the clinic for a meeting with the partners. Kristin went to the door and opened it to face Nikki Stanley, Charles Dimas, and Barry Lester. The three were dressed in black and carried their flashlights. Nikki had a whistle on a string around her neck and a clipboard in her hand.

"Hi," Kristin said, nodding at the men. Neither relaxed his face to soften the glum expression.

"We're on patrol," Nikki said sharply.

"I sort of guessed that," Kristin said. Jennifer came up beside her and Kristin instinctively put her hand on Jennifer's little shoulder, drawing her closer. "What can I do for you?"

"It's what you can do for yourself," Nikki said. "One of your lights is off on the side of the house."

"I thought they worked on a sensor or something," Kristin said, directing herself to the men. But they stood like sentinels forbidden to speak, men turned to stone waiting for their terms of silence to end.

"They are," Nikki said with a smirk. "You probably have a blown bulb."

"I'll tell Ted," Kristin said. "Anything else?"

"Yes. May we come in?"

"What for?" There was a nagging feeling in Kristin's stomach, an annoying tingle that stirred the fetus in her womb as well.

"We would like to show you something and suggest something," Nikki said. "It will take only a minute."

With obvious reluctance, Kristin stepped back and Nikki marched into the house, Barry and Charles following on her heels. Kristin stood by the door.

"Well?"

"We'd like to show you something in the office."

"Office?" Kristin closed the door slowly, her mind searching for what they would possibly criticize. Had she left a window open?

"Please," Nikki said, her lips twisting as if the word left a bitter taste.

"This way," Kristin said, leading them through the living room and down the corridor. She put on the overhead light fixture in the office and stepped back.

"You see the view you have of the lake here?" Nikki said nodding toward the window.

"So?"

"You just happen to have a view of that part of the lake that runs along the highway, the area from which the intruder entered our development," Nikki said and paused as if that were enough of an explanation. Kristin smiled with confusion and looked at the men, who did not smile back. The aura of seriousness emanating from Nikki washed over them, turning them into clones. It began to unnerve Kristin, who felt her heart start to pound.

"And?"

"But the desk is set up so that when Teddy or you sit at it, you have your backs to the window. If you just turn this desk around so that you take advantage of this view, you could conceivably spot someone intruding."

"Turn the desk around?"

"It's a simple enough move and a small concession to our needs. It would make you and Ted more of a part of the Neighborhood Watch. We all have an obligation to be sentries."

"Don't you think you're taking this a little too far, Nikki? I mean . . ."

The muscles in Nikki's face tightened.

"I'm surprised to hear you of all people say that. Angela Del Marco was your friend. Imagine if either you or Teddy had been sitting here that night, facing the window, and had seen the intruder. You might have saved her life."

Kristin shook her head and looked at the two men again, but they didn't crack a wrinkle.

"First of all, it was raining so hard, I doubt anyone would have seen someone sneaking up from the lake-shore, and, second, you're frightening everyone here into a bunker mentality."

Nikki snapped her head back as if Kristin had slapped her.

"Taking preventive measures and closing any gaps in our security is hardly a bunker mentality. Frankly, I would have expected more cooperation from you, the wife of one of our board trustees. If anything, you should be setting an example for the others."

Kristin felt something burst in her chest, followed with an explosion of heat that traveled up her throat and into her face.

"Really? Who the hell do you think you are coming

in here and dictating to me just how I should arrange my furniture? Turning this desk around would be stupid. Look where the lighting is. Look how the rest of the office is arranged. Don't lecture me, Nikki," Kristin fumed.

Nikki nodded. Kristin's outburst barely changed her facial expression. It was as if she had expected nothing less. She remained smug, confident, and undaunted.

"The lightbulb has to be replaced within twenty-four hours," she said firmly.

"Or?"

"Or you'll be cited, board trustee or not. When a resident doesn't follow the safety regulations in the CC and R's, she or he simply puts an additional strain and burden on our security guards and now the Neighborhood Watch patrol. Because you won't make a small change in your arrangement of the desk in here, the security patrol will have to be that much more concerned with this vulnerable place in our protective wall. That, eventually runs up our costs, costs which we all bear."

"I'll see that the bulb is replaced, but I won't start rearranging the furniture. It's a ridiculous suggestion," Kristin insisted.

"I'm sorry you feel that way."

"Don't let me read about it on your Neighborhood Watch report," Kristin warned.

Nikki smiled coldly and started away, Barry and Charles following. Kristin watched them go to the front door, where Nikki deliberately paused to jot something on her clipboard before leaving. Kristin's heart continued to pound for a few moments.

"Mommy," Jennifer said, tugging on Kristin's skirt. "Can we go back to the story?"

"What? Oh. Sure, honey. Bitch," she muttered under her breath, and then smiled at Jennifer and returned with her to the dinning-room table. They had just started again, when Jennifer cried out and pointed to the ceiling.

"What's that, Mommy?"

"What?"

Kristin looked up. The beam of a flashlight shining in through the front window slid over the ceiling.

"What the hell . . ."

She jumped up and ran to the front door, opening it and stepping out just as the patrol turned and continued down the street. Even under the state-of-the-art streetlights, the dark figures merged with the darkness and were lost in the shadows.

"You bastards!" Kristin screamed. Her voice echoed and died. She waited a moment and then slammed the front door closed, her heart pounding so hard now, she was afraid she might just faint. She put her hand on the ledge and took a deep breath. Memories of her miscarriage sent electrifying chills up and down her spine.

"Mommy," Jennifer said, her face lit with fear. One look at Jennifer forced Kristin to get control of herself quickly.

"I'm all right, honey. It's all right," she said and managed a smile. "Someone was just letting us know we had our curtains open too wide at night."

She closed them and turned back to Jennifer.

"Let's finish the story."

She returned to the table and focused her thoughts as hard as she could on the words and pictures, waiting with great anticipation for Ted's return, but he didn't return until nearly eleven.

After she had put Jennifer to bed, Kristin tried to

distract herself with some television and reading, but nothing worked. She kept gazing at the clock and listening for Ted's car in the garage. Finally, she relented and took one of the tranquilizers Doctor Hoffman had prescribed. It made her a bit groggy and she dozed off in her chair, not hearing Ted enter the house. However, she sensed his presence and woke abruptly, nearly leaping out of the chair.

"Easy," he said smiling. "I didn't mean to frighten you. I was just surprised to find you here. Sorry the meeting took so long, but we went into pension plans and—"

Suddenly, Kristin just started crying, the tears streaking down her cheeks.

"What's wrong, Kristin?" He knelt down quickly and took her hand.

"They . . . they came into our house."

"Who came into our house?"

"Nikki Stanley and her patrol," she said, wiping the tears off her cheeks. She quickly related what had occurred.

"Jesus," he said. "She has gone overboard."

"She's horrible. I don't want her near my house ever. Ever!" Kristin cried.

"Take it easy."

"You've got to say something, Ted. You've got to do something about that woman," Kristin demanded.

He nodded and stood up.

"It's late, but I'll call Philip in the morning and speak with him. I'm sorry this happened while I wasn't here."

"Can you imagine her dictating how we should arrange our furniture? Can you?"

He shook his head.

"Take it easy, Kristin. I promise I'll do something."

She relaxed and closed her eyes.

"If she puts this in her weekly report . . ."

"She won't. Come on, honey. Let's go to bed. You can't let yourself get so upset."

"I'm not letting myself. It's these people, this insanity that's taking over the development. You should have been here and seen their faces. Charles and Barry were like total strangers. They didn't crack a smile. They're so taken with themselves. I was frightened, Teddy. I didn't let them see it, but I really was!"

He nodded and guided her to her feet.

"And then afterward, for spite, I'm sure, someone directed a flashlight beam through the front window and frightened Jennifer. I suppose our curtains weren't closed properly. Can you imagine?"

She babbled about the whole episode all the way to the bedroom until she was under the covers. Teddy repeatedly reassured her and finally she closed her eyes, but the security guard's rattling of the doors to check on the locks snapped her lids open again.

"They're driving me mad," she said. "Get them away from our house. GET THEM AWAY!"

"Easy, honey, easy."

"I don't want them to check our home, Ted. Keep them off our property."

"Okay," he said. "Okay." He didn't want to remind her that it was development property. There was no way to prohibit the security patrol from stepping on the grounds, but maybe, until Kristin gave birth at least, he could keep them away from the house.

How the hell did this all happen? he wondered and then put it out of his mind so he could get some rest.

In the morning Kristin felt like she had a mind-numbing hangover. She actually studied herself in the mirror to see whether or not her forehead had grown out and protruded over her eyes. She was pale, her lids drooped, and the corners of her mouth dipped so she resembled a clown's sad face. She took as cold a shower as she could stand and put on more makeup than usual before joining Ted for breakfast and getting Jennifer started.

After Ted and Jennifer had gone, Kristin sat gazing out the rear patio door while she had a second cup of coffee. Poor Angela, she thought and recalled that Elaine Feinberg had been sitting in this very seat focused on the rear patio just the way she now was when she and Teddy had first come to look at the house. She vividly remembered Elaine's look of terror and words of warning when she had confronted her in the supermarket. Suddenly an idea blossomed.

Kristin went to the phone and called Michele Lancaster, the real estate agent. After what seemed an interminable cross-examination and effort to intercede, Michele reluctantly gave her Elaine Feinberg's new address. Without hesitation, Kristin grabbed her purse and a light jacket and left the house.

Carl Stark seemed to move deliberately slower when Kristin pulled up to the gate. He was reading something with his head down so long Kristin had to beep the horn. He looked up without expression, nodded and gazed at whatever he was reading for another few seconds before coming out of the booth. He walked with ponderous steps.

"Open the gate," she demanded.

"How long will you be gone?" he responded.

"Open the damn gate," she snapped. "Now!"

He stared at her long enough for her to assume he wasn't going to move.

"Open that gate or I'll drive right through it," she threatened and actually gunned her engine. His eyebrows rose.

"I'm just—"

"Doing your job, I know. Open the gate."

He turned and walked back to the booth. For a moment he just stared at her, daring her to do what she threatened, and then he opened the gate. Her wheels screamed as she shot through and accelerated, nearly missing the turn. Her heart was pounding so hard, she thought she might faint and crash. After a moment she calmed herself and slowed. All she needed was to get a speeding ticket, too, she thought.

A little over twenty minutes later, she parked in front of a cottage-size brown and white house that had the tired, anemic look of a structure five years beyond its time for restoration. The lawn had a sickly, pale green look with bald patches here and there. It was one of the poorer neighborhoods in Sandburg. Most of the homes resembled each other as if they all suffered from the same infectious neglect. In actual distance, Kristin was only fifteen or so miles from Emerald Lakes, but in quality and style of life, she might as well have been in the South Bronx. What a far cry from what Elaine Feinberg had enjoyed before her husband's death, Kristin thought as she emerged slowly from her car.

She walked over the cracked and pitted sidewalk and pressed the door buzzer button. She heard nothing and pressed it again. Feeling certain it didn't work, she knocked on the wooden door and waited. It was as if Elaine had been standing just to the side, for the door was thrust open without warning. The abrupt action not only stunned her, but seemed to suck in the air and her along with it. She gasped and then widened her eyes even more when Elaine stepped into the opening.

The woman's hair was disheveled. It looked as if she had been pulling on it in a rage of self-destruction. She wore no makeup; her face was ashen to the point that even the color in her eyes looked dulled and her lips were almost indistinguishable from the surrounding skin. Age, like a predator waiting for opportunity, had seized on her grief and despondency and etched deeper lines in her forehead and along the corners of her eyes. She wore a pair of dungarees and a sweatshirt with frayed sleeves. There was no recognition in her face.

"What do you want?" she demanded. "I don't want to talk about Jehovah or buy any magazines," she added before Kristin could reply.

"I'm not a saleswoman, Mrs. Feinberg. I'm Kristin Morris, remember?"

Elaine gazed at her skeptically.

"Morris. The people who bought your home in Emerald Lakes."

At the sound of the name, her face took on some color. A shot of crimson flashed across her cheeks when she grimaced.

"What do you want now?"

"I just wanted to talk to you. Please. I don't want anything else. I know you've had a terrible time. There's been some trouble at Emerald Lakes and I thought—"

"I know," she said, smiling for the first time, although it was a cold, bone-chilling look of glee. "I saw it on the local news."

"The woman was my neighbor."

"So? You're all neighbors in Emerald Lakes," she added with a sharp twist in her mouth.

"Please. Can we just talk a few minutes?"

Elaine considered and then stepped back.

"This isn't as pretty a place as my home in Emerald Lakes," she said. "And I'm afraid I haven't been much of a homemaker lately."

Kristin entered, looked around, and reflexively nodded in agreement.

"Why did you move here?"

"Why? They found it for me. It was part of the package, so to speak. I took it until my money comes from the sale of the home. The little money that's due me, that is," she added. "This is rent free. Actually," she said with a macabre laugh, "it's part of the penance, part of my sentence for Sol and me daring to challenge the homeowners association.

"But," she said, perusing Kristin for the first time, "you already know a little about that, don't you? Otherwise, why would you come here? Well, go ahead. Sit down if you don't mind the thrift store furnishings," she added, nodding at the well-worn, light brown sofa. As soon as Kristin sat, Elaine relaxed in the thick-armed, deep-pillow easy chair across from her. "You realize you're associating with a known undesirable."

"Why is it taking so long for you to get your money? I don't understand," Kristin said.

"Just some legal shenanigans to prolong the torment," Elaine replied. "But at least I'm out of there," she added with a sigh of relief.

"You really hated living in Emerald Lakes that much?"

"Not in the beginning. In the beginning Sol and I thought we'd found Nirvana. We embraced the lifestyle, the regulations, the security system. Actually, Sol liked Phil very much in the beginning, and we both felt sorry for him and Marilyn. Now," she said bitterly, "now I think the little boy was lucky to escape being Phil's son. It's a terrible thing to say, I know, but you'll have to excuse me. I'm not in the forgiving mood these days."

"What happened to you and Sol?"

"Happened?" She laughed. "Yes, I suppose you could say things happened to us. Sol started to take a more active role in the life of the development. Even though he wasn't a board trustee, he went to the meetings and started to voice opinions. Little Miss Napoleon, Nikki Stanley, never stopped reminding him he had no vote in executive session, so he decided to run against her. Nikki's campaign, if you can call it that, became somewhat bitter. There was a lot of arm twisting and threats. Sol was soundly defeated.

"But my husband was a proud, independent man. He didn't withdraw; he became more of a thorn in her back, and therefore, more of a problem for the executive board. Sol started to rile other homeowners up about some of the restrictions. He even began a petition. Few signed it, but he did try."

"Angela and I were doing something like that just before she was killed," Kristin said. Elaine nodded.

"I had a suspicion about that when I heard about the attack. Why would anyone, even an idiot, choose the most securely guarded development to burglarize when there are so many other beautiful homes nearby without half the danger of being caught?"

"Surely, your husband didn't take his life over the situation at Emerald Lakes."

"My husband did not take his own life," she replied firmly. "He was not a quitter. Why would he initiate a civil law suit against the homeowners association if he were going to give up? The action was never brought to court so he was still optimistic. And he was about to be a father. Is that the point in your life when you decide to end it all? We'd also discussed our future plans; we were going to sell and move out if we got no satisfaction from the courts."

"What did your husband do for a living?"

"He was the business manager for Marlin Enterprises. They make home construction materials like aluminum siding. Suddenly, he was being pressured at work. Phil Slater's doing, I'm sure," she said nodding. "Sol was fired a week before his death. The police like to remind me of that. They hang their hats on it; it hammers home their comfortable conclusion that he committed suicide."

"He did shoot himself, right?"

Elaine turned away and took a deep breath.

"Sol was not a gun person. He never hunted. I never knew him to have a gun."

"But surely the police checked that."

"It was an unregistered pistol, the kind no one can trace but is, unfortunately, easily available. That's what the detective said. I kept asking how would he know where to get it? He wasn't that sort of man."

"What was their response?"

"Desperate men do desperate things. Only his prints were on the pistol. He shot himself in his office. We were the only people in the house. He'd lost his job." She shrugged. "What could I say?"

"Was the detective an Oriental man? Japanese?"

"No, it was a redheaded man."

"Martin?"

"Yes, I think that was his name."

Kristin thought a moment.

"So what do you think really happened?"

Elaine stared a moment.

"I was in the bedroom. Sol was trying to protect me, keep me from getting too upset so I didn't know how bad our economic situation was. The bank was already threatening foreclosure; we had fallen behind on homeowners fees, as well as other bills. It was all there on the desk in black and white beside his slumped body," she said and took another deep breath.

"You want to know what I think? I think he fell asleep. They came into the house. They knew how to disarm the alarm at the front door. They brought the pistol; they put it in his hand and they pressed his fingers around it and made it seem as if he pulled the trigger. That's what I think," she concluded.

"Why do you say they?" she asked, thinking about Marilyn Slater's comments about the shadows. "Did you hear anyone come into the house?"

"No. I just heard . . . the gunshot. It was so loud. I screamed and for a few moments, I couldn't move. Finally I got up slowly and inched my way toward the office, calling his name. Then I saw him. I remember screaming and screaming. I went to the front door and screamed for help, and wonder beyond wonders, our super security guards were at the house in no time."

"Which ones?"

"Spier and Stark," she said and closed her eyes. "Then the police came and you know the rest."

Kristin nodded and gazed around at the dreary setting.

"Don't you have any family to go to?" she asked softly.

"Sol's family blames me."

"Blames you?"

"They think I instigated his battle with the home-owners and destroyed our economic well-being."

"But surely you've explained . . ."

"It's complicated. Somehow, they made me look like the bad one. You know how charming and generous Slater can be."

"What about your own family?"

"I have only a sister, who has problems of her own. She's in the middle of a vicious divorce involving custody of her two children. My mother's dead; my father's in a nursing home."

"Any friends here?"

Elaine laughed.

"Most of our friends were in Emerald Lakes." She sighed. "I'm just waiting to settle the financial matters and then I'll disappear in the woodwork, just as Phil Slater and his crew want. I'm tired and besides, they have all the cards . . . the power, the money, the influence. What do I have? I don't even have our baby," she said, her lips quivering. "I don't even have our baby."

Kristin rose quickly and went to her. Elaine clung to her for a few moments and then took a deep breath.

"It's not worth it. Whatever you hoped to do isn't worth it. If you're not comfortable being sheep, sell and move out," Elaine said.

"My husband still thinks he can change things. He became a member of the board."

Elaine pulled back.

"Member of the board? So soon?"

"Phil Slater appointed him to replace someone who had resigned."

"What do you want from me?" Elaine suddenly demanded, her face expressing the same look of paranoia Angela Del Marco's expressed when Kristin had told her about Ted's appointment.

"I just wanted to know the story, to see if there were any resemblances to what had just happened. They're out of hand there. They've formed a Neighborhood Watch patrol and—"

"What else do they want from me? Why did they send you here?" Her eyes were wide, the pupils brightening with illumination lit by the terror.

"No one sent me, Mrs. Feinberg," Kristin said, trying to remain calm. "I remembered our meeting in the supermarket that day and—"

"Get out!" Elaine screamed and pointed to the door. "Get away from me. Leave me alone. Leave me alone!"

"All right. Please. Don't get yourself upset. I'm telling you the truth," Kristin said, but she backed away. Elaine shook her head and muttered.

"Get out. Get away."

"Okay. I'm sorry. I didn't mean to disturb you."

Kristin went to the door. After she opened it, she turned. Elaine Feinberg was sitting with her shoulders against the chair, clutching the thick arms with such intensity, the muscles and veins in her neck and face tightened and flexed against her skin. She resembled a woman in the electric chair. The sight put a finishing chill in Kristin's heart and she retreated quickly, hurrying down the sidewalk to her car. She drove away without looking back.

14

◆

"YOUR DISPATCHER TOLD ME I could find you here," Kristin said.

Lieutenant Kurosaka turned from Detective Martin whose eyebrows rose to fold ripples of surprise in his forehead when he saw Kristin approach. He and Kurosaka were on the sidewalk in front of Rings and Things, concluding a preliminary investigation of a burglary at Sandburg's only jewelry store.

"Mrs. Morris." Kurosaka stepped away from Martin and the store owner, a tall, thin, mostly bald-headed man whose dark eyes were filled with bewilderment and tragedy. Kurosaka just nodded in his direction and muttered, "He was robbed and he doesn't have enough insurance."

"Oh. I'm sorry," Kristin said glancing back at the slumped, sad figure.

"So? What brings you here with such urgency?"

"I was on my way home from a talk with Mrs. Feinberg," Kristin said, "when I decided to stop and talk to you."

"Feinberg?"

"The woman whose husband allegedly committed suicide in the house we now own," Kristin said.

Kurosaka nodded. Nothing in his face revealed any reaction. His black eyes remained as unfathomable as ever.

"Allegedly?" he finally offered and relaxed his lower lip to the preamble of a smile.

"She never believed that was what happened. She told me Detective Martin investigated that death?"

"Oh. That was before I arrived, but I do know a little about it," he said, glancing back at Detective Martin. "Is there something new?"

"I wondered if you might find it interesting that the two residents of Emerald Lakes who challenged the homeowners association are both dead, and the two security guards who were on duty on both occasions were Spier and Stark."

"Not unusual or unexpected. Both events occurred at night when they're on their shift."

"They're not always on the night shift," she retorted instantly, anticipating his response.

"I see. You still think they're upset about being accused of misconduct?"

"It goes deeper than them, Lieutenant. There are some people in my development who are . . . shall we say, over the top. I really think they have some serious delusions of grandeur."

Kurosaka's face moved further along toward a smile.

"What Mrs. Feinberg just told me makes sense," Kristin continued. "Her husband did have money problems, but they had a great deal to look forward to, not the least of which was a child. All I'm asking you to do is to take another look at things. Go back and question Spier and Stark some more. Rattle some cages. Do what Columbo does," she added in frustration when he continued to simply stare. Finally, he smiled.

"My grandmother used to say a stopped clock is still right twice a day," Kurosaka said. Kristin grimaced with confusion. "Do not underestimate the apparent lack of movement," he explained. "Give me some time to reconsider some of the things you've said."

"Then you do suspect something too, don't you? Don't you?" she demanded without disguising her excitement.

"Let's just say I'm not drawing any conclusions just yet," he replied, "and leave it at that. I am aware of Mr. Feinberg's file," he offered, "but again, thank you for your assistance. Now, I must go back to this unfortunate incident. Oh," he said, turning back to her. "For the time being, don't mention this to anyone."

"I don't discuss it with anyone anymore," she said. "Not even with my husband," she concluded sadly. He nodded and returned to Detective Martin.

Buoyed somewhat by Kurosaka's small revelation, Kristin returned to Emerald Lakes. Spier was on duty when she drove up. Rather than simply opening the gate, he stepped out of the booth and approached. He carried his clipboard.

"What do you want?" she demanded. His mere presence intimidated her at this point.

"Mrs. Morris." He tipped his hat and then tightened the lines in his face. "Carl told me you were unwilling to tell him where you were going or how long you would be gone. When you do that, you only make our job harder."

"What is your job, Mr. Spier?" she responded with a firmness that threw him off balance.

"What?"

"Your job description. Let me hear it," she ordered.

"You open and close this gate and ensure that unwanted visitors don't make entry, correct? What else?"

"We patrol. We . . ."

"Serve and protect? Go on. What else? Whom do you work for?"

Spier didn't respond.

"It's a simple enough question, Mr. Spier," she said.

"I work for the homeowners association," he said sharply.

"I'm part of the homeowners association, so you work for me. I don't work for you. I tell you what I want; you don't tell me. Now open the gate."

His eyes were brilliant with rage and the corners of his mouth whitened, but he maintained a correct posture and swallowed hard. Then he smiled coldly and returned to his booth to open the gate. She didn't gaze at him; she drove through, her heart pounding, but on her face was an almost imperceptible smile of self-satisfaction.

After she calmed down, Kristin worked on her music for the remainder of the day. She found herself writing darker, deeper more intense melodies, but they were some of the best she had done. She greeted Jennifer when she returned on the school bus and then she began to prepare supper with Jennifer at her side, doing whatever Kristin would allow her to do to help. She was pretty good at setting the table. An hour before Teddy was due home, however, he phoned to say he wouldn't be able to be there for dinner. He had been asked to consult on an emergency operation. A seven-year-old boy had been shot in the eye with a pellet from an air rifle.

"How horrible. Will they save his sight, Ted?"

"It's possible, but it's going to be a tricky ordeal."

"And the surgeon asked for your help?" she said, not without pride.

"I'm not sure if I was chosen for my ability or because no one else in the office wanted the responsibility or wanted to give up the time," he replied.

"I'm sure it was because of your ability."

"Anyway, I thought I'd eat with the staff over at the hospital. Everything all right there?"

"Yes," she said quickly.

"I could go home and eat and hurry back, but it would be foolish."

"We're all right, Ted. Really."

"If you're sure," he said. After a pause he added, "I called you earlier today. You weren't taking one of your infamous nature walks, were you, Kristin?"

"No. I just ran a few errands," she said. She wasn't comfortable lying to him, but she didn't want to tell him about her conversation with Elaine Feinberg.

"All right. If I'm going to be very late, I'll phone. Give Jen a kiss for me."

"I will. Good luck."

"Thanks. Love you," he said and hung up.

Jennifer was upset Teddy wasn't coming home for dinner. There were so many things that had happened at school and she was exploding with the need to tell it all. Teddy was being a better listener than she was, Kristin thought. She couldn't keep her mind from wandering, despite her effort to be attentive. The moment darkness fell and the streetlights came on, Kristin's thoughts returned to Elaine Feinberg and Lieutenant Kurosaka's small, but significant revelation of doubt. If only she had one more thing to offer him, she thought, something concrete.

She went to the front window and gazed out at the

street. In an hour or so, the Neighborhood Watch patrol would begin. She wondered who was on duty tonight and if they would come rapping at her door with some new complaint or some other suggestion. The ringing of the telephone drew her to the receiver in the living room.

"Hello."

"Kristin," Teddy said, the tone of his voice so heavy that for a moment she didn't recognize him. "Where were you today?"

"What? Ted?"

"Where did you go?" he asked dryly.

"Why are you asking me that?"

"Phil Slater called my beeper number and I just got off the phone with him," he replied in a tired voice. "What are you doing, Kristin? What are you up to?"

"What do you mean? What did he tell you?"

"He said you went to see Elaine Feinberg and you got her very upset."

"How would he know that?" she wondered aloud. "She wouldn't call him to complain about me, Ted. She's terrified of him and the whole crowd."

"Never mind that, Kristin. Why did you go there?" he demanded with more firmness.

"I wanted to find out more about the death of her husband. And I'm glad I did. Mrs. Feinberg doesn't believe her husband committed suicide; she never did and she has good reason not to believe it, Ted."

"Kristin."

"You might as well know I went to see Lieutenant Kurosaka, too."

"What? Jesus."

"And he has some similar thoughts."

"What similar thoughts? What do you mean?"

"We'll talk about it when you come home. Why did Philip Slater call you?"

"He wanted to know what you were up to. He was afraid you were stirring things up. What similar thoughts? What did Lieutenant Kurosaka say exactly?"

"Why do you think Philip is afraid of what I might stir up?" she countered instead of answering his question.

"Why? Because there's enough negative publicity about our development since Angela's murder."

"How did he know I went to see Elaine Feinberg, Ted? Did he tell you she called him? Did he?"

"Whatever you did or said to her frightened her and she did call someone who called him, I think," Teddy replied.

"Because she thought he sent me," Kristin surmised.

"Whatever, Kristin. It doesn't matter. I thought you were leaving this alone. I thought you were going to let the police do the police work. You're at the end of your second trimester of pregnancy, just past that point when—"

"All right, Ted. Don't give me a lecture."

"I just can't believe this. Going to see Elaine Feinberg. They're all going to think you're crazy."

"Oh, that's it. It's not my health that worries you; it's still what the people in the development will think. You afraid I'll make headlines in the Neighborhood Watch report?"

"Kristin."

"I don't want to talk about this anymore on the phone, Ted. For all I know, the phone's tapped anyway. It's connected to the security booth, isn't it?"

"Jesus."

"I'll talk to you when you come home."

"Maybe the house is bugged," he said angrily.

"Maybe it is. We'll go on the rear patio and talk," she replied with deliberate seriousness.

"Okay. I'll be home as soon as I can."

"Good."

She hung up without saying good-bye. Her heart was thumping and her face felt as if she had drawn too close to a raging fire. She thought for a moment and then, fully aware of the irony, turned to the Emerald Lakes directory, flipping the pages to the emergency numbers. When she found what she wanted, she dialed the sheriff's department and asked for Lieutenant Kurosaka. She caught him just as he was leaving.

"Now you know what kind of hours we keep," he jested. "What can I do for you, Mrs. Morris?"

"Did you tell anyone about our conversation today?"

"What?"

"Philip Slater called my husband to complain about my visiting Elaine Feinberg," she said quickly. Kurosaka was quiet. "Elaine Feinberg wouldn't have told him."

"Perhaps you spoke to someone about it or referred to it or—"

"I didn't. I went directly to see you and then I came directly home and I've been here ever since. I haven't spoken to anyone but my husband on the telephone. Was I being followed? Was that it?"

"What makes you think that?"

"I don't know." She thought a moment, recalling the streets, her driving. "No. There was no one around when I came out of the house and I never saw a car behind me all the time. But I don't know. Does Philip Slater have eyes and ears everywhere?"

"Why did he call your husband?"

"To complain that I might be stirring up bad publicity for the development."

"He does worry about that," Kurosaka said. "Let me check something," he added. "For the time being, just remain calm. A woman in your condition shouldn't be involved in something like this," he said softly.

"I want to know how Mr. Slater knew I was at that house," she reiterated firmly.

"I'll be in touch," he promised.

After she hung up, she folded her arms under her breasts and opened the front door to take in some clear, cool air. She stood there taking in deep breaths so fast she nearly hyperventilated. Suddenly Philip Slater drove by, his eyes fixed straight ahead. Instinctively she pulled back into her doorway and watched him disappear around the turn toward the front gate. Then she stepped out again and looked up the street at his house.

Just seeing Philip Slater at that moment made her furious. She spun around and marched back into the house to get Jennifer.

"Where are we going, Mommy?"

"I want to visit Mrs. Slater, the nice lady who gave you all the dolls," she said.

"Can I look at the other dolls?"

"I'm sure you can, honey. Here, put on your Bugs Bunny jacket," she said.

As soon as she had slipped her into it, Kristin took her hand and led her out of the house and onto the street, marching with a determination that impressed Jennifer and kept her thousand and one questions in storage for the time being.

*   *   *

Marilyn Slater saw them coming. They were walking a straight line for the house, and even from this distance, she could sense the steadfastness in Kristin Morris's gait and intentions. She didn't know exactly what it was about, but she had suspicions because of the things Philip had said earlier.

Shortly after dinner, Philip had received a troubling phone call. She thought of it as troubling because Philip was rarely at a loss for words. But there he was stammering and cajoling someone, his face becoming more and more crimson until he was positively glowing with frustration and anger. She tried to ignore him, completing her after-dinner chores as silently as she could; but when she turned and saw him standing there fuming, she was overcome with dread.

"What is it?" she asked softly. He didn't turn; he didn't reply. After a moment he left the kitchen and went to his office, closing the door behind him. He was in there for nearly an hour. She sat in the living room looking through the television set, not hearing anything, not seeing anything. For weeks after Bradley's death, Philip would lock himself in his office for hours and when he finally emerged, he always looked as if he had been running miles.

If they would only comfort each other, she thought, it would ease the pain for both of them, but revealing his sadness and his despair was something Philip despised. Philip was far more comfortable with anger, and after he had directed his anger at an unreasonable God, a medical community that had failed them, and any other social agency he could think of, he focused on her.

Her weakness after the tragedy underlined the hereditary flaw that had brought about the medical crisis in the first place. After Bradley died, Philip's world simply became two places: Emerald Lakes and the outside. He built his walls; he constructed his chain fences; he installed his lights and employed his security guards to keep everything undesirable away.

Then he hardened even more and built another wall: a wall between them. She had tried to scale it, to penetrate it, to tear it down, but it was too thick and too high and he was too comfortable behind it. But in walling her out, he had walled her into her own prison and one way or another, she had to escape.

There were enough lights on in the Slater house for Kristin to assume Marilyn was home. She had the feeling that Marilyn might have been watching the street from the vantage point of that chair in the tinted window and had seen her coming anyway. Even so, it took three tries on the doorbell to get her to come to the door.

Marilyn Slater stood there with a look of exhaustion on her face. Her mascara had run, creating black teardrops under her eyes, and her normally perfect hair was tousled and ruffled as if someone had just given her a scalp massage.

"I'm sorry to bother you," Kristin began. She debated turning and fleeing the sight of this distraught woman. The dazed look in her eyes was a bit frightening. She gazed out at Kristin and Jennifer as if she had no idea who they were. "Are you all right?" Kristin followed.

Marilyn's lips quivered. Her gaze dropped to Jennifer, who was looking up at her with a mixture of fear and confusion, too. She clung tightly to Kristin's hand.

"What? Oh." Marilyn smiled and then she laughed. It was a chilling, maddening laugh as if Kristin had asked the most ridiculous question. "Come in. Please," she said. She stepped back. Kristin hesitated. She gazed down the street behind her, again considering a quick retreat. "It's all right," Marilyn added. "I'm okay."

"I just thought we could talk for a few moments," Kristin said. "But if it's a bad time . . ."

"No. I no longer distinguish between good and bad times anyway. All time is the same to me," she said and smiled at Jennifer again. "I bet you want to go look at my dolls, don't you? Come on," she said, reaching for her hand. Jennifer pressed herself back against Kristin.

"It's all right, honey," Kristin concluded. "Let's go look at the dolls."

They entered the house and Marilyn closed the door.

"I just cleaned up, but I could make us some coffee, if you'd like."

"No, thank you. I'm fine," Kristin said. Marilyn nodded, looked at Jennifer and smiled.

"Yes, you are. You're fine and that's wonderful. Let's go look at the dolls," she said and led them through the living room.

"You know what I have, Jennifer?" Marilyn said when they entered the doll room. "I have some clothes for my Chinese girl. How would you like to change her?" she said, showing Jennifer the doll and the clothes. Jennifer's eyes widened and her face lightened. She looked up at Kristin who smiled and nodded.

"Go on, honey. It's all right," she said. Jennifer finally released Kristin's hand and went to Marilyn who set the doll and the clothes down on the small table.

"Can you do it?" she asked. Jennifer nodded. "Go on then," she said guiding her to the chair. Then she straightened up and turned to Kristin.

"You want to talk about what happened to Mrs. Del Marco, don't you?" she asked.

"Yes, and Mr. Feinberg, too."

Marilyn nodded and relaxed her shoulders like someone who had been caught and trapped and finally had to confess.

"Let's go into the living room."

"We'll be right in here, honey," Kristin said, but Jennifer was already engrossed in her activity.

"You know," Marilyn began after they sat down, she in an oversize armchair and Kristin on the sofa, "I did what you wanted. I called the police after you figured out I had seen something. I told them about the two shadows."

"You definitely saw two shadows, not one?"

"First, one stepped out in front of Mrs. Del Marco. She stopped and then one came up behind her and the two closed in, clamped around her and pulled her into the darkness. I went to tell my husband, but I couldn't find him."

"What do you mean, couldn't find him?"

"He wasn't in the office and he wasn't in the bathroom. Later, he accused me of drinking too much."

"Drinking?" Kristin asked, her hopes dipping.

"Vodka," Marilyn said with some fanfare. She smiled. "Would you like a drink?"

"No, thank you."

"It sort of my embalming fluid," Marilyn said and laughed. "So I don't look as dead outside as I am inside," she added softly.

"Were you drinking the night Angela was attacked?"

"I had one drink, but I still saw them," she added firmly. "And then later, I looked in the garage and saw Philip's boots were soaked. He had been outside. I wasn't soused. He hadn't been in the house when I looked after all."

"Why did he lie?" Kristin asked quickly.

"Philip doesn't lie. He doesn't think I'm worthy of knowing the details about the things he does. There are, shall we say, gaps between us, long, wide gaps. You look like you don't understand. I understand why. I'm sure you and your husband are quite different."

Kristin smiled, uncomfortable with these intimate revelations.

"Sure you don't want a drink?" Marilyn asked.

"No, thank you."

Marilyn nodded, disappointed.

"I went to see Mrs. Feinberg earlier today," Kristin said. "And she told me she didn't believe her husband had committed suicide."

"Oh, he did. I saw the ambulance and I remember when Philip got the phone call."

"No. I don't mean that. I mean, she thinks he might have been murdered."

Marilyn Slater stared as if she were waiting for the punch line.

"The shadows again," she finally said.

"Did you see them that night, too?"

"No, but I have seen them before. You absolutely sure you wouldn't like a drink? It helps sometimes when you're talking about these things."

"Yes, I'm sure. Thank you. Anyway," Kristin continued, "someone told your husband I went to see Mrs. Feinberg and he was upset enough about it to call my husband and complain."

Marilyn nodded.

"Do you know who called him?"

"No, but I know someone called and got him very angry. He locked himself in his office. He used to do that a lot after Bradley died," she added, and then she pressed her lips together quickly as if she had just uttered a blasphemy. "Philip doesn't like me talking about Bradley."

"Why can't you talk about him?" Kristin asked.

"It keeps the tragedy alive."

"But he was your child. You want to keep his memory alive, don't you?"

Marilyn's lips quivered.

"I do it secretly," she whispered. "I go down into the basement where all Bradley's things are kept and I look at his pictures."

"You shouldn't have to do that in secret. I don't mean to poke my nose in where it doesn't belong, but I think that's wrong."

Marilyn nodded.

"Can you think harder about what you saw the night Angela was killed? Maybe there was something about the shadows. Were they tall? Did you see uniforms?"

Marilyn shook her head.

"Did they just pop out of the darkness or did they come up the street?"

"Out of the darkness."

"But there were two? There were definitely two?"

"Yes, there were two."

"Look, Mommy," Jennifer said, stepping into the doorway between the living room and doll room. She held up the doll.

"That's very good, honey. She looks beautiful."

"She does," Marilyn said.

"Can I dress this doll, too?" Jennifer said, and held up the doll that reminded Marilyn of Bradley.

"Oh, you found him," she said. "It's time to change his clothes, too." Marilyn rose. "Let me show you where I keep them," she said. Kristin watched her return to the doll room with Jennifer. Then she turned and looked toward the rear of the house, thinking.

I shouldn't be doing this, she thought as she rose from her seat, especially in my condition. But she continued anyway and walked out the living room and down the hall toward what she knew was Philip Slater's office.

She didn't know what she hoped to find, but she felt compelled to explore. Perhaps there would be something to indicate who had called Philip earlier to reveal her visit with Elaine Feinberg.

The office door was slightly ajar and there was a small lamp lit on the desk. The shutters were drawn tightly closed and the small, weak layer of illumination deepened shadows and thickened the darkness in the corners. Kristin paused, listened for Marilyn Slater, and then pushed the door open enough for her to enter the office.

Once inside, she felt her heart begin to pound. Despite his absence, Philip Slater's intimidating presence somehow lingered. It was clear that he spent most of his time in this room. The air still carried the sweet yet manly scent of his cologne. Everything on his desk was precisely and neatly arranged with practically geometric correctness.

Kristin turned slightly to her right and her heart skipped a beat. She actually gasped. Philip Slater's overcoat hung on the pole hanger and for a moment, she had the impression he was actually standing there. She caught her breath and walked past the table where there was a model of a house. She hesitated at the desk as if she were about to commit a more serious violation and then went around to the chair to gaze at the papers and notes on the shiny dark oak surface.

There were telephone numbers with names she didn't recognize scribbled on the notepad to her left. She did recognize Ted's beeper number, however, and that sent a chill through her. She lifted the cover of the long pad to her right and studied some of the notes. It was obvious they all had to do with construction jobs.

Disappointed, she gathered more courage and opened the bottom right drawer. It had files neatly aligned. She knelt down and lifted each one gently into the light to read its heading. Building and electrical codes followed architectural proposals and bids on construction projects. Everything looked innocuous. Her quick, clandestine search was proving futile.

She stood up and gazed around the office. The narrow door of the only closet caught her interest so she went to it and opened it quickly. She saw the light switch and flipped it to reveal shelves of old building plans and stacks of files. One shelf caught her interest because she saw the words *Covenants and Conditions*. Closer examination revealed it was a library of CC and R's from other developments, some as far away as California.

Then her gaze dropped to the floor under this set of shelves and her heart was washed in a wave of chilled blood. There, unmistakably, was the cover of Angela's file with the words scrawled across it in a black magic marker ink: *Declaration of Independence*.

Slowly, she bent her knees and lowered herself to a squat position. She reached out to pick up the file cover. But before she did so, she heard the closet door being pulled completely open and she looked up to see Philip Slater standing there, gazing down at her.

Even with the shadows draped over his face, she could see the luminous gleam of rage in his eyes.

He said nothing.

She started to stand.

He stepped forward and thrust his arm out, hand clenched in a fist, to strike the lightbulb. Kristin screamed as the glass shattered around her. Then she saw the door shutting. She moved too late and the door clicked in place, casting her in complete darkness. She heard the key snap the lock and she screamed again and pounded the door.

"Let me out of here! Stop this!" she cried. She paused, expecting complete obedience. When it didn't come, she felt the panic seize her. She groped for the handle and ran her palm over the metal, searching for a way to open the door from the inside, but she found nothing.

She folded her small hands into fists and pummeled the door, screaming as loudly as she could. Pain shot down her neck and settled into a knot at the base of her spine. Then it spread with electric speed around her hips and over her abdomen, dropping into her pelvis. She crumbled to the floor, gasping, desperately trying to calm herself.

She felt just the way she had before her miscarriage.

"Oh, no," she moaned. "Please. No."

She took deep breaths and rocked, waiting, hoping for the pain to subside. Gradually, in tiny increments, it did, but instead of standing again, she leaned over and gently lowered herself to the floor of the closet, keeping her body folded in a fetal position because it was more comfortable that way. She waited and listened.

It was deadly silent and so dark.

What is he doing? she wondered.

"What do you think you're doing?" she muttered.

And then she remembered Jennifer and the panic that had receded exploded with such force and fury, she thought she would fly apart, her head, her legs and her arms going off in different directions. It burned into her heart. It was so hot, she couldn't even cry; the tears evaporated before they could emerge.

She lifted herself into a sitting position and brought her lips as close to the doorjamb as she could and then she pleaded.

"Please . . . let me out. Please . . . don't hurt my daughter."

Silence. Darkness.

There was only the sound of her own imagination, raining down terror.

15

Kristin heard Philip yelling. It was muffled at first, but then it became clearer and louder as his reprimanding of Marilyn grew more intense. He was blaming everything on her.

"If you hadn't said anything to that woman, none of this would have happened. Your insane babbling has finally caused us serious trouble. Are you satisfied, Marilyn?"

Apparently, Marilyn offered no resistance, verbally at least. Kristin heard only Philip. She was listening hard for Jennifer's cries. She expected her to be nearly hysterical by now but she heard nothing.

The berating continued. Philip's voice rose in pitch until he was shrieking, his voice resembling that of a man who had cornered himself and was exploding with frustration. This was followed by a deep, silent moment, like the eye of a storm passing, and then Kristin heard Marilyn's shrill scream of pain. It sounded like he was dragging her by the hair down the hallway.

"Get over here! Get the hell in there," Philip commanded. "Go on!"

That was followed by some scuffling. Kristin

couldn't imagine what Jennifer was doing exposed to all this, but she knew she had to be petrified.

"My baby," she muttered. "My baby." She pulled herself into a sitting position, her ear still to the door.

"Let me go, Philip! You're hurting my arm. Please, leave me be," Marilyn Slater pleaded.

Apparently, he was twisting her arm, dragging her back to the office.

"And how am I supposed to do that? How am I supposed to leave things be? You let her come in here and sneak into my office when I left explicit instructions that you were not to speak to that woman. I told you she was up to no good, didn't I? Now look what you let her do."

"I didn't know she went into your office, Philip."

"Sure. You didn't know. What do you know, Marilyn? You know how to suck on that vodka pretty well. That's what you know."

From the sound of their voices, Kristin knew they were just outside the closet door now. She rose and began pounding again.

"Let me out of here. Open this door immediately," she ordered, swallowing back her fears and pain.

"You have to let her out, Philip."

"Don't tell me what I have to do, Marilyn."

In the short moment of silence, Kristin could almost hear him thinking, scheming.

"This is the story, Marilyn," he began. "She broke into our home. You came home and then found her in my office planting that file to make it look like I had something to do with what happened to Angela Del Marco, understand?"

"What file?"

"Never mind what file. You just say she was carrying a file in her hands when she entered the house," he ordered.

"That's ridiculous, Philip," Marilyn said just loud enough for Kristin to hear. "Why would she do that?"

"You just back up my story or . . . or I'll have you committed."

Through the locked closet door, Marilyn heard Philip Slater go to his telephone.

"Spier. Call the police and then call for the security car and come up here. I've intercepted a break-in at my house. No. Everything's under control for the moment."

"You're not going to get away with this, Philip," Marilyn said. "You better just let her go home."

"Shut up. Just shut up and don't say anything to anyone, understand?"

Kristin heard the key turn in the lock and the door was finally open. She faced an intimidating Philip Slater, who loomed before her, his shoulders raised, his hands clenched in fists. He seemed swollen in size, gigantic and formidable, a statue in granite blocking her way.

"Just sit right down on the floor," he ordered. "The security and the police will be here soon."

"You're insane," Kristin said softly, her intensity and volume building. "How dare you lock me in this closet? I heard what you plan to do. Marilyn's right. Who do you think will believe such a stupid story?"

"Most everyone in the development will believe it, that's who," he replied confidently. "They all know about your activities, your attitude, the things you and Angela Del Marco were planning to do to bring down all that I've built here. So shut up and sit down."

"You attacked Angela, didn't you, you and your private little army," Kristin accused, maintaining her defiance.

"I told you to sit on the floor," Philip said calmly, pointing.

"I will not." Kristin looked to the office doorway. "Where's my daughter?"

"Daughter?" Philip Slater's confident, strong demeanor weakened a bit.

"Yes. Do you think everyone's going to believe I broke into a house with my child beside me? Even your gullible followers will wonder. What was it supposed to be, a family outing?"

"Marilyn," he began, turning, "why didn't you tell—"

Marilyn wasn't standing there.

"Marilyn!"

Kristin started to step out of the closet, but he held up his hand to block her path.

"Stay where you are, I said. I could just as easily add you came at me and I had to defend myself," he threatened. Then he looked to the doorway again. "Marilyn!"

As if she had been standing just outside and waiting, Marilyn appeared, smiling.

"Yes, Philip?"

"You damn idiot. Why didn't you tell me she brought her little girl along? Where is she?"

"In the room with the dolls, safe," Marilyn said, still smiling.

"Get her, for crissakes."

"There's no reason to frighten her more than you already have, Philip. You might as well sit at your desk and stop yelling at everyone."

"Did you hear me?" He started toward her. "I said—"

Marilyn Slater brought her right arm around and revealed the pistol in her hand. Philip froze.

"What the hell do you think you're doing with that?"

"Nothing much," she replied, still smiling softly. Kristin saw the glint of madness in her eyes and didn't move, but Philip seemed blind to it. He regained his composure quickly and held out his right hand.

"I told you to get the little girl, didn't I? Now give me the pistol and do what I say for once."

"What do you mean, do what you say for once? I always do what you say, Philip. I've done everything you've wanted me to do since we were married and even after Bradley's death, haven't I? Oh, maybe I drank some vodka now and then even though you didn't want me to do that, but that's all. I've been a good wife and a good mother."

"Right," Philip said smirking. "A good mother."

"I was. I didn't do anything wrong. It wasn't my fault," she said shaking her head, her lips quivering. "You shouldn't blame me. He shouldn't blame me, should he?" Marilyn asked Kristin.

"Of course he shouldn't."

"I don't want to talk about that now, Marilyn. This isn't the time. Give me the pistol and get the little girl. Now," he snapped. Marilyn shook her head.

"We should have talked about it more, Philip. Ignoring his memory was like burying Bradley twice. He's been terribly alone. We were all he had and when we stopped ourselves from thinking of him, he had no one. That's why he cries so much, even now."

"Cries so much?" He shook his head and smirked. "You're crazy. When this is over, I definitely will have you committed."

"No, Philip. I'll commit myself." She looked at Kristin. "I'm sorry," she said. "Philip, always gets his way."

"Marilyn," Kristin said, "you can stop him."

"No. He always manages to get what he wants, one way or another. Don't you, Philip?" she said and raised the pistol, but instead of pointing it at him, she pointed it at her right temple and said, "Ten."

The explosion was so loud, it seemed to shake the very foundation of the house. Marilyn's blood and flesh and bone splattered over the wall to Kristin's right and then Marilyn's body appeared to float to the floor, her arms out, her head recoiling from the violent intrusion.

Philip Slater was as shocked as Kristin was and stepped back, raising his arms as if to ward off a blow. Kristin screamed and shot forward, thinking only of Jennifer.

She ran down the hallway, through the living room and into the doll room. At first she didn't see Jennifer; then she spotted her cowering in a corner, clutching one of the dolls and shivering with terror.

"Mommy!" she moaned.

Kristin reached out and Jennifer ran into her arms.

"It's all right, honey," she said embracing her tightly. "It's all right."

"I want Daddy."

"We'll call him. We're going home now. Come on, sweetheart."

She took her hand and led her out of the doll room, but when they turned through the living-room doorway toward the front entrance, she found Philip Slater had regained his composure and was blocking their way.

"My security is coming," he said. "You'll need this." He thrust the pistol toward her. Kristin shook her head and pulled Jennifer closer as she retreated. "Take it," he demanded. "Take it!"

Jennifer started to cry.

"No," Kristin said. "If I have a gun in my hand, they will shoot me. That's what you want."

Impatient, Philip stepped forward, seized Kristin's hand and shoved the pistol into her palm, literally folding her fingers over the handle. Then just as the Emerald Lakes security patrol car pulled into the driveway, Slater opened the door and smiled at Kristin.

"You broke into my home," he said. "My wife heard something and got our pistol. There was a struggle and you shot her." He nodded toward the pistol. "Your fingerprints will confirm that."

"NO!" Kristin cried and dropped the gun as if it had turned blistering hot in her hand. She heard the car doors slam.

"Through the kitchen. Out the back door," Philip said nodding. "It's your only chance."

Kristin considered. Spier and Stark were approaching the house. They might shoot her anyway and put the gun in her hand. And what would they do to Jennifer?

Kristin had no choice. She turned and did what Philip Slater capriciously suggested: charged down the hallway and into the kitchen. She practically lunged at the rear door, snapping the lock open and hurrying herself and Jennifer out into the night.

Lights, triggered by motion, dropped a pool of illumination like a net around them. It blinded her, but Kristin continued running with her horrified daughter clutching her hand. At the hedges that bordered the yard, Kristin caught the heel of her shoe in a go-pher hole and went flying into the bush. The branches were like wires, tearing and scratching at her blouse and arms, but the bush broke her fall and she was able to prevent herself from striking the ground too hard.

"Mommy!"

"I'm all right, honey."

Kristin struggled to her feet. Her shoulder ached from the impact of her palm on the earth when she broke her fall, but she ignored it. Voices were echoing in the kitchen of the Slater house. They would be out the rear door in moments. Kristin seized Jennifer's hand again and they crossed quickly into another yard and around a neighboring house, where the lights, also triggered by motion, glared as brightly. She continued through the yards, ignoring the pain from the scratches and cuts along her forearms. Her thighs began to ache and she vaguely realized that she had twisted something in her hip as well when she had fallen.

"Where are we going, Mommy?"

"Home," Kristin said. "We've got to get home and call Daddy."

They came around the side of a house and stepped into the street. Kristin looked back and saw the Slater's front door wide open, the security car's bub-ble light turning. She swallowed her hysteria once more and walked as quickly as she could, almost oblivious at this point to the prongs of pain which had begun to emanate from her pelvis and lower ab-domen. Jennifer was too frightened to utter a sound. She followed along as quickly as her little legs would carry her.

They turned up the driveway to their front door.

Kristin opened it quickly and stepped into the house, pausing for a moment to catch her breath.

"I want Daddy," Jennifer said.

"Yes, honey. We're calling him right now," Kristin said and started down the steps to the living room. When she turned toward the kitchen, however, she noticed the patio door had been slid open. She stopped.

"Mommy?"

"Shh, honey. Wait."

Panic seized her again, crawling up and over her ankles, spiking through her thighs. She felt incapable of movement, cemented to the floor by a surge of fear that shot through her heart.

A noise in the hallway drew her attention to the shadow gliding along the wall. Without waiting, she turned herself and Jennifer around and hurried across the living room, up the steps and out the front door.

"Where are we going, Mommy?"

"Out of here to find help," she muttered and turned left. But as they started down the street, heading toward the front gate, the evening's Neighborhood Watch patrol led by Nikki Stanley came around the corner. They had obviously been told something. Nikki blew her whistle and Kristin heard, "There they are!" The whistle sounded again.

Kristin veered to her left over the Dimases' front lawn, around the side of their house. Lights went on throughout the house and in every house along the street, illuminating backyards, side lawns, and folding back the shadows to eliminate every possible nook and cranny for hiding.

People were shouting behind them. The whistle was blown and blown. Doors slammed. The sound of the security patrol car squealing to a stop was like a shrill scream through the night. Kristin felt her legs wobble, the pain cutting up and down the inside of her thighs and sticking her in the side with the sharpness of a knife. She gasped, turned this way and that, frantic and terrified that she would make the wrong move and deliver herself and her child into the hands of Philip Slater's crazed vigilantes.

They were close behind. She could hear the footsteps over the walks and lawns. People were calling to each other. In one house, the alarm was triggered. More doors slammed. Beams of flashlights sliced the darkness like random stabs into the night.

"Which way?" she heard Spier call.

"Behind the Dimases," Nikki Stanley replied.

Kristin turned to her right and crossed through the Meltzers' yard. The agony was too intense and Jennifer was hysterical. She had slowed so that Kristin was practically dragging her along. Desperately, she searched for an avenue of escape and focused on the small tool shed just to the right.

"Shh, honey. Just follow Mommy," Kristin said opening the shed door.

Jennifer resisted being dragged into the hole of darkness. Visions of rats and other creatures were scrawled across the screen of her imagination.

"Please, honey. We've got to hide from the bad people for a few minutes, Jen. Come on," she coaxed and pulled her in beside her. Then she closed the shed door, leaving them in coffin-like darkness.

"I'm afraid, Mommy."

"It's all right. Shh," Kristin whispered, and knelt down as best she could to embrace her. Jennifer whimpered, but was too frightened to cry loudly. Kristin held her tightly and they waited and listened.

Footsteps went past. There was more shouting. A beam of light hit the shed, but quickly moved off.

"Split up," she heard Spier say. "I'll go west."

"Right," Stark replied.

Kristin held her breath and waited. Then she inched the shed door open and peered out. The yard was clear. Off to the right, people were shouting and flashlights continued probing through the darkness.

"I want Daddy," Jennifer wailed.

"Me too, Jen."

There was still too much activity around her house and she had to assume that whoever had been in there waiting for her might still be.

"Let's go home, Mommy."

"We will. We've got to take a little walk first, honey."

She led her out and decided to go toward the lake where they might safely wait for things to calm down. Surely it wouldn't be too much longer before Ted came home anyway. There was just enough illumination from the stars and the reflection off the water to provide a direction.

"We'll be all right. They won't find us. Soon, Teddy will be home. It's going to be fine," Kristin babbled, cheering herself on, encouraging herself as if she were a schizophrenic. Jennifer was as much terrified by Kristin's actions and words as she was by the pursuit of these angry people.

They cut through some brush, under some trees and down a path, when suddenly Kristin stopped. A shadow that was clearly the silhouette of a man loomed before them. He had to have seen and heard them, yet he hadn't moved. He waited patiently. Kristin looked back. She saw the flashlights twisting and turning in the night, blocking any effective retreat.

"Mrs. Morris?"

She grabbed Jennifer and stepped back into the darkest shadow.

"Who is it?"

"Easy, Mrs. Morris. It's all right."

He stepped toward her until she could see his face.

"Thank goodness," she gasped.

Detective Martin smiled.

"Are you all right?"

"No. I'm exhausted. You know I'm pregnant and my daughter is terrified. These people have gone crazy."

"Yes, ma'am. It's not a very pleasant situation, not for anyone."

"Why were you waiting in here like this?" Kristin asked as she wiped Jennifer's face.

"I intercepted a call and drove up. When I saw which way they were all running, I just assumed you might be headed down here. What's going on exactly?" he asked.

She caught her breath and told him about Marilyn Slater and what Philip was planning to do.

"She actually shot herself?"

"Yes and when he handed me the gun . . ."

"I understand."

"So I ran out of the house and he has everyone thinking I'm to blame. He either participated or had something done to Angela Del Marco," she continued without catching her breath. "I found our notebook in his office closet."

"Don't say? He kept that there?" Detective Martin nearly laughed.

"Let's go back. I want to call my husband," she said.

"They're really wild back there, ma'am. I suggest we go this way," he said, nodding toward the lake.

"What?"

"Toward the lake," he said, gesturing more emphatically.

"Why? You can stop them. You're a policeman. We'll go back."

"No, ma'am. We can't go back. We'll go this way now," he insisted. When she didn't move, he reached out and seized her right elbow. "This way, Mrs. Morris."

"Why?" she asked, but took a few steps under his pressure.

"Keep going, Mrs. Morris. That's it. Follow the path. Go on," he coaxed, pushing her from behind now.

"Why are you doing this? We can go back; we'll call my husband."

"Right there, Mrs. Morris," he said pointing to a rubber raft on the shore.

"What? You want us to go to the other side of the lake?" she asked, trying to make some sense out of his instructions.

"Sure."

"But why?"

"It'll look good. Make some sense," he replied.

"I don't understand."

"Simple. You found this boat and thought it would be the best means of escaping the madness," he said.

"What do you mean? I found this boat?" A dark realization like a shadow of ice fell over her heart. She took a step back, tightening her grip on Jennifer's little hand.

"Get in the boat, Mrs. Morris. *Now,*" he demanded. It all came raining down over her in a cloudburst of understanding. "You're with him, aren't you? You . . . you were the one who investigated Sol Feinberg's supposed suicide, too, but he hadn't committed suicide, had he?"

"Get in the boat, Mrs. Morris."

"Why? Why would you want to help a madman?"

"Well, his money's not mad, Mrs. Morris. He's got a lot more than he needs. Whereas me? I come from a family that could only dream about living in Emerald Lakes. Maybe I'll move into your house someday soon," he added.

"You can't get away with this. Lieutenant Kurosaka—"

"Get in the boat, Mrs. Morris. If I have to tell you again, I'll shoot the little girl," he added, pointing his pistol at Jennifer, "and we'll just blame it on one of those crazed Neighborhood Watch patrolmen." Instinctively, Kristin pulled Jennifer to her. She felt her daughter's silent sobbing. "I mean it," he added. She heard the sound of a gun's hammer being clicked back.

Exhausted herself, she put Jennifer into the raft obediently and got in beside her.

"Why do you want us in here?"

"We'll see how well you two can swim," he said. "In your hysteria," he continued, creating the fabricated scenario, "you overturned."

Swimming in her condition wasn't impossible, but saving Jennifer at the same time . . .

"Please. We don't care about this place. He can have what he wants. We'll move away. We'll sell the house for practically nothing. We'll—"

"All that will happen anyway, Mrs. Morris. You shouldn't have been so damn determined and so damn independent. Team players are all Mr. Slater wants in Emerald Lakes," he said, and started to push off and get in the raft himself when suddenly, a gunshot cracked.

Detective Martin snapped his head back. His eyes widened with surprise, but as he fell back, he propelled the raft forward. He slid into the water behind them, dropping as if he were being dragged down by a shark. Kristin screamed and out of the darkness came Lieutenant Kurosaka.

"Hold on, Mrs. Morris," he cried just as Harold Spier appeared behind him.

Kristin shouted, but to her surprise Spier ran past Kurosaka toward the shore and leaped into the water like a professional life guard. With a few quick, long strokes, he reached the raft.

"Easy, Mrs. Morris," he said. "Just sit back."

The powerful man hooked his arm over the side of the raft and dragged it back to the shore. Then he helped Kristin and Jennifer out under Lieutenant Kurosaka's approving eyes. Carl Stark came running from the left to join them.

"What the hell's going on?" he asked. "I heard the gunshot."

"Help me drag Martin's body out of the water," Spier replied in response. Kurosaka moved forward to offer Kristin his hand and guidance as she continued to step over the rocky terrain.

"Are you all right, Mrs. Morris?"

"I don't know," she replied. "I'm too numb and confused at the moment."

"Understandable," he said. "Let me help." He went to lift Jennifer and she started to cry.

"It's all right, honey," Kristin said. "Lieutenant Kurosaka is our friend. I think," she added in a whisper. The real life events had become a nightmare of such twisted proportions she didn't trust her own eyes and ears anymore.

Kurosaka lifted Jennifer into his arms and started up the path.

"Can you walk, Mrs. Morris? I can send for the paramedics."

"I'd rather just walk," she said. "I don't want to stay here a moment longer than I have to."

"Very good."

She started behind him when Stark came alongside. He took her arm to guide her around some bushes. She turned sharply and looked at him.

"Just part of the job," he said.

She almost laughed, but she saw he meant it.

When they stepped out of the darkness and onto the street, they confronted a clump of residents gathered at the front of her house, their flashlights directed downward, some off. Another patrol car had arrived and the two uniformed officers approached Kurosaka, who directed them back to the lake.

At the driveway Kristin turned and looked at her neighbors. Nikki Stanley appeared to have shrunken in size. She resembled a naughty little girl who had been caught misbehaving. Her face was filled with almost as much confusion and fear as Kristin's was.

"What's going on?" Vincent McShane asked. He looked at his neighbors. "I thought we were chasing the intruder who shot Mrs. Slater." The sweat on his forehead glued down the strands of his hair. His, as well as most everyone else's face, was swollen and flushed.

"Everyone just go home," Lieutenant Kurosaka said. "It's all under control for the moment." When none of them moved, he added. "Don't worry. You're all safe."

Those appeared to be the magic words. The clump broke apart and the residents retreated to their homes in silence, Nikki and Jean the last to walk away.

Another patrol car arrived. Kurosaka said they should wait for him in front of Philip Slater's home. He continued to carry Jennifer to the house. Once inside, he set her down gently on the sofa.

"You'd better rest a minute, Mrs. Morris. I'll call your doctor."

"My husband," Kristin said.

"He's on the way," Kurosaka assured her, and went to the phone.

Kristin sat beside Jennifer and embraced her. Then she closed her eyes and when she opened them again, she found herself on her bed with Teddy sitting beside her, clutching her hand to his forehead, his head bowed. Doctor Hoffman stood beside him, smiling down at her.

"She's conscious," he said. Teddy lifted his head quickly.

"Kristin."

He embraced her and held her for a long moment before sitting back.

"What happened?"

"You passed out, mostly from the exhaustion and excitement, I imagine," Doctor Hoffman said. "Your vitals are all good and the baby's fine. A bit confused and shaken up, I bet, but fine," he added with a smile.

"Jennifer?"

"She's asleep," Teddy said. "I washed her face and got her in her P.J.'s but I don't think she realized it."

"The poor thing."

"How are you feeling?"

"I don't know. I ache in new places, but I'm

afraid to move." All of it came rushing back over her. "Oh Teddy, it was terrible. Marilyn Slater shot herself right before my eyes and he tried to blame me and then they were all after us and Detective Martin—"

"I know, honey. I know."

"You should just rest, Mrs. Morris," Doctor Hoffman said. "There will be plenty of time to review it all in the morning."

"But the security guards. I thought . . . they helped us," she said, still with a note of skepticism.

"Yeah, they did."

"It wasn't them. It was that detective. Teddy—"

"Easy, honey. Doctor Hoffman's right. You've got to relax now."

"I'm relaxed. Now that I'm home," she added, "and Jennifer's all right. But I can't relax until I understand, Teddy."

He looked up at Doctor Hoffman who nodded.

"Lieutenant Kurosaka says our security guards are just overzealous, partly because of the way Philip Slater ran the complex and their firm. The real villain was his partner, Detective Martin, as you know. He began by doing private investigations for Slater, who then paid him handsomely to correct what he considered to be flaws in his perfect development. Police internal affairs planted Kurosaka with Martin because there were suspicions of his extracurricular activities for some time, not just with Philip Slater, either. Martin killed Sol Feinberg just the way his wife believed. Slater hired him to do it. Then, the two of them killed Angela. They wanted to make it look like a rape and mugging, but that was Martin's undoing. He's a secretor."

"What does that mean, Teddy?"

"A secretor is someone whose blood type can be determined from body fluids other than blood. Now, with DNA fingerprinting, if the assailant has left his own body fluids behind, such as semen, the police can identify him."

"But why wouldn't Detective Martin know that?"

"I'm sure he did, but he never dreamed he would be a suspect. He wasn't a very good policeman anyway. Now, of course, he's singing like one of the caged birds Philip Slater gives to his residents."

"Poor Marilyn," Kristin muttered.

"Why don't you try to get some sleep now, honey. I'll stay right here."

"I'll stop by in the morning," Doctor Hoffman said. "But I really think you're fine. You're a lot stronger than you think, despite what happened to you before," he added.

"I guess if she can go through this all right, she can deliver a baby, huh, Doc?"

"Piece of cake," Hoffman said. He patted Kristin's hand and turned to leave.

"I'll just walk him out, honey," Teddy said. She nodded. He kissed her cheek and they left.

She opened her eyes and gazed up at the ceiling.

It was almost eleven-thirty. Kristin wondered if the security guards would be checking doors tonight. She closed her eyes and never heard a thing until morning when she woke to the sound of Jennifer calling her name. Still in her pajamas, Jennifer stood at the side of the bed.

"As soon as she opened her eyes, she called for you," Teddy explained. "I had to bring her in here to show her you were all right."

"Oh, honey, Mommy's fine."

She started to sit up, but the ache in her thighs declared its determination not to be ignored. She swallowed a groan but glanced frantically at Teddy.

"Mommy needs to rest a little more, honey." Jennifer looked like she might start to cry again. "I know what," Teddy said quickly, "why don't you and I make Mommy breakfast this morning. You show me where everything is, okay?"

"Okay," Jennifer said. It tempted her away from Kristin's side.

"It's going to be hard for a little while," Teddy admitted, shifting his eyes toward Jennifer.

"We'll get through it," Kristin said.

"I'm sorry I didn't listen more when you first came up with your worries," he said. "You were right, Kristin, and I, who should be an expert when it comes to seeing things, was blind. Thank God you're all right. I would have hated myself if anything had happened. Can you forgive me?"

She smiled.

"I'll work on it," she said.

He kissed her.

After he left with Jennifer to prepare breakfast, Kristin took a deep breath and got herself into a sitting position. She gazed through the window at the lake. It was as beautiful as ever this morning, but last night it might have become Jennifer's and her watery grave.

She wondered if they could continue to live here, even if she wanted that anymore.

And then, for the first time, she felt the baby kick and cried out with surprise.

Teddy and Jennifer came hurrying back.

"The baby just kicked," she said. "There! He did it again."

"He?"

Teddy sat on the bed and put his hand on her stomach. Then he smiled.

"Can I feel too?" Jennifer asked.

"Of course, honey," Kristin said.

The three of them sat there, hands on Kristin's stomach, waiting for the reaffirmation of life and the promise that came with it.

EPILOGUE

"THAT BRINGS US TO THE Neighborhood Watch report,"
Teddy said, and sat back in his desk chair. Behind
him, through the open curtains, the board of trustees
could see the moonlight gleaming on the surface of
Emerald Lake. Although it was the middle of the
summer, the water was so still it looked like ice.

Nikki Stanley cleared her throat and glanced up
quickly from her notepad.

"I have only one item," she said apologetically.

"Well, that's a relief," Vincent McShane quipped.
Sid Levine smiled and Teddy nodded. Paul Meltzer,
who was chosen as a replacement for Philip Slater in
a special election, looked unsure of himself and only
relaxed his lips in anticipation of Nikki Stanley's item.

"Go ahead, Nikki," Teddy said.

"The Cosens, Wildwood Drive, number 3071. Their
red maple is almost eight inches too high. According
to section thirty-one—"

"That is a beautiful tree," Paul Meltzer said, and
then pressed his lips together as if he had said something blasphemous.

"It is," Teddy said. "It's so cheerful to come upon it."

"It's too high," Nikki said. "There's a specific code

describing acceptable heights for trees, bushes, and hedges. It was enacted to protect the neighbors' views and—"

"But where this is located, it doesn't affect anyone's view," Teddy said. He looked at Sid who first glanced at Nikki and then at Vincent McShane.

"That's true."

"Nevertheless—" Nikki began.

"If the purpose of the code is to protect views and this tree doesn't affect views, why worry about it?" Teddy said.

"Someone else," Nikki replied, "whose tree does affect a view will have a right to complain when we ask him to cut down his."

"Maybe we can point out the difference, show him the logic," Teddy said softly. "We're not so big that we can't sit down over a cup of coffee and reason with each other."

Nikki slapped her notepad shut.

"If we're going to conduct ourselves that way, then what is the point of having a Neighborhood Watch report?" she snapped.

"To know with whom we should have that cup of coffee, Nikki," Teddy said.

Nikki tightened her lips. Sid, Vincent, and Paul nodded in agreement.

"Well," Teddy said, sitting forward, "if no one has anything else . . ."

"Let's adjourn," Vincent McShane said, rising.

"So moved," Sid Levine said.

The board members left Teddy's office.

"Can I offer anyone coffee?" Kristin said as they emerged. She was sitting on the sofa with the new baby in her arms and Jennifer beside them.

"None for me, thanks," Sid replied. "I promised Jean I'd come right home."

"Me, too," Vincent said.

"You promised Jean, too?" Paul quipped. Everyone laughed but Nikki.

"How's the new baby? Keeping you up nights?" Vincent asked Kristin.

"He's like his father—when he's hungry, he can't wait."

Everyone smiled. Nikki even looked a bit more relaxed. She stared at Kristin a moment and then led the others to the front door.

"Looks like a beautiful night," Teddy said, standing in the doorway.

Everyone muttered agreement. He watched them walk away, Vincent going up the street and the others down.

"So, Mr. President," Kristin said when he closed the door and stepped down to the living room. "How did your second official meeting go?"

"Quite well, I thought." He looked at Jennifer. "Guess who's coming home tomorrow, sweetheart?" he said.

"Who, Daddy?"

"Mr. Sniffles," Teddy said.

The smile on his daughter's face filled him with a warm glow.

"No problem?" Kristin asked.

"Not really. You'll read all about it in the next report to the residents," he added.

Kristin laughed and the baby started to cry.

"Bobby's hungry again!" Jennifer declared.

"So, what else is new? Keep your eye on your brother, honey, while I go warm the formula," Kristin said placing the baby in the cradle.

Teddy watched her for a moment. Then he looked at his children. He smiled to himself.

It was good to be living in Emerald Lakes, good to be living in a place where his family was comfortable and secure. How far would he go to protect it? he wondered. He thought for a while and decided it was best to leave it unanswered.

For now.

Visit the
Simon & Schuster Web site:

www.SimonSays.com

**and sign up for our
mystery e-mail updates!**

Keep up on the latest new releases,
author appearances, news, chats,
special offers, and more!
We'll deliver the information
right to your inbox—
if it's new, you'll know about it.

SIMON & SCHUSTER
A VIACOM COMPANY
www.SimonSays.com